THE RING OF DEATH

Recent Titles by Sally Spencer from Severn House

THE BUTCHER BEYOND
DANGEROUS GAMES
THE DARK LADY
THE DEAD HAND OF HISTORY
DEAD ON CUE
DEATH OF AN INNOCENT
A DEATH LEFT HANGING
DEATH WATCH
DYING IN THE DARK
A DYING FALL
THE ENEMY WITHIN
FATAL QUEST
GOLDEN MILE TO MURDER
A LONG TIME DEAD
MURDER AT SWANN'S LAKE
THE PARADISE JOB
THE RED HERRING
THE RING OF DEATH
THE SALTON KILLINGS
SINS OF THE FATHERS
STONE KILLER
THE WITCH MAKER

THE RING OF DEATH

Sally Spencer

This first world edition published 2010
in Great Britain and in the USA by
SEVERN HOUSE PUBLISHERS LTD of
9–15 High Street, Sutton, Surrey, England, SM1 1DF.
Trade paperback edition published
in Great Britain and the USA 2010 by
SEVERN HOUSE PUBLISHERS LTD

British Library Cataloguing in Publication Data

Spencer, Sally.
  The Ring of Death.
  1. Police – England – Yorkshire – Fiction. 2. Serial murder
  investigation – Fiction. 3. Detective and mystery stories.
  I. Title
  823.9'14-dc22

ISBN-13: 978-0-7278-6868-8   (cased)
ISBN-13: 978-1-84751-218-5   (trade paper)

All Severn House titles are printed on acid-free paper.

Severn House Publishers support The Forest Stewardship Council [FSC],
the leading international forest certification organisation. All our titles that
are printed on Greenpeace-approved FSC-certified paper carry the FSC logo.

Mixed Sources
Product group from well-managed
forests and other controlled sources
www.fsc.org Cert no. SA-COC-1565
© 1996 Forest Stewardship Council
FSC

Typeset by Palimpsest Book Production Ltd.,
Grangemouth, Stirlingshire, Scotland.
Printed and bound in Great Britain by
MPG Books Ltd., Bodmin, Cornwall.

PROLOGUE

For most men, suddenly finding themselves in this position would be a terrifying experience, Andy Adair thought.

As their minds slowly came back to life – as they began to hazily remember the blow to the back of the head which had robbed them of their consciousness – they would already be finding it hard to breathe.

And then – as they realized they were tied securely to a chair, and had a hood over their heads – they'd crap their pants.

But not him!

He was not that run-of-the-mill kind of man.

He was a *hard* man.

He didn't focus on the pain from his head-wound, because he had been trained to *ignore* pain.

He didn't waste his time wondering how he'd got into this situation.

None of that mattered.

What *was* important now was what happened *next*.

And the simple truth was that – in a *hard man* sort of way – he found the whole situation amusing.

The Enemy – and he was sure it was a *single* enemy – had put the sack over his head in an attempt to induce what Adair's instructors had called sensory deprivation.

And certainly that would work with some men.

It had worked with the wogs he himself had interrogated in the Middle East, during the Aden crisis, for example.

It had worked with the Catholic scum he had helped break down in the Northern Ireland conflict.

But it was not about to work with *him*.

And it was from that knowledge of his own sense of control over the situation that the amusement stemmed.

Because, even now, that invisible Enemy was probably studying him for signs of growing fear – and was being sadly disappointed.

He could hear the Enemy breathing, short, shallow breaths designed to conceal his presence.

But that wouldn't work, either.

Not with a man who'd been *trained* to listen.

Not with a man who'd spent so much time on the *other side* of the sack.

Slowly and silently, Adair started to count.

One hundred . . . two hundred . . . three hundred . . .

This was another technique he'd been taught in the army, and it had two purposes. The first was to enable him to calculate how long he had been held – which might come in useful later. The second was keep his mind occupied, so that no *unnecessary* thoughts came into it.

He had reached six thousand, seven hundred and twenty-six when the Enemy – admitting defeat, even if he didn't yet realize it himself – finally broke the silence.

'Don't you want to know *where* you are?' the man asked.

'Bloody amateur!' Adair thought, in disgust.

'Don't you want to know *why* you're here?' the Enemy continued.

Pathetic! This feller wouldn't have lasted ten minutes in the hands of the Ulster Proddies.

'I want some information,' the Enemy said.

'Is that right?' Adair asked.

His captor spoke with a convincing Lancashire accent, he noted, but that proved nothing.

A lot of Irishmen who'd spent a few years in the area could put on the local accent when they needed to. And when you were working for the Irish Republican cause – when you were the *enemy within* on the English mainland – you did need to put it on, because you knew that sounding like a local was one of the best disguises you could adopt.

'I want some information, and you're going to give it to me,' the Enemy said.

And now there was a hard edge – an almost iron-clad certainty – to his voice, which, despite everything, made his captive start to feel perhaps just slightly unnerved.

'I'll give you some information, Paddy,' Adair said.

He spoke harshly, perhaps to show the Enemy he was not to be intimidated, and perhaps, also, to bolster up his own courage a little.

'And that information,' he continued, 'is that when I get out of here, your life won't be worth living.'

'I want to know exactly what went on at Moors' Edge Farm,' the Enemy said. 'And I want the names of the men who organized it.'

'Wrong question!' Adair thought, slightly knocked off balance.

Or, at least, he corrected himself, not one of the questions he'd been *expecting*.

'You can get stuffed,' the hooded man said.

He concentrated on his breathing, forcing it to be regular and calm, knowing that would help steady his pulse and his heart-beat.

The threats would come soon, he told himself.

'*I can hurt you, you know. I can hurt you in ways you could never even imagine.*'

That was what *he* would have said in this situation. That was what he *had* said, in situations just like it.

But there were no threats. Instead, all he heard was a match being struck, followed by a roaring sound.

And then he felt the pain in his arm – an agonizing pain as the flesh was burnt away.

He screamed, and the immediate pain stopped, though a secondary pain – less intense but no less horrendous – continued.

'In case you're wondering what I'm using, it's a blow-lamp,' the Enemy said casually. 'Nasty things, blow-lamps. They can burn their way through a solid oak door in less than a minute – so just imagine what this one could do to you.'

Adair let his head slump to one side, as if he'd lost consciousness, though it was a hard act to maintain when all he really wanted to do was scream again.

'If you're faking it, you're just wasting your time and mine,' he heard the Enemy say. 'If you're *not* faking it, I'll just wait until you come round, and then start again. Because I *will* have the information I require.'

Adair could still hear the blow-lamp spitting out its flame in the background. Nothing he'd ever been taught – nothing he'd ever had to endure – had prepared him for this.

He remembered something else his instructor had said.

'*In general, you need to dominate the Enemy, even when*

he seems to have the upper hand but there are a few *occasions when it might serve you best to put on a show of cooperating.'*

'All right, I'll tell you what you want to know,' Adair said, pretending to be panicked, yet not really *having to* pretend any more.

'Start with the names,' the Enemy ordered him.

'There's a man called Wally, who I met in a pub called the Flying Horse,' Adair began. 'I don't know his other name, but he's about thirty-five and—'

As the flame brushed against his arm, he stopped speaking and started to scream again.

'Do you think I'm a complete bloody fool?' the Enemy asked, contemptuously. 'Wally, who you met in the Flying Horse! That won't do at all. I know who all your friends and acquaintances are. What I *don't* know is which of them are involved in what's been going on at Moors' Edge Farm.'

It was hard to think with the pain, Adair thought.

So very, very hard.

But he had to try. He had to find some way to get through to this Paddy – to reach some sort of temporary compromise. Then, later – when this was all over – he'd track him down. And that would be when the bastard would learn what *real* pain was.

'I . . . I . . . could give you a couple of names, and you could get more names from them,' he said.

'I want the names of everybody involved,' the Enemy said unrelentingly. 'And I want them from *you!*'

'Be reasonable,' Adair said, aware that his tone had become a whine – and no longer caring. 'If I give you *all* the names, I'll have no future in this town.'

'You still don't get it, do you?' the Enemy asked.

'Get what?' Adair asked tremulously.

'It's no longer a question of you having a future *in this town.* You have no future *anywhere.* And why do you think that is?'

'I . . . I don't know,' Adair croaked.

'You have no future because when you've told me all I need to know, I'm going to kill you.'

He had never *really* been a hard man, Adair realized – not in the way that *this* man was hard. He felt tears forming in his eyes and snot start to trickle over his upper lip.

'Please!' he sobbed.

'After what you've done, there can be no pity and no mercy,' the Enemy said coldly. 'The best you can hope for now is a *quick* death. And that's what you'll get, once you've given me the information. It won't be a gentle death – you've lost the right to that – but at least it will soon be over.'

The threats could still be no more than part of the interrogation technique, Adair told himself.

They could be no more than part of the interrogation technique . . . they could be no more than part of the interrogation technique . . . they could be no more . . .

'I'm waiting,' the Enemy said.

'Tom Harding,' Adair gasped.

'That would be Thomas W. Harding, who lives at 93 India Road, Whitebridge?'

'I . . . I don't know if that's his exact address, but, yes, he does live in India Road.'

'Good,' the Enemy said approvingly, as if, despite his initial reservations, he was now starting to consider Adair a promising pupil after all. 'Next name?'

'John Bygraves.'

'John Bygraves of Waverley Avenue?'

'I don't know,' Adair sobbed. 'It might be Waverley Avenue, but I just don't know.'

'It's Waverley Avenue,' the Enemy said. 'Next?'

Adair spilled out another twenty names before he finally said, 'That's it. I swear to you, that's all of them.'

And even then, the Enemy was not satisfied.

'Describe exactly what went on,' he said. 'Paint a picture for me.'

'Paint a . . . paint a picture?'

'That's what I said.'

Adair did his best. As the details – some he had all but forgotten – spilled out of his mouth, there was a corner of his brain which was reciting a babbled prayer that this might be enough – that despite what he had said earlier, the Enemy might find it in his heart to show a little mercy.

'Is that all?' the other man asked, when the chronicle came to end.

'That's all,' Adair promised.

A slight pause.

'Are you sure?' the Enemy asked. 'Because if you *can* remember something more, it *will* keep you alive just a little while longer.'

'Look, you don't have to . . .' Adair began.

And then, as the metal claw ripped across his throat, tearing away the flesh and lacerating his windpipe, he said no more.

ONE

The pub landlords of Whitebridge feared the clever young men from the brewery's planning and design department in much the same way as landlords in former times must have feared a visitation by the plague. Daily, they lived in trepidation of the knock on the door which would announce the arrival of these callow youths, whose eyes gleamed – like vultures swooping down on a particularly juicy prey – and whose imaginations were positively exploding with exciting ideas for improving the place. For the landlords knew – as did their customers – that once these fashionably suited vandals had crossed the threshold, the boozer they had known and loved was all but doomed.

Walls would be torn down, in order to open the place up. Windows would be enlarged, letting in more of the outside world which the drinkers had come to the pub precisely to forget. But worse, even, than this destruction, was the *reconstruction* which followed it.

The pub needed a *theme*, explained these smart-arsed designers who did most of their own drinking in cocktail bars. It needed an *image*. And so it was that pubs built in the age of Victoria suddenly found themselves lumbered (and that was the *right* word, in every sense) with mock – and totally structurally unnecessary – seventeenth-century oak beams. So it was that pubs which had never had any connection with the coaching inns of earlier times had their walls festooned with horse brasses, harnesses, and long thin coaching horns.

The Drum and Monkey, having so far been spared this fate, was, to its regular customers, an island of placid stability in a world of frantic change. They *liked* the idea that the landlord felt that his main task in life was to sell beer. They felt comfortable with the fact that there was a best room there for those who wanted it, and a public bar for those who didn't. And some of them took an almost guilty pleasure in knowing that when a serious crime had occurred, the corner table in that public bar would invariably be occupied by a team of detectives which had once been led by DCI Charlie Woodend and was now headed by DCI Monika Paniatowski.

Though no serious crime was yet known to have occurred, two of Paniatowski's team were sitting at their customary table that lunchtime.

The elder of the pair, Detective Inspector Colin Beresford, was in his early thirties. From a distance, he managed to maintain the fresh-faced appearance of a much younger man. Closer up, it was his eyes you noticed – eyes which showed the strain of having carried a heavy responsibility, and a concern that he had somehow failed to carry it as well as he might have done. The eyes did not actually *tell* an observer that after years of struggling to take care of a mother suffering from Alzheimer's disease he had reluctantly decided to put her in a nursing home, but the observer would not have been the least surprised to learn that this was, in fact, the case.

The younger man was in his early twenties. His slim aesthetic features seemed as if they should belong to a high-flying college lecturer rather than a detective constable, and, in fact, Jack Crane, with his 1st Class Honours degree in English Literature, could easily have been a university lecturer had he decided to follow that particular path. But he had instead chosen the grimy streets over the dreaming spires – and it was a rare day on which he regretted his choice more than once.

The third member of the team was in the ladies' toilets, examining herself in the mirror. What she saw reflected back at her was a face which it would have pleased most women to possess, and which – on a good day – she even found perfectly acceptable herself.

Her hair was blonde and silky, her eyes blue, intelligent and penetrating. Her nose, reflecting her Central European background, was a little larger than those normally handed out in Lancashire, but it was strong rather than dominating, and the men in her life – not that there had been any of *them* recently – had often admitted to finding it very sexy. Her lips were wide and inviting, her chin was resolute without being square.

She stepped back from the mirror, lit up a cigarette, and

stood perfectly still as the acrid smoke curled its way around her lungs.

'Yes, not bad,' she told the reflection in the mirror. 'Not bad at all.'

And then – realizing she'd actually spoken the words *out loud* – she quickly glanced around to see if there was anybody there to hear her.

Colin Beresford watched his old colleague (and new boss) emerge from the toilets and walk towards him.

It hadn't been easy for Monika, taking over from the legendary Charlie Woodend, he thought. In fact, he amended mentally, it had been bloody *hard*.

Stepping into Charlie's shoes would have been a formidable task for any *man*. For a woman – the very *first* woman DCI in the division – it had been an ever greater obstacle. And the transition hadn't exactly been helped by the rumours buzzing around Whitebridge Police HQ that Paniatowski owed her promotion less to her own ability than to her previous relationship with the chief constable.

All of which meant that, even though Paniatowski had handled her first major investigation with a flair and intuition which would have made Charlie Woodend proud of her, most of the bobbies in Whitebridge HQ were still unconvinced she'd been the right choice for the job.

'I'm just getting a round in, boss,' Beresford said, as Paniatowski resumed her seat. 'Another vodka?'

The DCI thought about it. 'I've had two, so far, haven't I?'

'That's right.'

'Then I'd better pass on a third. I've got a meeting with the chief constable this afternoon.'

Beresford frowned. 'Did he say what it was about?'

'No, he didn't. There wasn't even a hint.'

The inspector shook his head, slightly mournfully. 'Not good,' he pronounced.

'Not good,' DC Crane repeated, puzzled. 'But if you don't know what it is that the chief constable wants to talk about—'

'If it was good, he'd have made the purpose of the meeting clear beforehand, so the boss had time to think about what she wanted to say,' Beresford interrupted. 'Since he's playing

it close to his chest, it's much more likely to be an ambush
than a meeting of minds. Isn't that right, boss?'

Paniatowski looked down regretfully at her empty vodka
glass. 'That's right,' she agreed.

The sign on the office door said 'Dr A. Beatty', and as he sat
down opposite the man the sign referred to, DS Cousins found
himself wondering what the 'A' stood for.

Allen?

Ambrose?

Archibald?

Arsehole?

It probably wasn't the last of these, Cousins decided – but
it certainly *should* be!

He didn't like Dr A. Beatty. Didn't like him because he
was one of those deluded men who thought that if he brushed
hair over the bald spot in the middle of his head, no one would
notice the baldness. Didn't like him because his lips had a
habit of twitching slightly – signalling, almost – about half a
second before he actually spoke. But most of all, he didn't
like him because Beatty was the psychiatrist who he'd been
coerced into meeting with once a week.

Beatty's lips did their slight twitch. 'You're on time this
week,' he said. 'That's a good sign, Paul.'

'Is it, Amadeus?' Cousins asked innocently.

The lips twitched again, as if Beatty were thinking of
correcting Cousins, then the doctor glanced down at the file
on his desk and said, 'How long is it now since your wife
died, Paul?'

'It's all in that file,' Cousins told him.

'I know it is, but I'd still like you to tell me.'

Cousins shrugged. 'Two years, three months and six days.'

'And how do you feel about that?'

'How do you think I feel? I've over the bloody moon about
it. I'm so happy I have to keep pinching myself to make sure
I'm not just dreaming.'

Beatty shook his head, reprovingly, though not so vigor-
ously as to disturb his carefully arranged hair.

'You agreed to attend these sessions only when you were
told they were a pre-condition to your returning to your normal
duties. Isn't that correct?' he asked.

'Too bloody right it is.'

'But what you seem to have failed to have grasped is that that pre-condition required more than you simply turning up at my office, though, as I said earlier, the fact that you have become more punctual *is* a good sign.'

Cousins said nothing.

'You are required not only to be here, but to make a positive effort to *work* with me,' Beatty continued. 'And if you fail to do that, Paul . . . well, we both know what the consequences will be, don't we?'

'You're threatening to have me sent on sick leave again.'

'I'm not *threatening* anything. That is not my role. I will merely write an objective assessment of these meetings, and your superiors will make the decisions about your future.'

Cousins sighed. 'All right,' he said, 'I was totally devastated by my wife's death.'

The doctor gave him a disapproving look. 'Too easy,' he said.

'What do you mean – too easy?' Cousins demanded.

'You're talking in platitudes,' the doctor replied. 'You're using words – mere clichés – as a way of blocking out your true emotions.'

'They might be clichés to you, but they're not to me,' Cousins said angrily. 'I *was* devastated. She was the only woman I ever really wanted, and I'd lost her.'

'And who did you *blame* for that?'

'I didn't blame anybody,' Cousins said, perhaps a little too quickly.

'Everybody blames somebody – or something – in cases like that,' the psychiatrist persisted. 'Did you blame God, perhaps?'

'I'm not sure I believe in God,' Cousins told him. 'And even if I do, I don't think he's interested enough in me personally to punish me by planting cancerous cells in my wife's body.'

'Then perhaps you blame the doctors?'

'They did all they could.'

'Or your wife herself? That's quite common.'

'No,' Cousins said, with a sudden ferocity. 'Not her!'

The doctor smiled, knowingly. 'Then that only leaves you, doesn't it?' he asked.

'That's right. It only leaves me.'

'And how are *you* responsible?'

Cousins shrugged. 'I don't know. Maybe if I'd made her go to see the doctor earlier . . .'

'I've seen her medical record. Even if she *had* gone earlier, it would have made very little difference.'

'Or maybe if I'd been a better person, a more considerate person . . .'

'How would that have helped?'

'I don't know, but maybe if I'd spent less time at work she wouldn't have got sick.'

'Are you saying your wife was unhappy with your marriage?'

'Not exactly unhappy – but maybe she sometimes felt a little neglected. It's an occupational hazard among bobbies' wives.'

'So there are times when you think that your wife developed cancer through your *neglect*?'

'Maybe.'

'There's no scientific evidence for that ever having happened, you know.'

'And can science prove that it *doesn't* happen?'

'Not definitively, no, but then there is very little in this world that can be definitively . . .'

'Well, there you are, then.'

'You didn't have any children, did you?'

No, they didn't. She'd wanted them. And so had he, in a way. But he'd wanted to get established in the Force first, so they'd put it off and put it off until it was too late.

'I said, you didn't have any children, did you?' the doctor repeated.

'It's all in the file,' Cousins said morosely.

The psychiatrist raised an eyebrow.

'Work with me, Paul. You have to *work with me*,' he said.

Cousins sighed again. 'We didn't have any children. We had a cat and a dog. And *they're* both dead, as well.'

'It's the question of *why* you didn't have any children that I'd rather like to take up—' Beatty began.

'I said they're both dead as well,' Cousins interrupted him. 'The cat was run over by a car.'

'I see, but to get back to question of children . . .'

'Don't you want to know who I blamed for that? Aren't you interested in finding out if I can detect the hand of God in the conspiracy to have poor little Ginger flattened under the front wheels of a Vauxhall Victor?'

'Well, no, not really. As I said, I think one of the funda-mental points we need to discuss . . .'

'Don't you even want to know if I blamed *myself*?'

It was the psychiatrist's turn to sigh. 'All right, Paul, if it will make you feel any happier, I *will* ask you that question,' he said, reluctantly.

The seconds ticked by . . . ten . . . twenty . . . thirty . . .

'Well?' Beatty demanded.

'You haven't asked the question yet,' Cousins pointed out, in an eminently reasonable tone. 'Come on, Dr Beatty – work with me!'

The psychiatrist sighed again. '*Do* you blame yourself for Ginger's death?' he asked finally.

'He was a bloody cat,' Cousins said slowly, as if talking to someone he had suddenly decided was particularly dim. 'He liked to play "chicken" with passing cars, and one day he lost. So of course I don't blame myself. What do you think I am? Some kind of nutter?'

TWO

This was perhaps the fourth or fifth meeting that Monika Paniatowski had had with the chief constable since she'd become a DCI, and it didn't seem to her as if they were getting any easier.

Part of the problem, of course, was that at another time – and in another county, the other side of the Pennines – she and George Baxter had been lovers.

But that wasn't the only reason, she admitted to herself.

The other part was that there was a big difference between talking to the boss as a detective inspector – a reliable number two in a team – and talking to him as a chief inspector – whose job it was not only to deliver reports, but also to protect herself and her people.

And protecting herself and her people was what this particular meeting was about – she was almost convinced of that now.

'Ever since Sergeant Walker was reassigned, you've been working without a bagman,' Baxter said, confirming her suspicions.

'Ever since Sergeant Walker tried his best to sabotage my investigation and I managed to get *rid of* him, I've been working without a bagman,' Paniatowski paraphrased silently.

'I haven't been involved in any investigation which has been major enough for me to *need* a bagman,' she said aloud.

'Then this is the ideal opportunity for you to *get* a new bagman – while you have the time and leisure to show him the ropes and train him into the job,' Baxter said.

'How much training will he need to carry my bag?' asked Paniatowski – knowing there was much more to the job than that, and knowing that *Baxter* knew there was much more to it, yet still finding herself unable to come up with a better argument.

'Every other DCI I have working for me is screaming out for extra manpower,' Baxter mused. 'Why aren't you?'

Because bringing new people into the team was dangerous,

Paniatowski thought. Walker had done all he could to wreck her first major case – and with it, her career – simply because she was a woman. And he was only the tip of the iceberg. There are half a dozen other sergeants who, if they'd been given the opportunity, would have acted exactly as he did.

'DC Jack Crane is acting as my bagman at the moment, sir,' she said. 'And he's very good at it.'

'He's a baby!' Baxter said dismissively.

'He's twenty-four, sir.'

'Like I said, he's a baby. But then that's an advantage, as far as you're concerned, isn't it – because babies are so much easier to handle?'

It wasn't a question of being easy to handle, Paniatowski thought – it was a question of trust. Jack Crane had gone out on a limb for her in the Szymborska murder case, and she knew she could rely on him.

'So *you* get to pamper DC Crane, while *I* get to keep experienced sergeants kicking their heels when I could be offering them the chance of a role they could really get their teeth into,' Baxter said. 'Is *that* how it works?'

No, that didn't seem fair, Paniatowski conceded – at least from the chief constable's point of view.

'Who've you got in mind?' she asked, resignedly.

'DS Cousins,' Baxter said.

'Cousins!' Paniatowski repeated. 'But he's—'

'Been out on sick leave,' Baxter interrupted her.

'Sick leave! Yes, strictly speaking, I suppose he has. But it's not exactly a septic toenail which has been keeping him away from . . .'

'And now the police shrink has assured me that he's ready to return to normal duties.'

'You know what a major case is like, sir,' Paniatowski protested. 'You know the kind of pressure the team's under. And any team's only as strong as its weakest link.'

Baxter shook his head sadly. 'You disappoint me, Monika,' he said.

'And why's that?' Paniatowski demanded.

'Because I would have thought you'd have learned more working under Charlie Woodend than just how to solve murders – I thought you'd have learned a little humanity.'

Paniatowski felt as if she'd been punched in the stomach.

But it was a fair punch, she acknowledged – a punch she probably deserved.

'You think Cousins is up to the job?' she asked.

'I'd never have put him forward if I didn't,' Baxter said, with just a hint of rebuke still evident in his voice. 'He was a fine officer before his wife died, and the shrink thinks there's every chance he'll be a fine officer again. But I'm not *ordering* you to take him.'

'No, sir?'

'No. But if you don't want Cousins, I'll leave the decision as to who's assigned to your team to Chief Superintendent Horrocks. And *he* won't allow you to pick and choose.'

It was blackmail, Paniatowski thought. But at least it was blackmail from a decent man who was basically on her side.

'Cousins it is, then,' she said.

Baxter nodded. 'Good,' he said.

Louisa Paniatowski, half-English, half-Spanish by birth (and just a little bit Polish by adoption) was busy poring over her history homework when Monika arrived home at half-past six.

She gazed up at her mother with a look of mild disapproval in her eyes, and said, 'Why aren't you at your judo class, Mum?'

Paniatowski shrugged helplessly. 'I thought you might appreciate my company.'

'I always *do* appreciate your company,' Louisa replied. 'But judo is a *commitment*, you know.'

So earnest, Paniatowski thought fondly. So like Bob, her long-dead father, in so many ways.

But it still didn't do to let her get *too* cocky.

'I'm a black belt,' she reminded her daughter. 'A fifth dan. Do you know how many other women there are in England who could say that?'

'Not a lot,' Louisa conceded. 'But since there are some men who are *tenth* dans, that means you've still got a lot to learn.' She smiled, as if she was suddenly worried that her mother might think she was being too critical. 'Besides,' she continued, 'if you don't go to your classes now – when you're *not* investigating a major murder case – when *will* you go?'

'I can strike a balance between my work life and my home life,' Paniatowski said, noting how defensive she sounded, even to herself.

'Like Uncle Charlie did?' Louisa asked innocently.

'I have the greatest respect for Uncle Charlie, as you well know,' Paniatowski said severely.

'But . . .?' Louisa asked.

'But he was what you might call an old-style kind of bobby – one who had to be in the thick of everything himself.'

'You, on the other hand . . .' Louisa said, with an amused smile playing on her lips.

'I, on the other hand, am a more modern, forward-looking police officer – one who knows how to delegate and how to guide her team from a distance.'

'If you say so, Mum.'

'I *do* say so.'

Louisa nodded, as if she quite accepted her mother's point.

'By the way,' she said, 'I was talking to Mrs Tait, my form teacher, today.'

'Oh yes?'

'Yes. And Mrs Tait's been reading this article in the *Times Educational Supplement* which apparently says that any child without her own colour television in her bedroom is at a . . . at a . . .'

'At a what?'

'I'm trying to think of the exact words. At a distinct educational disadvantage! That's it! So bearing in mind that you don't want *me* to be at a "distinct educational disadvantage," can we go out and buy me a colour telly on Saturday?'

Paniatowski found she placed her hands on her hips – a motherly gesture she'd once promised herself she'd never adopt.

'You surely don't think I'll fall for that, do you?' she asked.

'Why not?' Louisa wondered.

'Because it's so obviously a load of old rubbish!'

'True,' her daughter conceded. 'But you can't blame me for trying. After all, if you can believe you're any different from Uncle Charlie, you might believe anything.'

THREE

Five forty-two a.m.

If the night-duty room had been London or New York – big cities in which, reputedly, crime never slept – then the sound of the telephone bell slicing its way through the empty early-morning air would have been almost anticipated. But this wasn't either of those places. It was Whitebridge, a *small* city, where even the most industrious of cat-burglars was safely tucked up in bed by half-past three, and where, between the last fight on the doorstep of a closing pub and the first fight at an early morning bus stop, *nothing* happened.

Sergeant Kendrick, somewhat started by this sudden intrusion on his peace and quiet, laid aside his newspaper – with the crossword still only half-completed – and picked up the phone.

'Whitebridge Police Headquarters,' he said. 'Can I help you?'

'Oh my God, it was horrible!' gasped a man's voice on the other end of the line.

'What was horrible, sir?' Kendrick asked, using a measured, authoritative voice in which he could not quite suppress the hint that if he was, in fact, talking to a crank, he would not be at all surprised.

'I know murder's *supposed* to be horrible,' the man gabbled. 'But not like this. It was awful. I mean, it was just *awful*.'

'Calm down, sir,' Kendrick said soothingly. 'You'd better give me the details. An' you can start by tellin' me your name.'

It took less than a minute to persuade Kendrick both that the caller – a Mr Toynbee – was genuine, and that the crime he described really *was* awful.

'It . . . it wasn't the fact that his throat was cut that was the worst,' Toynbee moaned down the line. 'It was the other thing – the way he'd been—'

'Quite so, sir,' Kendrick interrupted, doing his best to hide his own revulsion from the caller. 'Listen, Mr Toynbee, what I want you to do now . . .'

'I'm not going back there,' Toynbee screamed. 'You can't *make* me go back there!'

'I wouldn't dream of it,' Kendrick reassured him. 'In fact, I'd like you to stay just where you are now, until the police arrive. Have you got a kettle?'

'A kettle?' the other man repeated, as if the words were meaningless to him.

'A kettle,' Kendrick repeated.

'Yes, I . . . I'm looking at it now.'

'Then brew yourself a cuppa. An' be sure to put lots of sugar in it. Will you do that for me?'

'Yes, I'll do that,' Toynbee promised.

'And don't worry,' Kendrick told him. 'We'll have somebody with you in a matter of minutes.'

'Will it help?' Toynbee asked, with a pleading note in his voice.

'Sorry?'

'The tea! Will it help?'

'Should do,' the sergeant said.

But he was thinking, 'God knows if *anything* will help after what you've been through.'

Five forty-seven a.m.

The first thought that flashed through Colin Beresford's mind as he groped for the bedside phone was that the call was from his mother's nursing home, and that they were calling to inform him that she had died in the night. The second thought was if any such merciful release *had* occurred, whoever was in charge would probably have waited until a civilized hour before ringing him.

'Beresford,' he mumbled into the phone, as he tried to focus his mind on what he had now decided would undoubtedly be police business.

'I'm right in assuming you're the inspector on call, aren't I, sir?' asked the voice at the other end of the line.

'Considering you just woke me up, you'd bloody better be!' Beresford growled.

And the moment the words were out his mouth, he was

thinking, 'Christ, it doesn't take long for a little bit of power to turn your head, does it?'

The man on the other end of the line was silent, perhaps wondering what he should say next.

'Yes, I'm the inspector on call,' Beresford told him. 'Who am I speaking to?'

'Sergeant Kendrick, sir.'

'Sorry for biting your head off, Kendrick. I'm not at my best at this time of the morning.'

'Very few of us are, sir,' the sergeant said, forgivingly. 'Thing is, we just had a report of a murder, an' as bizarre as the circumstances seem, I think it's on the up-an-up.'

'Then you'd better give me the details.'

Kendrick reeled them off, and when he'd finished, Beresford said, 'And you're sure this isn't just some kind of sick joke?'

'Not *sure*, no,' the sergeant said cautiously. 'But the caller didn't sound as if he'd *invented* it. And to be honest with you, I don't think I *could* invent that kind of thing myself.'

And neither could I, Beresford agreed silently – not however hard I worked at it.

'All right, I'll take things from here,' he said.

'Would you like me to ring *ma'am*?' Kendrick asked.

From the way he said the last word, Beresford guessed that the sergeant was no big fan of Monika's – and immediately felt better about speaking roughly to him earlier.

'No, I'll ring her myself,' he said. 'You just make sure there are enough uniforms at the scene to lock things down.'

'Got it,' Kendrick said.

'And one more thing,' Beresford continued.

'Yes, sir?'

'The next time you speak to me about my boss, make sure you use her full title.'

'Got that as well,' Kendrick said, suddenly sounding sullen.

Five fifty-three a.m.

'You were quick off the mark,' Kendrick said, surprised at the speed with which DS Cousins answered his phone. 'Were you already up?'

'I haven't really been to bed,' the other man replied. 'I don't sleep much, these days.'

Aye, that's what I heard around the station, Kendrick thought.

'Thing is, Paul, there's been a murder, and I've had to assign it, at least in the short term, to the Polack's team,' he said aloud.

'*Had to* assign it?' Cousins repeated.

'They were next on the rota. I had no choice in the matter.'

There was a pause, then Cousins said, 'So if you've already called DCI Paniatowski, why are you calling me?'

Kendrick gave a mental shrug. 'You're down on the list to be joinin' that team soon, so I just thought you might like to get in on the ground floor.'

There was another pause at the other end of the line, then Cousins said, 'I want you to know I appreciate this, Harry.'

'You what?'

'Ever since I came back off sick leave, most of the fellers I used to work with have been steering clear of me. So I appreciate the vote of confidence you've just given me.'

It was scarcely that, Kendrick told himself. He still thought of Cousins as a raving loony, but the man *had* been a good bobby once. And if it came to a choice between helping Cousins pull the strings behind the investigation, or leaving the whole thing to a foreign-born bitch who probably couldn't find her own tits without the help of a road map, the sergeant knew which *he'd* prefer.

'I won't forget this. I mean it,' Cousins said.

He sounded so pathetic, Kendrick thought with disgust – a bit like a whipped dog which comes crawling back for another beating.

'Think nothing of it, Paul,' he said. 'After all, if us old-fashioned bobbies can't depend on *each other* to hold back the tide, who can we depend on?'

FOUR

At six-oh-nine Paniatowski was already behind the wheel of her red MGA, her first cigarette of the day clamped in her mouth, a cup of instant coffee jammed between her seat and the gearstick mounting.

She drove at speed through a town which was only just waking up – her siren contributing to that awakening – and by six-seventeen, as she reached the roadside sign which thanked her for visiting Whitebridge, she was already lighting a second cigarette from the stub of her first.

All evidence of civilization quickly petered out as soon as she left the town behind. Now there was only the moors ahead of her – a vast expanse of purple heather waving gently in the breeze, and short bitter grass that even the hardy moorland sheep found tough work.

A startled rabbit ran across the road, and she stamped down on the brake pedal to avoid hitting it. A family of voles scurried for cover at the sound of her engine. It was going to be a lovely morning, she thought, looking up at the sky and observing the peewits, as they hovered above her.

Was she making a deliberate effort to absorb the harsh beauty of the moors, she wondered.

And if so, why?

Perhaps it was an attempt to inure herself – in advance – to the horror which was awaiting her.

She slowed as she approached the clump of silver-birch trees where the body had been discovered. There were already vehicles at the scene – two patrol units and a third, unmarked, car – but there was no sign yet of either Dr Shastri's Land Rover or an ambulance.

As she pulled in behind one of the patrol cars, she saw a man walking quickly towards her. He was square-bodied and dressed in a blue suit which was a few years out of style. His dark hair was turning grey, and the stubble on his chin was almost white.

He could have been in his mid-fifties and wearing his age

well, or in his mid-forties and carrying it badly, Paniatowski thought. Then she recognized him – and realized that it was the latter.

When he'd reached the MGA, the man came to a halt.

'DS Cousins, ma'am,' he announced.

'Yes, I know,' Paniatowski said neutrally.

'I realize I'm not officially a member of the team yet,' Cousins continued, 'but the duty sergeant rang me, so I thought I might as well turn up and see if I could be of any use.'

The duty sergeant rang me! Paniatowski repeated silently.

'Mate of yours, is he?' she asked.

'No, not particularly, ma'am,' Cousins replied, sounding puzzled.

But was he *really* puzzled at all? Paniatowski asked herself.

Or was he, rather, part of the conspiracy of old-time sergeants determined to see that the new DCI did not succeed?

'You're getting paranoid,' she thought.

But then, as the old joke went, it was hard *not* to be paranoid when everybody was against you.

She studied Cousin's face for signs of deviousness, and could find none.

But what did that prove?

Detective Sergeant Walker had seemed straightforward enough, too – even as he was attempting to plunge the dagger deep into her back.

'I want the crime scene secured,' she said crisply.

'That's already been done, ma'am,' Cousins said. 'There are four uniforms in place now, and they know where the reinforcements are to be deployed when they arrive.'

Paniatowski nodded. 'In that case,' she said, 'let's go and look at the body, Sergeant.'

'The stiff was found by Mr Toynbee, who's the owner of the kennels just down the road,' Cousins said, as they walked. 'That's the reason he was out so early in the morning.'

'What is?'

'His dogs. He likes to give them a walk first thing.'

'So you've spoken to him?' Paniatowski asked, worried that Cousins might *already* have started the undermining process.

'Yes, ma'am – but only briefly. I've told him to stay in his office until you'd talked to him. I've also advised him that if he wants to see his operating licence renewed, he'd be wise to speak to nobody else first.'

'That's *good* advice,' Paniatowski agreed.

They entered the woods. The trunks of the silver-birch trees glistened in the sunlight which was seeping through their foliage. The ground still smelled of that damp earthiness brought on by being soaked in morning dew. Somewhere in the near distance, a bird was singing.

'Watch out for that pile of vomit, ma'am,' Cousins cautioned, pointing into the grass. 'Mr Toynbee spewed up his load when he saw the body. And I can't say that I blame him.'

The trees, closely packed near the road, thinned out as they advanced into the wood, and soon they reached a clearing where the body had been dumped.

'Jesus!' Paniatowski said, feeling the bile rise to her throat at her first sight of the corpse.

She'd been briefed for this moment. She'd known what to expect. But *knowing* wasn't the same thing as being *prepared* – and it was clear to her now that she hadn't been *prepared* at all.

Much of the flesh on the dead man's lower right arm had been burned away, but she'd seen worse in her time, and that wasn't the problem she had with this corpse. Nor did the fact that he was completely naked really bother her – though, in the overall picture, it certainly didn't help.

What had got to her – what had brought up the bile – was that he had been posed on his hands and knees, and though she'd been briefed on that, too, the actual sight of it still shook her.

Why should it affect her like this, she wondered.

What was so especially horrific about him being in this position?

It was, she supposed, that more than anything else that had been done to him, this act seemed to rob him of all humanity.

'Can't have been dead for more than seventy-two hours, or the rigor would have worn off and he'd be flat on the ground,' Cousins said, matter-of-factly.

'Get a grip, Monika!' Paniatowski ordered herself. 'Show this new sergeant of yours what you're really made of!'

'But he must have been posed in that position – *fixed* in that position – until rigor set in,' she said, keeping her voice as flat and analytical as she possibly could.

Cousins nodded. 'That's true, ma'am.'

Paniatowski walked around the body. The victim had been in his mid-thirties, she guessed, and had been in very good shape physically. His throat had been ripped open, but there was no sign of blood on the ground in front of him. What there *was* on the ground, though, was a driving licence, wrapped up in a see-through plastic envelope.

'He wasn't killed on this spot,' she said, feeling slightly better now.

'No, ma'am, he wasn't.'

'And it can't have been easy to transport him here.'

Cousins nodded again. 'He wouldn't have fitted in the boot of a car like that. The killer will have needed at least a small van to shift him.'

'So why do it that way?' Paniatowski wondered. 'Why didn't the killer move him before rigor set in? Why would he deliberately make it so much more difficult for himself?'

'The only plausible explanation is that he wanted us to find his victim in exactly the position we *did* find him in,' Cousins said.

'Because he wanted his victim to be humiliated, even in death?'

'That would explain why he took all his clothes off him,' Cousins said. 'He's a well-built enough feller, but it's hard for anybody to look dignified when they're stark bollock naked.'

Paniatowski knelt down and examined the driving licence. 'If this is his, then his name's Andrew Adair, and he lives at 32 Palmerston Terrace,' she said. 'But we don't know for certain that it *is* his, do we?'

'No, but it's more than likely,' Cousins said.

Yes, it was, Paniatowski agreed. The killer had gone to a lot of trouble to protect the driving licence, and what would have been the point of that if it had belonged to anyone but the dead man?

'Which raises another important question,' she said aloud. 'Why is he making it so easy for us to identify his victim?'

'Now there you've got me, ma'am,' Cousins confessed.

'As soon as we've got a photograph we can use, I want it shown to the residents of Palmerston Terrace,' Paniatowski said.

'But not to the residents of number 32?' Cousins suggested tactfully.

'No, not them,' Paniatowski agreed. 'If he has any family, I don't want them seeing him until Dr Shastri has done what she can to make him look a little more human.'

'You shouldn't expect too much, ma'am,' Cousins cautioned.

Paniatowski felt her heckles rise. '*Why* shouldn't I expect too much?' she demanded. 'Because, when all's said and done, Dr Shastri's only a *Paki*?'

'No,' Cousins replied, with just a hint of rebuke. 'Because it wouldn't be an easy job for any doctor – even one *as good as* Dr Shastri. And she's not Pakistani, ma'am – she's Indian.'

'You're right, of course,' Paniatowski said, with an apology in her voice, if not in her words.

She took her cigarettes out of her pocket – noting as she did that her hands had stopped trembling – and held the packet out to Cousins.

The sergeant shook his head. 'I've given up, ma'am.'

'Wish *I* could,' Paniatowski said. She slotted a cigarette into her own mouth, lit it up, and inhaled deeply. 'I'm going to talk to the owner of the kennels,' she continued. 'Mr Toynbee, is it?'

'Yes, ma'am. Harold Toynbee.'

'So until Inspector Beresford turns up, you'll be in charge here, Sergeant. All right?'

'Fine with me, ma'am,' Cousins said.

The kennels were surrounded by a high wire-mesh fence, and when Paniatowski rang the bell at the gate, the sound was greeted by a series of barks and howls. A man, wearing cord trousers and a rough tweed sports coat with leather patches on the elbows, emerged from a square single-storey brick building, quite close to the entrance, and Paniatowski held up her warrant card for him to see.

'DCI Paniatowski,' she said. 'Are you Mr Toynbee?'

'That's me,' the man admitted.

He was around forty-five years old, Paniatowski guessed. He was a hale and hearty man, with the kind of ruddy complexion which indicated a clear preference for the outdoor life – though on that particular morning the ruddiness was somewhat tinged with grey.

Toynbee unlocked the gate. 'You'd better come into the office, Chief Inspector.'

He led Paniatowski across the yard to the brick building, while all the time the dogs continued their howl of disapproval.

The office itself was divided into two halves. In one half – the business part – there was a desk and a bank of filing cabinets. In the other half – the showroom part – there were two display cabinets filled with winners' cups of various sizes, and whatever wall space was available had been covered with framed certificates.

'That was awarded for Best in Breed at Crufts, three years ago,' Toynbee said, pointing automatically at one of the larger cups in the display cabinet.

'Very impressive,' Paniatowski said.

'We'd have come away with Best in Show, too, if the judges hadn't already decided, before the show even opened, to give the cup to one of the bigger breeds that year,' Toynbee added sourly. 'Course, they *say* they hadn't decided at all. They *say* they always go into it with an open mind. But everybody knows that . . .' He pulled himself up short. 'I'm sorry, I'm babbling. But when I got up this morning, I never expected I'd find a . . . find a . . .'

'Why don't we sit down?' Paniatowski suggested.

'Sit down?' Toynbee repeated. 'Good idea.'

He walked around his desk and plopped down into his chair. He was still in a state of shock, Paniatowski thought, as she took the seat opposite him, but that was more than understandable.

'I've seen dead bodies before,' Toynbee said, as if he felt the need to defend himself. 'Course I have. I helped lay out my own granny. But this was . . . this was something else.'

'Did you get a look at his face?' Paniatowski asked.

'I did,' Toynbee said, almost guiltily. 'I . . . I actually knelt down so I could see it more clearly. I don't know *why* I did that. Do *you* know why I did that?'

'I take it you didn't recognize him,' Paniatowski said.

'God, no! If I'm this cut up over a complete stranger, imagine how I'd have been if it had turned out to be a mate.'

'So you've never heard of Andrew Adair?'

'Don't think so.'

'What time did you find the body?'

'Must have been half-past five. Something like that, anyway. That's when I normally walk the older cockers. No traffic around at that time, you see. Means they can have a good run off the leash.'

'So you arrived here at the kennels at what time, exactly?'

'Didn't *arrive* at all. Never left.'

'I'm sorry?'

'They're valuable dogs, are my cockers. Leave them unguarded, and you could guarantee some thieving bastard would have them away. So somebody always stays here overnight – either me or one of my kennel lads.' He jabbed his thumb in the general direction of the door opposite the office entrance. 'There's a bedroom, bathroom and small kitchen in there. It's comfortable enough.'

'Then you were here all night?'

'That's right. Why?'

'I noticed that when I arrived, the dogs kicked up a hell of a fuss,' Paniatowski said. 'They didn't happen to do the same thing sometime in the night, did they?'

'As a matter of fact, they did,' Harold Toynbee said. 'They had a real howling fit on them at around two o'clock and . . .' He caught his breath, as if he had just realized something that he should have understood a long time ago. 'That'll be when it happened, won't it? That'll be when the bastard dumped the body?'

'How long did this howling fit of theirs last?'

'Twenty or maybe twenty-five minutes.'

'But you didn't get up to investigate whatever it was that was making them so upset?'

'No, I didn't.'

'Why not?'

Toynbee shrugged. 'Last night was a bit extreme, but they often get worked up like that. If there's a fox on the prowl – or even a hedgehog – they can go bloody mad. That's why I had to move the kennels out of town. People were complaining about the racket, you see.'

'Do you always take the dogs into the woods?' Paniatowski asked.

'As a general rule, yes. They like to have a bit of a root around under the trees.'

'And you said the reason you take them out at that time of day is that there's very little traffic around?'

'That's right. On that walk, I can go for days without seeing a single car. Although . . .'

'Although . . .' Paniatowski encouraged.

'Although, a couple of times this week, I have seen a blue Bedford six-hundredweight van driving along the road.'

'The killer will have needed at least a small van to shift him,' Cousins had said.

'You think that might be what the killer used to move the body?' Toynbee said.

'It's a possibility,' Paniatowski admitted. 'Which direction was he travelling in?'

'From Whitebridge to Whalley.'

'Did you get a look at the driver's face?'

'I'm afraid not. On both occasions, I'd gone into the woods by the time the van drew level with me.'

'So you didn't get the number, either?'

'No, he was too far away. And anyway, why would I have bothered to take the number? As far as I was concerned, it was just an ordinary vehicle going about its business.'

'So there was nothing unusual about the van at all?' Paniatowski asked hopefully.

'Well, the driver did seem to be going rather slowly, considering there was a clear road ahead of him,' Toynbee mused.

'Any minute now, it's going to start making sense to him,' Paniatowski thought.

'He was driving slowly so he *wouldn't* draw level with me until I'd gone into the woods, wasn't he?' Toynbee asked.

'Yes, I rather think so.'

'He didn't want me to see his face or be able to take his number.'

'Correct.'

'What he *did* want to do was to make sure that I went into the woods every day.'

'It's certainly looking that way,' Paniatowski agreed.

'Because the bloody swine had me marked down to find the body from the start!' Toynbee exploded.

'Yes,' Paniatowski said softly. 'I rather think he had.'

FIVE

When Monika Paniatowski returned to the scene of the crime, she found it transformed.

An ambulance had arrived, and the two-man crew, having nothing else to do for the moment, were leaning against the side of their vehicle, smoking No. 6 Tipped cigarettes and drinking vacuum-flask-coffee from plastic cups.

Three more patrol cars had appeared, and the uniformed officers who'd been disgorged from them now formed a ragged – though undoubtedly effective – cordon around the edge of the woods.

A battered Land Rover, belonging to Dr Shastri, was parked next to the ambulance, but there was no sign of the good doctor herself, which meant she was probably already in the woods, examining the body.

And finally, there was DI Colin Beresford, standing and watching the whole operation like the conscientious bobby that he was – ensuring that even though there was only the slightest chance that anything *could* possibly go wrong, nothing actually *did*.

'I think the killer may have used a blue Bedford six-hundredweight van to transport the body,' Paniatowski told her inspector.

Beresford whistled softly. 'Christ, if you're right about that, boss, it's a real break at this early stage of the investigation,' he said. 'But what's led you to that conclu—'

'I'll explain later,' Paniatowski said briskly. 'What I want *you* to do, straight away, is to get back to headquarters, assemble your team, and put them right on it.'

Beresford nodded. 'Got it, boss.'

'I need to know who in the Whitebridge area owns a van like that,' Paniatowski continued. 'I want all the owners checked out, and I also need to know if any vans matching that description have been stolen in the last few days.'

'Right,' Beresford agreed.

'I also want the whole of the Whalley road, from Whitebridge to Whalley, thoroughly canvassed. Because though it's highly unlikely that anybody was out and about on it at the ungodly hour of five-thirty in the morning, it's just *possible* they were. And *if* they were, I want to know if they've seen the blue van or its driver any morning this week.'

'But if he only dumped the body this morning . . .'

'I'll explain that later, as well,' Paniatowski said. She looked around her. 'Where's DS Cousins?'

'Gone,' Beresford said.

'Gone?' Paniatowski repeated.

'He said he had a lead that he had to chase up. I thought he must have been acting on your instructions.'

'Well, he bloody well wasn't!' Paniatowski said.

So, despite initial appearances, it was going to be just like Walker all over again, she thought bitterly – another sergeant who resented the fact he had to work for a female DCI, and was already doing all he could to kick her legs from underneath her!

'I'm sorry, boss, I didn't know,' Beresford said. 'He seemed so sure of himself.'

'Yes, his sort always did,' Paniatowski thought.

'It doesn't matter,' she said. 'I'll take charge here. You get back to HQ and start looking for that blue van.'

She turned, and walked into the woods, to be confronted, once she'd reached the clearing, with a sight which almost made her think she was hallucinating.

The corpse was where she had left it, still on its hands and knees, still in the grip of rigor. But projecting from under it were a pair of coffee-brown feet clad in golden sandals, which were in turn attached to a pair of legs wrapped chastely in a flowery sari.

'Ah, so you have arrived, my dear Chief Inspector,' said a voice from somewhere beyond the legs.

Paniatowski walked over to the corpse, and crouched down next to it.

'You look just like a mechanic, examining the underside of a car, Doc,' she said.

'Indeed I do,' Dr Shastri agreed. 'But, of course, a good car mechanic is more much skilled than a simple Indian doctor.'

Shastri extricated herself from the awkward position with the grace and smoothness of a dancer. And when she stood

up, her sari fell back into its natural folds and looked as fresh
as if she had just put it on.

'This is a most interesting case you have brought me,
Monika,' she said. 'The death is easily explained. The poor
man had his throat slashed with what I would guess was some
kind of metal hook. It is what happened to him *after* death
which really fascinates me. He was immediately draped over
some kind of object, in order to mould him into the shape he
is currently assuming.'

'And you're sure this was done *immediately*, are you?'
Paniatowski asked.

'Perhaps not,' Shastri conceded. 'But it was certainly done
within half an hour of death, or there would be clear signs of
livor mortis in the lower extremities.'

'I see,' Paniatowski said thoughtfully. 'So the victim was
draped over this object . . .'

'I would guess it was a packing case of some kind, though
I cannot be definite about that. But what I strongly believe is
that it was neither a random action nor a random object. I
think the killer chose a box – or whatever it was – of just the
right height, in order to produce this pretty little human statue
of his.'

'Why?' Paniatowski asked.

Shastri laughed, and it was like the gentle ringing of golden
temple bells. 'There you go again,' she said.

'I'm sorry?'

'You're asking me to play the detective for you. But I can't.
I do not *know* why the killer did it – unless, perhaps, he is
addicted to the game of necrophilia leapfrog. All I can tell
you is *what* happened.'

Paniatowski grinned. 'I've known you too long to fall for
that line,' she said. 'You've got your own theories. I'm sure
of it.'

'Actually, on this occasion, you are only half-right at best,'
Shastri said. 'I did think, at first, that it may have been done
to humiliate the dead man . . .'

'That's what my sergeant and I thought,' Paniatowski said.

And just where *was* her bloody sergeant? And just what
was he bloody well *doing*?

'Certainly stripping him naked could be seen as wishing to
humiliate him,' Shastri continued, 'but why stop there? Why not

then subject him to what most men would call the *ultimate* humiliation?'

'Which is?'

'Poor, ignorant Indian that I am, I do not know the term an English layman would use to describe it, but we in the medical profession would call it "cutting his knackers off".'

Shastri was quite right, Paniatowski thought. For most men – and this had been a fine strapping specimen of a man – castration would have been the ultimate humiliation.

'In what little time your demanding police force allows me, I have been studying medieval English church tombs,' Shastri said. 'You know the kind of thing I mean, don't you? A supine statue of a knight in armour, sometimes with his lady by his side.'

'I know the kind of thing you mean,' Paniatowski replied, mystified.

'It is perhaps a little morbid of me, but then I am engaged in a morbid profession,' Shastri continued. 'And I do find it fascinating, because each tomb tells its own story to those who have the ability to read it. If the knight has his hands clasped in prayer, it tells us one thing about him. If there is a dog at his feet, it tells us another. In other words, it is all carefully constructed, so that to those who understand, it will mean something.'

'And you're saying that this has been carefully constructed to send a message to someone?' Paniatowski asked.

'Exactly so.'

'But what's the message, and to whom is it being sent?'

'Ah, now we are straying beyond my realms of competence again,' Shastri said.

SIX

The stretcher had not been designed to transport frozen, kneeling men, and the two-man ambulance crew struggled to manoeuvre the corpse into such a position that it would not fall off on the journey through the woods.

'It will be a most interesting post-mortem to perform,' said Dr Shastri, as she watched the process. 'I have not yet decided whether to conduct it with him as you found him or to turn him over on his back, so he looks like a dead hamster.'

Was she really as flippant as she sometimes seemed, or was it just a defence mechanism, Paniatowski wondered.

And then she remembered how wonderfully sensitive Shastri had been when telling her the results of Bob Rutter's post-mortem, and she had her answer.

'You could always break his arms and legs before you went to work on him,' she suggested, playing the doctor's game.

Shastri clicked her tongue disapprovingly. 'Oh dear me, no, that would never do,' she said. 'I am a scientist, not a pork butcher.'

The ambulance men raised the stretcher. The corpse wobbled slightly, but seemed to be about as stable as could be hoped for.

Paniatowski and Shastri formed part of the cortege as it made its way from the clearing to the waiting ambulance.

'I'd like your report on the victim as soon as possible,' Paniatowski said, as they reached the road.

'How unusual to hear you say that,' Shastri replied, with a smile. 'Normally, you are in no hurry at all.' She sighed. 'Do not worry, I will work through the night if needs be. I am quite resigned to my slavery. It is a fate which befalls all police doctors.'

'And you love it,' Paniatowski told her.

An old green Ford Cortina pulled up, and a square man in a blue suit climbed out of it.

'I was wondering if, once this case is over, you and Louisa would like to come to my house for afternoon tea,' Dr Shastri said.

'We'll talk about it later,' Paniatowski said, more abruptly than she'd intended to, as she watched Sergeant Cousins slam his car door and begin to walk towards her.

'Ah, there is trouble in Paradise,' Dr Shastri said, perceptively. 'And that being the case, I will remove myself from the scene as quickly as possible.'

She turned and walked towards her Land Rover, nodding to Cousins as they passed one another.

When he'd drawn level with Paniatowski, the sergeant came to a stop and said, 'I'm back, ma'am.'

'I can see that you're back, but where the bloody hell have you been?' Paniatowski demanded.

Cousins shrank slightly away, as if surprised by the sudden and unexpected vehemence of the attack. 'I was following a lead, ma'am.'

'A lead?'

'The dead man's tattoo.'

'Tattoo?' Paniatowski thought. '*What* tattoo?'

'You see, I knew immediately that it must mean the victim was, or had been, a member of a—' Cousins began.

Paniatowski put up her hand to silence him. The tattoo – if there actually *was* one – might be interesting, but there were other, more important, matters to be dealt with first.

She looked around her. There were a number of unformed constables still within earshot, and it wouldn't have been right for them to hear what was about to follow.

'Let's go up the road a little,' she suggested, though from her tone it was clear that it wasn't a suggestion at all.

'If that's what you want, ma'am,' Cousins said, mystified.

'It *is* what I want,' Paniatowski replied emphatically.

They walked until they were fifty yards away from the woods, then Paniatowski came to an abrupt halt and said, 'So you saw this tattoo, and then you thought that you'd just go swanning off, did you?'

Cousins shrugged. 'Inspector Beresford had arrived by that point, and there didn't seem to be much for me to do here.'

Looking back over her shoulder, Paniatowski saw that both

the ambulance and Dr Shastri's Land Rover were in the process
of executing three-point turns.

'You're my *bagman*,' she told Cousins.

'I know that, ma'am.'

'And what that means is that you carry my bag and perform
any other minor duties I assign to you. What it *doesn't* mean
is that you have the right to go off chasing what *you* consider
to be leads, without telling me first!'

The ambulance drove passed them, quickly followed by the
Land Rover. Paniatowski gave an obligatory wave to Shastri,
but the doctor, as if to keep herself above minor police wran-
gles, had her eyes firmly focused on the road.

Paniatowski turned her attention back to Cousins. The
sergeant was looking troubled.

'Can I speak frankly, ma'am?' he said earnestly.

'Why not?' Paniatowski asked herself. 'If we've got problems, let's get them out in the open.'

'Go ahead,' she told the sergeant.

'I don't imagine you were exactly as chuffed as little apples
when you heard I'd been assigned to your team,' Cousins said.

'Don't you?' Paniatowski asked, deadpan.

'No, ma'am, and I expect that had something to do with
the fact you're naturally wary of anybody who's spent some
time in the nut house.'

'Show a little basic humanity, Monika – just like Charlie
would have done,' Paniatowski advised herself, echoing
Baxter's words.

'You were in hospital,' she said. 'In much the same way as
you would have been if you'd broken a leg.'

'If you don't mind me saying, ma'am, I don't think you're
being entirely honest with me – or with yourself,' Cousins said.

'And suppose I *do* mind you saying it?' Paniatowski
countered.

'Then I'm very sorry to have offended you, but it had to
be said anyway. Look, ma'am, we both *know* they don't put
you in a *straitjacket* in any *normal* hospital. We both *know*
they don't lock you away in a *padded cell* in a *normal* hospital.'
A totally unexpected smile came to his face. 'That's a little
nut-house humour, ma'am,' he explained. 'I was never in a
padded cell. You have to pass *exams* in lunacy before you get
one of them.'

'I don't like having the piss taken out of me, Sergeant!'
Paniatowski said angrily.

Cousins bowed his head. 'You're right, ma'am, I was taking
the piss, and I shouldn't have done,' he admitted contritely.
'But I was trying to make a serious point.'

'Then make it!'

'When my wife died, I went to pieces,' Cousins said, with
a poignancy in his voice that Paniatowski found almost unbear-
able. 'I couldn't cope. I couldn't make decisions. Choosing
what to have for breakfast was a major challenge for me, so
I ended up having nothing at all. That's when I realized I had
to get help. That's when I understood that I needed to be in
a place where all my decisions were taken for me, and where
there was someone paid to listen to me pour out my misery
and – eventually – offer me constructive ideas on recovery.
That was all that was involved – no straitjackets, no electric
shocks – just time and peace.'

The wave of guilt which swept over Paniatowski almost
drowned her. When Bob Rutter – the love of her life – had
been found dead at the foot of that steep hill, she'd almost
gone insane herself. And maybe she would have, if Charlie
Woodend – despite being devastated by Bob's death on his
own account – hadn't nursed her through it.

'I'm so sorry,' she said.

'For what, ma'am?'

'For thinking, even for a moment, that . . .'

'I'm sure you'll have taken a more charitable view of my
condition than a lot of my closer colleagues did – and they're
the ones who should have been making the allowances,'
Cousins said graciously. 'The point is, I may have been lost
for a while, but now I've found myself again.'

'I believe you,' Paniatowski said.

'But I don't think that's the *only* problem we have
over working together, ma'am,' Cousins continued. 'You
see, I've been on the force longer than you have, and that
means—'

'That means you know how to do my job better than I do
myself,' Paniatowski interrupted, as her pity drained away and
anger gushed in the fill the vacuum.

'No, ma'am, it means I've had more of a chance to observe
your career than you've had to observe mine. I saw how you

worked when you were DCI Woodend's bagman. You took chances. You went out a limb. What I did this morning – following my instincts – is just the sort of thing you'd have done when you were *Sergeant* Paniatowski. I'm right about that, aren't I?'

'Maybe,' Paniatowski conceded.

'So why do you fly off the handle with me? I think it's because you're worried that I'll turn out be another Inspector Walker.'

'*Sergeant* Walker,' Paniatowski corrected him.

'So you haven't heard,' Cousins said.

'Heard what?'

'Walker's been promoted, probably as a result of the part he played in solving the Linda Szymborska murder – or, at least, the part he *claims* to have played.'

They couldn't accept it, could they, Paniatowski thought angrily. The brass – and that probably even included George Baxter – simply *couldn't* accept that she could have solved that murder without the help of a man.

'The thing is, ma'am, I'm *not* Ted Walker,' Cousins said. 'I don't mind working for a woman – as long as she's good at her job.'

'And I am?'

'Yes. As far as I've been able to tell, from the outside looking in, you're *very* good,' Cousins said.

'And how about the fact that I'm several years younger than you?' Paniatowski asked sceptically.

'There was a time when I saw myself as a rising star in the Central Lancs Constabulary,' Cousins said, almost musingly, 'a time when I thought I was destined for great things. But I was just fooling myself. I simply haven't got what *you've* got, and what young Beresford – sorry, Inspector Beresford – *will have* some day. I'm not senior officer material.'

'Then *what* are you?'

'What I am is a bloody good bagman – probably the best you'll ever work with. I take my job seriously – always have done – and now . . . well, now, it's just about all I've got left. So I'd be grateful, ma'am, if you'd give me the chance to show you just what I can do.'

Though he managed to hide the fact well, this whole

conversation had been no more than a plea for acceptance on Cousins' part, Paniatowski thought.

'Welcome to the team, Sergeant,' she said, meaning it.

'Thank you, ma'am,' Cousins replied – meaning it too.

SEVEN

So far, they'd been able to keep a lid on the investigation, Paniatowski thought, as she looked at her team, sitting around the table in the Drum and Monkey. So far, the press hadn't even got a whiff of the fact that the body of a naked man had been found in the woods. But that wouldn't last – because in a town like Whitebridge, nothing was *ever* secret for long.

Still, for the moment at least, they had a breathing space: a time in which they could operate without the local – and probably national – reporters breathing down their necks; a time in which half of Colin Beresford's team of junior detectives w*eren't* out on wild-goose chases, investigating calls from people who were probably cranks, but who just might *not* be.

'Let's review what we've got so far,' she said. 'Would *you* like to start, Inspector Beresford?'

Beresford nodded. 'First of all, we've identified the victim,' he said. 'The driving licence left at the scene of the crime . . .'

'Or rather, the place where the body was actually found,' Paniatowski corrected him.

'. . . or rather where the body was actually found,' Beresford agreed, 'belonged to an Andrew Adair, of 32 Palmerston Terrace, and we've been able to establish, by talking to other residents of the street, that the victim is in fact Adair. Further inquiries have established that he's been living there for around six months, that he was the sole resident of the property, and that he seemed to keep pretty much to himself.'

'What about the van that's been seen near the woods twice this week?' Paniatowski said.

'A blue six-hundredweight Bedford van was stolen from the centre of town four nights ago, and was recovered near the Empire Mill this morning,' Beresford said. 'Unfortunately, before the thief abandoned it, he set it on fire.'

'And we've no idea who this thief might be?'

Beresford shook his head. 'Nobody saw him nick it, and nobody saw him burn it.'

Paniatowski turned to Cousins. 'Tell us what you've found out, Sergeant.'

'When I was examining the body in the woods, I noticed that the dead man had a tattoo on the inside of the right arm,' the sergeant said. 'It wasn't very elaborate – just two words in a foreign language. It was all Greek to me, of course,' he laughed, 'though I later found out it wasn't Greek at all, but Latin.' He laid a single sheet of paper on the table. 'These were the words.'

'*Utrinque Paratus*. Ready for anything,' DC Crane said, before he could stop himself.

'I didn't know you spoke any Latin, Jack,' Paniatowski said. 'Where did you learn it?'

'Where else but at bloody *school*,' Crane thought, furious with himself for inadvertently revealing the extent of his education. 'I studied it at advanced level and got a bloody A!'

'I can't *speak* it, as such, ma'am,' he said aloud. 'I've just somehow picked up a few phrases. *Nil illegitimus carborundum* – that's another one I know.' He was wittering, he thought, but didn't know how to get out of it. 'It means, "Don't let the bastards grind you down",' he finished lamely.

'Fascinating,' Paniatowski said, in a tone which clearly implied it wasn't. 'Shall we get back to "Ready for anything", Sergeant?'

'Yes, ma'am,' Cousins agreed. 'It's apparently the motto of the Parachute Regiment, so thinking it was probably a fair bet that the dead man had been a Para himself, I rang up an old mate of mine in the War Office. He was a bit cagey at first, as you can imagine, but once I'd promised to keep his name out of it, he said he'd have a peek at Adair's file and pass on any information that didn't actually endanger national security.'

'And what information *did* he pass on?' Beresford asked.

'That Adair left the army six months ago, after serving for twelve years,' Cousins paused for a second, 'and that he was one of the Paras involved in the Bloody Sunday shootings in Londonderry.'

If Cousins had been expecting this revelation to be something of a bombshell, he was not disappointed. Bloody Sunday had shocked the whole country, and just the mention of it – in connection with someone involved in their investigation – was enough to reawaken that shock in the team now.

The afternoon of Sunday the 30th of January 1972.

A demonstration of Irish Catholic civil-rights marchers, in Derry.

The demonstrators – thirty thousand strong by some accounts – had been planning to march to the Guildhall, but the army has set up barricades to prevent that, and instead the marchers are diverted to a place called Free Derry Corner.

Some of the younger demonstrators break away from the main group, and start hurling stones at the barricades, but there is nothing new – nothing unusual – in this.

Unconfirmed reports begin to filter into army headquarters that an Irish Republican Army unit has sent a sniper into the area, and that some of the marchers are carrying nail bombs on their persons.

The tension mounts.

Nerves, already frayed, become ragged.

At seven minutes past four, the Paras are sent into the heart of the demonstration, with orders to start making arrests.

What happens next is still disputed. The soldiers say they came under fire, but the marchers themselves – as well as the spectators and the journalists sent to cover the event – disagree. What is beyond dispute is that the Paras fire a hundred rounds of ammunition straight into the crowd.

Thirteen demonstrators are killed – some of them shot in the back as they run away, one as he waves a white handkerchief and tries to help a wounded friend.

The official report, published only eleven weeks later, confirms the army's version of events, but there is not a Catholic in the whole of Ireland who doesn't see it as a whitewash.

'So you think this murder is related to Bloody Sunday, do you?' Beresford asked, breaking the silence that had fallen over the team.

'Be a bit of a coincidence if it wasn't, don't you think?' Paul Cousins replied. 'I mean, it's not as if Adair's *just* been murdered, is it? He's been tortured, and then stripped naked.

Whoever killed him must have really bloody hated him. And what else could he possibly have done in his life to have brought so much hatred down on him?'

But still Beresford did not seem convinced.

'The thing is,' he said, 'there have been IRA executions before, and they've never gone in for anything as elaborate as that. What they normally do is make the victim kneel down and then shoot him in the back of the head.'

Cousins shrugged. 'Then maybe you're right, sir. Maybe it's not punishment for his part in Bloody Sunday. But in that case, what the hell is it?'

A good question, Paniatowski thought. Dr Shastri had speculated that the killer had posed his victim in that way in order to send a message, but had had no idea what that message might be.

And Dr Shastri was not alone in that!

Paniatowski didn't see the uniformed constable enter the bar, and it was not until he was standing directly opposite her that she even knew he was there.

'Sorry to disturb you, ma'am, but the chief constable would like to see you,' the constable told her.

'Did he say what it was about?'

'No, ma'am, he didn't. He just said that I'm to drive you back to headquarters right away.'

Paniatowski knocked back her remaining vodka, and stood up.

This was the second time in two days she'd been summoned to George Baxter's office, she reminded herself. The first time it had been in order to have Paul Cousins foisted on her. That, it was true, seemed to be working out much better than she'd ever expected it to – but she didn't think she could be so lucky twice.

The moment Paniatowski entered Baxter's office and saw the man sitting across the coffee table from him, she knew that her worst fears had been realized.

The visitor was wearing a herring-bone suit which probably came from one of the best bespoke tailors on Savile Row. He had silvery hair, cut in a deceptively simple way, which shone as if it were *real* silver, and his glowing pink skin was almost entirely free of wrinkles.

He looked the perfect English gentleman, Paniatowski thought.

So smooth, so sophisticated and – above all – so civilized.

And that was exactly what he was – on the surface. But underneath that well-tailored suit and immaculate grooming there lurked a dark savage beast that knew no pity or remorse – that would do whatever was necessary to get its way.

She hated this man, she despised him, and – though she would not admit it, even to herself – she was also, perhaps, a little frightened of him.

The chief constable stood up. 'Ah, Monika,' he said, with a false heartiness which revealed just how uncomfortable *he* was with the situation. 'I believe you already know Mr Forsyth, who works for the Ministry of . . .' He paused and looked down at the other man. 'Which ministry did you say?'

'Just *the* ministry,' Forsyth replied, enigmatically.

Baxter ran his fingers through his mop of ginger hair.

'Mr Forsyth would like a chat with you, Monika,' he said awkwardly.

'A *chat*?' Paniatowski repeated.

'That's what you said, wasn't it?' Baxter asked the seated man.

The corners of Forsyth's mouth crinkled into a half-smile. 'I believe what I actually said was "a *cosy* chat",' he replied.

'So if you'll excuse me . . .' Baxter said, still addressing Forsyth.

'Of course,' Forsyth agreed.

Baxter crossed the room in one direction, his chief inspector in the other. As they met in the middle, the chief constable gave Paniatowski a look which said that the last thing he wished to do was leave her alone with Forsyth, but the matter was out of his hands.

Paniatowski kept on walking towards the coffee table. She didn't *want* to do it. What she *wanted* to do was turn around, leave the room, and not stop until she was outside the building and could gulp in some clean, fresh air, free of Whitehall poison. Yet there was no choice in the matter, and on legs which were tingling so much they might almost have been trembling, she *forced* herself to continue until she came to a halt next to Baxter's chair.

Forsyth did not stand up and offer her his hand, though it

was not any lack of manners which had prevented him from doing so. Like everything else about him, his manners were impeccable, and what held him back was the knowledge that if he offered her his hand, she would not take it.

As the chief constable stepped into the corridor, closing the door behind him, Forsyth said, 'Do please sit down, Chief Inspector.'

Paniatowski sat, because, she told herself, not to do so would show Forsyth just how disturbed she was.

'As if he doesn't *already* know!' she thought, angry with herself.

Forsyth reached into his briefcase, and produced two silver hip flasks and two small glasses. He placed the glasses on the table, unscrewed one of the hip flasks and poured its contents into the first glass.

'Single malt,' he said.

He unscrewed the second flask, and poured the clear liquid into the second glass.

'Vodka,' he told her. 'Zubrowka.'

'Am I supposed to be impressed by that?'

'*I* would be, in your position. Many experts consider Zubrowka to be the finest vodka in the world, and I happen to know that it's *your* favourite tipple.'

'You *know* that, do you?' Paniatowski asked.

'For a fact,' said Forsyth, with all the certainty of a man who was never wrong, because if he *was* wrong, the rules were quickly re-written to make him *right*. 'Yes, your favourite tipple. But you can't get your hands on it often, can you, Monika – because it's very much in demand with the bigwigs in the Polish Communist Party?'

It was all games with this evil bastard, Paniatowski thought. And the frightening thing was that, half the time, they worked.

Forsyth took a sip of his malt, and smacked his lips appreciatively.

'You're not drinking,' he said.

'No, I'm not, am I?' Paniatowski agreed.

'I haven't seen you since you were a mere sergeant, DCI Paniatowski,' Forsyth said amiably. 'If you remember, we met when you were working with Cloggin'-it Charlie Woodend, on that rather nasty little business down at the old Haverton Army Camp.'

Paniatowski said nothing.

'You *do* remember, don't you?' Forsyth asked.

'I remember,' Paniatowski said. 'And I also remember that other *rather nasty little business*, when you personally blocked the criminal prosecution of half a dozen snivelling ex-public schoolboys who worked for the War Department, and who should definitely have been banged up for a long, long time.'

'Ah yes,' Forsyth agreed. 'But I was only involved on the periphery of that little affair, and I must admit, I'd quite forgotten it.'

'You're a liar!' Paniatowski said.

Forsyth smiled. 'Don't you think you're being a little harsh, Chief Inspector?' he asked mildly.

'A man like you doesn't forget,' Paniatowski told him. 'You hoard every dirty trick you've ever pulled in some festering corner of your mind, and when you've got a little time free you re-live each and every one of them, and tell yourself what a splendid patriot you are.'

For a moment it looked as if Forsyth would lose his equanimity, then his face settled back into its bland mask

'As much as I might enjoy these gentle sparring sessions of ours, we both know that they're of no real consequence,' he said, his voice hardening almost imperceptibly. 'We both know, in fact, that I'm here for a purpose, that eventually I will tell you what I want you to do to fulfil your part in that purpose, and that you will do it – because you have no choice in the matter.'

He was right, Paniatowski thought. Even Charlie Woodend had had to bend to the might of the Secret Service.

'Tell me what you want,' she said.

'I want you to investigate the murder of Andrew Adair as you would investigate any other murder. But I want to be kept abreast of all your findings.'

'Why?' Paniatowski asked.

'That's really none of your concern,' Forsyth said dismissively.

'It might help my investigation to know why you're interested in him,' Paniatowski pointed out.

'Possibly it would,' Forsyth conceded.

'But you're still not going to tell me?'

'No.'

'I assume he was working for you.'

'If it makes you happy to assume that, my dear chief inspector, then by all means feel free to do so.'

'But you're still not going to tell me in what *capacity* Adair was working for you?'

'Since I've refused to even confirm that he *was* working for me, that seems highly unlikely.'

'So let me see if I've got this straight,' Paniatowski said. 'You want me to catch the killer for you, but you don't want to tell me anything that might assist me in catching him?'

She looked down at her hand, and was surprised to discover that, without even realizing it – and certainly without appreciating it – she had drunk the vodka that Forsyth had poured for her.

Seeing the look of self-disgust on her face, the spy smiled briefly at his small triumph.

'As I think I've already explained, in terms simple enough for anyone to understand,' he said, 'what I *want* you to do is treat this particular case as you would treat any other, except that you will be keeping me appraised of the details.'

The air in her office was thick with cigarette smoke when Paniatowski entered it, a clear indication that her team were as worried as she had been by the unexpected summons – though they, as yet, had no idea what they should be worried *about*.

'Do you remember a feller from London called Forsyth, Colin?' she asked her inspector.

'Forsyth?' Beresford mused. 'Silver hair, plummy voice, God's gift to espionage?'

'That's the man,' Paniatowski agreed. 'He's back with us again.'

'Well, bugger me,' Beresford said.

He'd said the words as if Forsyth was no more than a mild irritant, like a wasp at a picnic, Paniatowski thought. But that was because Colin didn't know Forsyth as she did – had never had a real glimpse of the black depths of the man. And perhaps it was as well that he *didn't* know – that she should have to bear the true strain of Forsyth's presence alone.

She briefly outlined what the spy had told her.

'If Sergeant Cousins is right, and we are dealing with the IRA here, then what Forsyth is doing is using us as human mine-detectors,' Paniatowski said, growing angrier by the minute. 'We find his target, get blown to hell so he knows where it is, then he moves in. Well, I won't have it! I won't put my team at risk like that!'

'With respect, ma'am, the only way you can avoid that situation is by doing no *investigating* at all,' Sergeant Cousins said. 'And though I don't know you as well as the others do, I can't see you going for that option at all.'

He was right, of course, Paniatowski thought. She couldn't just walk away from an investigation. But if there had to be risk, she could at least make sure that it was as low a risk as possible.

'I want your lads confined to purely routine tasks that can't possibly get them into trouble,' she told Beresford. 'Any serious investigating will be done by me.'

'By *us*,' Beresford said firmly.

'That's right,' Cousins agreed, 'by *us*.'

'Count me in, too, ma'am,' Crane said.

'I don't want you involved in the actual investigation, Jack,' Paniatowski told the detective constable.

Crane looked hurt. 'That's not fair, ma'am.'

'What I want *you* to do is to watch Forsyth,' Paniatowski explained.

'Watch him, ma'am?'

'We need to know what game he's playing. We have to find out why he won't tell us exactly what job Adair was doing for him. And that means watching him.'

'You want me to watch a *spy*?' Crane asked, incredulously. 'You want me to *follow* a man trained to spot the KGB?'

'He's not that kind of spy,' Paniatowski said. 'I don't get the impression that he's ever been one of the pieces on the chessboard of espionage.'

'Then what *is* he?'

'He's the bastard who moves the pieces around – and sacrifices them without a second's thought. He wouldn't spot a KGB agent if he had his rank tattooed on his forehead – and I doubt he'll spot a fresh-faced young detective constable, either.'

'Spying on the spy master,' Colin Beresford said reflectively. 'If it goes wrong, we could all get screwed to the wall.'

'Meaning we shouldn't do it?' Paniatowski asked.

'Meaning I don't think he's left us much choice in the matter,' Beresford replied.

EIGHT

The press briefing room was one of the 'innovations' introduced by the previous chief constable, a man more interested in the way crime was reported than why it was committed or how it was solved. The room itself was located just off the main foyer of police headquarters. It was oblong, and had two entrances – one at the back for the hacks, one at the front for the officer who would be giving the briefing. The officer in question gave the briefing from a raised podium, which the chief constable thought gave him increased authority, but had always made Charlie Woodend feel like a shameless politician running for office.

Monika Paniatowski had never liked these press conferences, and liked them even less since the Linda Szymborska murder investigation had attracted national press attention, and, in the process, had made her a minor celebrity. Some of her colleagues, she knew, envied her this celebrity status – some of them would given their right arm to have had a little of it themselves – but, as she saw it, a detective's job was to detect, and anything which got in the way of that was to be avoided!

'Don't get your kickers in a twist about it, boss,' Colin Beresford had advised her, when she'd complained about it to him. 'Fame is a fleeting thing, and will soon fade away.'

And maybe it would, she thought, as she mounted the podium and looked down at the assembled journalists and the two camera crews from regional television stations – but there was no evidence of it fading away quite yet.

Unless, of course, she wasn't the reason they were there at all, she thought, with sudden concern. Because it was *just* possible there had been a leak in police headquarters – *just* possible that what had brought them all crawling out of the woodwork was some knowledge of the bizarre nature of the murder – and that really was the *last* thing she wanted.

She faced her audience with much greater calm and self-assurance than she would have been able to display even a month earlier.

'This morning, at around five-thirty, the police were called to a piece of woodland just off the Whalley road,' she said. 'There they discovered the body of a man, who has since been identified as Andrew Adair. Mr Adair was thirty-six years old and died as a result of wounds inflicted to his throat. We are treating his death as suspicious.' She paused for a second. 'That's all I have to say at the moment. I am now willing to take questions, though – as always – I am not prepared to say anything which I feel may prejudice my investigation.'

As she'd been speaking, she'd also been scanning the audience for potential problems, and had soon found one sitting right there on the front row.

Mike Traynor – staff reporter for the *Lancashire Evening Chronicle*, and stringer for at least two of the more sensational national newspapers.

Mike Traynor – his collar drowning in dandruff, his foxy eyes searching for a weakness in her statement that he could use as the basis of an attack.

Their history was short, but bitter.

Paniatowski would never forgive him for the way he had questioned her conduct of the Szymborska case – her first investigation as a DCI.

Traynor, for his part, would never forgive her for solving the case so successfully that he'd been forced by his editor to publish a grovelling apology.

But it was not Traynor who made the initial attempt to breach her defences and trick her into admitting to something she'd rather have kept herself. Instead, the initial salvo was fired by Lydia Jenkins, rising star of the local radio station.

'So Adair's throat was *slashed*, was it?' Jenkins asked, innocently.

'Slashed!' Paniatowski repeated silently. 'Yes, you could call it that. In fact, it wouldn't be an exaggeration to say it had been ripped to bloody shreds!'

'As I told you, Lydia, he died as a result of injuries sustained to his throat,' she said aloud. 'And I'm afraid that's as far as I'm prepared to go at the moment.'

'Was he a local man?' asked Bill Haynes, a journalist from the *Telegraph*, the *Chronicle*'s main rival.

Now *that* was a question she'd been expecting, Paniatowski

thought. Local papers were always most interested in local people. In fact, the formula was quite simple – the death of one local man equalled the death of two other Lancastrians, four northerners, fifty southerners or a hundred foreigners.

'He was living locally, but originally he came from Oxfordshire, and had recently been a serving member of the armed forces,' Paniatowski said.

Mike Traynor raised his sweaty paw in the air for permission to speak, and Paniatowski nodded to him.

'Was there anything unusual about the crime?' Traynor asked.

'We like to think that murder is *always* unusual,' Paniatowski told him. 'We'd be in a pretty poor state of affairs if it wasn't.'

But she was thinking, 'Does he know anything the others don't know? Has his snitch on the Force leaked the fact that Adair was naked, and was positioned on his hands and knees?'

'Yes, murder *is* unusual,' Traynor agreed reasonably. 'What I meant was, are there any particularly unusual *circumstances* surrounding this murder?'

Did he know? Did he bloody *know*?

'What is it you're expecting, exactly?' Paniatowski asked. 'Evidence of witchcraft, perhaps? Nazi memorabilia scattered all over the area? Singed grass where an alien flying saucer landed?'

'Well, no,' Traynor said uncomfortably, as the reporters on either side of him sniggered quietly. 'I just wondered if maybe . . .'

He didn't know a thing, Paniatowski thought, with relief. Not a bloody thing.

'There are other aspects to the case which are unusual,' she conceded, 'but I'm certainly not prepared to release the details yet. Are there any other questions?'

All the other reporters had their eyes fixed on Mike Traynor, waiting to hear what his comeback would be.

Traynor himself seemed to be blissfully unaware of their interest – or of his own humiliation – and instead appeared to be casually lighting up a cigarette.

But that was only on the outside. Inside, he was boiling with rage.

He would fix this bitch good and proper, he promised himself. He would fix her if it was the last thing he ever did.

*   *   *

The houses which made up Palmerston Terrace had been erected hurriedly, in the previous century, to accommodate the families who had abandoned the countryside in order to work in the booming cotton industry.

Each house had been built with two rooms upstairs and two rooms down. The focal point of these dwellings had been the kitchen, in which a blazing fire – kept burning even during the summer months – served both to warm the cottage and heat the oven in which most of the cooking was done. The front room – the parlour – was reserved for weddings and funerals, until the family grew to such an extent that it was no longer possible to cram any more kids in the bedrooms upstairs, at which point it became an extension dormitory. There was a back yard which contained the washhouse and the cottage's only tap, and a smaller building which the authorities referred to as the 'sanitary closet' and the people who actually used it called 'the lavvy'.

Over the years, the houses had been modified somewhat. Most of them now had an inside bathroom – at the expense of one of the upstairs bedrooms – and electric stoves had replaced the old coal-fired range. But the exteriors of the cottages had changed little, and any of the original inhabitants, staring up at them from the cobbled street, would have felt quite at home.

No. 32 Palmerston Terrace was where Andy Adair had spent the last few months of his life, and so had ceased to be merely one house sandwiched in the middle of a row of identical houses, and had become the focus of interest of the police investigation.

Not that there seemed much of anything to be actually interested *in*, DS Cousins thought, as he watched his team carefully combing through Adair's personal effects.

Adair had owned one good suit, two jackets and three pairs of trousers, all of which were hung neatly in the wardrobe. His socks, vests and underpants had been stored in drawers, with military precision and neatness. If he had been a reading man there was no evidence of it in the cottage, and if he had been a writing man he was clearly one who did not retain his correspondence.

In other words, Cousins told himself, the team knew no more about the man now than they had when they had first entered the cottage.

He looked out of the parlour window and saw two middle-aged women standing together on the opposite side of the street. They both had brooms in their hands – as if they felt the need to justify their presence – but it was clear that their interest was less in sweeping than it was in watching how events were unfolding in No. 32.

Cousins stepped out of the front door and walked across the street to where they were standing.

'Are you in charge?' asked one of the women, before he had a chance to speak himself.

'Yes, I am,' Cousins confirmed.

'So what's going on?' the woman demanded.

'Oh, you've got a cheek, you have, Edna,' the other woman said, though she did not actually *sound* disapproving.

'The way I look at it, Betty,' the first woman said, 'is that if you never ask, you'll never find out. So what *is* goin' on?' she asked Cousins a second time. 'Is it true that feller's been murdered?'

'Yes, I'm afraid it is,' Cousins replied.

'Oh, what a shame!' said Betty, as she did her best to cover her look of salacious curiosity with a veneer of regret.

'Well, who would ever have thought it?' asked Edna, as she, too, attempted to form the appropriate expression of shock and concern.

'Did you know Mr Adair well?' Cousins said.

'Didn't know him at all,' Edna replied. 'He kept himself to himself. Didn't talk to the neighbours . . .'

'He was always pleasant enough to *me* when I spoke to him on the street,' Betty pointed out.

'*Pleasant enough* isn't the same as *talkin*',' Edna said sharply. 'You've got to be accurate when you're speakin' to the police.' She paused for a second. 'Now where was I?'

'Pleasant but not talkative,' Cousins prompted.

'That's right. He didn't have mates callin' round on him, either, an' single men – without a wife to put her foot down – *always* have their mates callin' round on them. Still,' she lowered her voice as if she were about to impart a great secret, 'he *was* a southerner, you know.'

'So I believe,' Cousins said. He made a half turn. 'Well, since he kept himself to himself so much, and there's nothing you can tell me about him . . .'

'I never said I couldn't tell you *nothin'*,' Edna said hastily.

An amused smile flickered briefly across Cousins' face, but was gone by the time he was looking directly at the women again.

'I'm listening,' he said.

'Mr Adair kept odd hours,' Edna told him.

'Odd?'

'It was a rare day he opened his bedroom curtains before eleven o'clock in the morning – not that I was looking, you understand.'

'Of course I understand,' Cousins agreed. 'You weren't *looking*, but you couldn't help *seeing*.'

'Well, exactly,' Edna agreed, folding her arms across her ample bosom, as if she was glad that had been made clear.

'On the other hand, he was out very late,' Betty said, making her second attempt to get a foothold in the conversation.

'What do you mean by "late"?' Cousins asked.

'He never came home until the pubs closed,' Betty said.

'Sometimes he was even later than that,' Edna added, quickly recapturing the initiative.

'How could he be later than that?' Betty asked sceptically. 'Once the pubs are closed, there's nowhere else to go, and men *always* make their way home. It's a well-known fact, is that.'

'A well-known fact it may be, but I'm tellin' you that he sometimes didn't come home until four or five in the mornin'.'

'How would you know that?' Betty challenged.

Edna looked embarrassed.

'I sometimes have to get up in the middle of the night to ... you know,' she said, with some reluctance. She turned to her friend, though perhaps turned *on* her friend would have been more accurate. 'An' don't you go pretendin' you don't do the same, Betty Openshaw, because *all* women of our age have the same problem.'

'I never said a word,' Betty countered, adding, almost under her breath, 'but I *am* four years younger than you.'

'Anyway, I'd sometimes look out of my window and see him walkin' up the street.'

'Walking up the street *how*?'

'Puttin' one foot in front of the other,' Edna replied, clearly puzzled by the question.

'What I mean is, was he staggering from side to side, as men often are when they come home late?'

'No, he wasn't,' Edna said, as if she'd just received a revelation. 'I always *assumed* he'd been out on the batter, but now I think about it, he didn't seem drunk at all.'

They had arranged to meet at a pub called the Pig and Whistle, mainly because neither of them was known there.

The newly promoted Inspector Walker arrived first, and thus had ample opportunity to study Mike Traynor as the journalist crossed the bar.

And the man didn't look happy, Walker thought. He *definitely* didn't look happy.

Traynor dropped down into the chair opposite Walker with all the grace of a dumped sack of potatoes.

'The bitch!' he said. 'The bloody bitch!'

Walker, who never failed to draw pleasure from others' discomfort – even if the 'other', in this case, was an ally of his – couldn't resist grinning.

'I take it that you're talking about our dear Detective Chief Inspector Paniatowski,' he said.

'She's getting better at giving these press conferences, you know,' Traynor complained.

'Some people might think that was a good thing,' Walker said, still extracting as much fun out of the moment as he could.

'Some people might think it, but I'm not one of them,' Traynor said. 'The thing is, she's developed this trick of sounding as if she's being frank and open. And she's got *so* good at it that most of the morons who pass themselves off as journalists are taken in. But not me. Not Mike Traynor.'

'So she didn't tell you anything useful?' Walker asked.

'No,' Traynor agreed. His eyes narrowed. 'And neither have you.'

It was Walker's turn to start feeling uncomfortable. 'That's because there's nothing to tell at the moment. Whatever happened out in the woods, *Ma'am*'s keeping a tight lid on it.'

'I pay you for information, not excuses,' Traynor said tartly.

How things had changed, Walker thought. Only a few weeks earlier, when the journalist had been unsure of him, their relationship had been like a courtship, with Traynor making all of the running.

'If DCI Paniatowski's not doing her job properly, then it's your duty as a member of the police force – and the well-being of that force is where your loyalty truly lies – to make the general public aware of that failing. And, of course – though I know this wouldn't sway you one way or the other – there might be a bit of money in it for you.'

That was what Traynor had said back then.

But now the journalist was like a man who, having coaxed his bride to the altar, no longer saw the need to make any effort. Now, in Traynor's eyes, his police source was no more than a drudge – bought and paid for.

Many a man would have been hurt by such a change in attitude, Walker thought, but the truth was that it didn't really bother him *what* Traynor thought of him, as long as the money kept coming in.

Besides, he told himself, whatever the journalist might think, *he* was still the one in control, because if Traynor *really* started to annoy him, he could always arrest the bastard on some trumped-up charge. If he did that, of course, Traynor would try to drag him down, too, based on the bribes he'd paid out. But without the money as evidence, it would just sound like sour grapes – and they'd *never* find the money, however hard they looked!

'I'll try and get you something with a bit more meat to it,' the inspector told the journalist, 'but since it's going to be harder work and more risk for me, it will naturally cost you a little more than usual.'

'Don't push it,' Traynor threatened.

'And don't you try bullying me,' Walker said. 'Or *bullshitting* me, either. You'd sell your own granny to raise the money you needed to bring *Ma'am* down – and we both know it.'

'I'll pay well for good information,' Traynor conceded. 'But you'd better make sure it *is* good.'

'Like I said, I'll do what I can,' Walker replied. 'Are you stopping for a drink?'

Traynor shook his head, and clouds of dandruff fell to his collar like a gentle early snow.

'There's no time for boozing today,' his lips said. 'I've got to get back to the office.'

But what his *eyes* said was, 'The way I feel about you at

this minute, I'd rather cut my own arm off than have a drink with you.'

Walker watched Traynor walk to the door, then was suddenly aware that someone else was standing next to the chair that the journalist had just vacated. He turned, and saw that the new arrival was a man who had silver hair and was wearing an expensive-looking herringbone suit.

'Would you mind if I joined you, Inspector Walker?' the new arrival asked mildly.

'Yes, I bloody well would mind,' Walker growled.

'Really?' the man with the silver hair said.

'Really!' Walker repeated.

'I'm sorry you feel like that,' the silver-haired man replied. And then he sat down anyway.

NINE

The cafe was a greasy spoon, located just off the market square. The moment he entered the door, DI Beresford had it tagged. It was the sort of place that only invested in a single teaspoon, and even *that* was kept chained to the counter – an establishment in which the dishcloths were rinsed out once a week, whether they needed it or not. It was *not*, in other words, somewhere he would normally have considered going in to – except when leading a police raid – but it was where Sid Eccleston had insisted they meet, and so there he was.

'I use this place as my office,' Eccleston said, as he rolled himself a wafer-thin cigarette on the grimy Formica tabletop. 'Yes, surprising as it might seem to you, I run my entire business empire from a humble little place like this.' He winked at Beresford, as if he were about to teach him a valuable lesson. 'It helps cut down on the expenses, you see, Inspector.'

And any cockroach you can catch is probably yours to keep, Beresford thought.

Eccleston was around forty-five years old, the inspector guessed, and was one of those men who took little pride in their personal appearance – the state of his teeth was ample evidence of that – but who were wildly impressed with what they thought they'd accomplished in life.

'When the Calcutta Mill closed down, most of the lads I'd worked with blew their redundancy payments in the first few months,' Eccleston said, in a self-satisfied manner. 'They just pissed it away! They bought new cars, and big television sets. They had fitted carpets laid in their front rooms, and took their families off to Spain for their holidays.'

'But not you,' Beresford said, as he knew he was expected to.

'But not me,' Eccleston agreed emphatically. 'Them old workmates of mine thought they'd soon get *new* jobs in *new* mills, but I knew that kind of job was never coming back to Whitebridge.' He paused, and looked down at the mug in front of him. 'You're not expecting *me* to pay for these teas, are you? I mean, when all's said and done, I am giving up my valuable time to assist you in your inquiries, so it wouldn't be unreasonable to expect the police force to provide the liquid refreshment.'

'Well, our expenses are very tightly controlled, and don't normally run as far as providing cups of tea for witnesses,' Beresford said, deadpan, 'but since your time *is* so valuable, I think we can make an exception to the rule on this occasion.'

'That's all right, then,' Eccleston said. 'Now where was I? Oh yes, I knew the jobs were never coming back, so I invested my redundancy money in a couple of terraced houses, and started renting them out immediately.'

'It was that easy, was it?'

'Simplicity itself, if you're smart enough to grasp an opportunity when it's presented to you. See, there's plenty of newly-married couples living in the in-laws' back bedroom, and desperate to get out. But they don't have the capital for it, do they? Then I come along and offer them an escape – and if the place I rent them is a bit old-fashioned, or has a touch of damp, they're not going to complain as long as I'm not charging more than they can afford to pay.'

'You make yourself sound almost philanthropic,' Beresford said.

'Here, there's nothing bent about me,' Eccleston, as if he'd just been insulted. 'I'm a simple, honest Whitebridge man, born and bred.'

'Of course you are,' Beresford agreed. 'I certainly never meant to suggest otherwise.'

'Anyway, when them first two properties started turning a profit, I bought a couple more,' Eccleston continued, somewhat mollified. 'And ask me how many I've got now.'

'How many have you got now?' Beresford asked.

'Fifteen! All of them occupied, and all of them bringing me in a regular income.'

'And one of them was occupied by Andy Adair,' Beresford said, getting to the real point of this meeting.

'That's right, it was,' Eccleston agreed. He frowned. 'That place could be a bit of a problem to me, now, couldn't it?'

'Could it?'

'Well, yes. I mean, my tenant's been *murdered*. Admittedly, it could have been worse – he could have been killed on the actual *property* – but even so, some people are a bit squeamish about renting a house that was once occupied by a man who met a violent death.'

'Some people are *over-fussy*,' Beresford said.

'You've hit the nail right on the head,' Eccleston agreed enthusiastically. 'Some people *are* over-fussy. Still, knowing that doesn't really help matters, does it?' He sighed. 'If I want to get anybody in that house soon, I'm going to have to lower the rent, you know.'

'You'd have thought, wouldn't you, that before Adair allowed himself to get killed, he'd have considered the inconvenience that he would be causing you?' Beresford said dryly.

'What?' Eccleston asked, obviously puzzled. Then he gave a thin laugh. 'Oh, I see. It's a joke.'

'That's certainly one way of looking at it,' Beresford agreed. 'How did Adair happen to rent the house from you?'

'He came recommended.'

'Who by?'

'By a lad called Harry Quinn, who I've known for years. They'd done a bit of soldiering together. Harry said Adair was a good sort, and I was prepared to take his word for it.'

'And was he a good *tenant*, as well as a good *sort*?'

'A perfect one. Always paid his rent on time, and if there were any repairs needed doing round the house, he'd do them himself, instead of bothering me – like most of my bloody tenants do.'

'Where did he work?' Beresford asked.

'Work?' Eccleston repeated.

'Work,' Beresford agreed.

'Do you know, now you mention it, I've absolutely no idea.'

'So as far as you're aware, he might have had no job at all?'

'It's possible.'

'Then weren't you taking a bit of a chance by renting the house to him in the first place?'

Eccleston grinned. 'No chance at all. Taking chances is not the way I operate. He paid me three months' deposit in advance. In cash!' Eccleston suddenly looked a little concerned. 'That needn't go down in your report, need it?'

'Why? Because you haven't declared the money he gave you?'

'Look, lad, I'll buy the teas,' Eccleston said hastily.

Beresford smiled. 'That's very generous of you.'

'Think nothing of it. And as to that other matter . . .'

'Yes?'

'I meant to declare the income, but I somehow haven't quite got round to it. So if you could just give me a couple of days to get my records up to date . . .'

Beresford frowned. 'I don't know,' he said dubiously. 'That's asking a lot, that is.'

'And if there's anything I can do in return . . .'

'How many of your houses have young children living in them?' Beresford asked.

Eccleston shrugged. 'I don't know. Seven or eight.'

'And how many of those houses with young children in them have had damp-proof courses installed?'

'That's hard to say, off-hand.'

'Take a guess,' Beresford suggested.

'Well, none, I suppose,' Eccleston admitted.

'So you knowingly house children in damp dwellings, do you?'

'Doesn't do them any real harm,' Eccleston protested.

'Bollocks!' Beresford said. 'Look, I'll make a deal with you.'

'What kind of deal?'

'Get damp-proof courses installed in all your houses within the week, and you'll hear no more from me about undeclared income.'

'Do you know how much a bloody damp-proof course costs, Inspector?' Eccleston asked, outraged.

'No, I don't,' Beresford admitted. 'But do *you* know how thorough the Inland Revenue can be, once they start going over your books? And do *you* know that if they *do* find evidence of tax fraud, you could actually go to prison?'

'I'll get them damp courses installed,' Eccleston promised.

'You'd better, Mr Eccleston,' Beresford replied, 'because I'll be checking up on you.'

The man with the silver hair had been sitting opposite Inspector Walker, in what appeared to be comfortable silence, for at least five minutes.

Walker himself was sipping moodily at his beer, and

wondering why he was tolerating the man's presence. There was, he supposed, no reason at all why he hadn't told him to just sod off – except that he didn't look like the kind of man you *could* tell to sod off.

'Have you got a name?' he asked finally.

'Of course. How rude of me not to have introduced myself before,' the silver-haired man said. 'My name's Forsyth.'

Walker grimaced at his accent. 'Foreigner, are you?' he asked.

'No, as a matter of fact, I'm from London.'

'That's what I said – a foreigner,' Walker replied, feeling a little better for having scored a point. 'So what can I do for you, Mr Forsyth?'

'I couldn't help noticing that you were just in earnest conversation with Mr Traynor of the *Lancashire Evening Chronicle*,' Forsyth said.

'In earnest conversation? I was *talking* to him, if that's what you mean. Not that that's any of your business.'

'Ah, but it is my business,' Forsyth said mildly. 'You see, I work for the government.'

'So what? I can talk to *whoever* I like, *whenever* I like. It's still a free country, isn't it?'

Forsyth laughed, dismissively. 'A free country?' he repeated. 'You're surely not still naive enough to believe that fairy tale, are you, Inspector?'

Enough was enough, Walker decided. Though his instincts were screaming against it, it was time to show this man just whose patch this was.

'I believe it enough to believe that I've got the right to tell you to bugger off,' he said.

A bit clumsy, that, he thought, but at least he'd got his message across.

Except that, apparently, he hadn't. Because instead of getting up and leaving, as he was supposed to, Forsyth was doing no more than shaking his head slowly from side to side.

'I *could* go,' the Londoner said. 'And I will – if you insist. But you'd be making a big mistake to let me.'

'Would I? Why?'

'Because I know a great deal about you, and what I know can be used either against you or for your benefit.'

'That's a load of bollocks,' Walker said.

Forsyth sighed. 'Really? Tell me, Inspector Walker, do you know where your wife is living at the moment?'

'Leave my wife out of this,' Walker said aggressively.

'Which means, I take it, that you have absolutely no idea at all where she is,' Forsyth replied. 'But, you see, I have. Mrs Walker, née Horrocks, is living in sin with a door-to-door insurance salesman . . .'

'Everybody knows that!'

'. . . in Plymouth. Last night the two of them went out for a Chinese meal. He had safe old steak and chips, but she, being of a more adventurous nature, chose sweet and sour pork. They went to bed at a quarter past eleven, and were hammering away at the bedsprings until a quarter to twelve, which is quite an impressive performance for a couple in middle age.'

'You're making all that up,' Walker said.

'Don't you believe *any* of it?' Forsyth asked with a smile. 'Or is it just the *last part* you find hard to accept?'

'I don't believe any of it. I could make up stories about *your* wife, and you'd have no way of knowing whether or not I was telling the truth.'

'Then let's talk about something which you *can* verify,' Forsyth suggested. 'You did your national service in Korea, where you were commended once for bravery and twice hauled before a disciplinary board for breaching standing orders. You drive a Ford Escort, which is now so battered that it is worth considerably less than the payments you still owe on it. You have two hundred and thirty-two pounds in your deposit account at the Linen Bank, and forty-one pounds sixty-three pence in your current account.' Forsyth paused. 'Need I go on?'

'He did that all without notes,' Walker thought, with amazement. 'He's probably got half my life story in his head.'

'How long have you been collecting information on me?' he demanded, angrily.

'Only since this morning,' Forsyth replied. 'So imagine what I could come up with if I *really* started digging.'

'What exactly do you want?' Walker asked, defeated.

'Since the Linda Szymborska murder investigation, you have been feeding information on police activities to Mr Traynor . . .'

'If I have told him anything – and I'm not *admitting* I have – then it's only been in the interest of the Force and—'

'For which you have been paid, the money going into a

bank account you opened in the name of Charles Hudson, especially for that purpose. Would you like me to quote the account number?'

'So that's it then, is it?' Walker asked. 'You take what you know to the chief constable, and I get the chop?'

'Oh no, nothing like that,' Forsyth assured him. 'Far be it from me to nip the promising career of an outstanding policeman like you in the bud.'

'I could do without the sarcasm,' Walker said.

'I'm sure you could,' Forsyth agreed.

The two of them fell silent for perhaps half a minute, then Walker said, 'So what is it you want me to do? Stop talking to Traynor?'

'Quite the contrary,' Forsyth replied. 'It is in the interest of my department that you *continue* talking to Traynor – but only as long as you feed him the information that I *want* you to feed him.'

'And who'll benefit from that?'

'I will,' Forsyth said, then added hastily, 'and, of course, the government, which works tirelessly in *all* our interests.'

'What about *Ma'am*?' Walker asked.

'I think you must be referring to DCI Paniatowski. Am I right?'

'You know you are. Will *she* benefit from it?'

'That will depend,' Forsyth said, in measured tones. 'If she's a good girl, and does exactly what's expected of her, she could benefit from it considerably. If, on the other hand, she decides to plough her own erratic furrow, then it could well be her downfall.'

Ma'am couldn't play the good girl if her life depended on it, Walker thought, as he did his best to suppress a grin.

'If it's for the good of the country, then I'll cooperate in any way I can,' he told the other man.

'I would have expected no less of you,' Forsyth replied.

TEN

The Prince Albert bar of the Royal Victoria Hotel had done its very best to imitate the decor and atmosphere to be found in the bars of the more exclusive London gentlemen's clubs, and while it would not have fooled anyone who actually belonged to one of those clubs for even a moment, it was highly regarded by Whitebridge society.

The Prince Albert was where the town's more successful lawyers congregated after a hard day of tying the legal system in knots. It was the preferred venue for meetings of the Freemasons and the Chamber of Commerce. And, that particular early evening, it was where the smooth and enigmatic Mr Forsyth had chosen to drink his pre-prandial dry sherry.

Watching him, from a table in the corner of the bar, DC Crane found himself wondering what it would be like to be Forsyth – to send agents out into the field, knowing there was a chance they would never return; to order the elimination of people he considered to be a danger to the state; to . . .

Or maybe it wasn't like that at all, Crane thought. Maybe that kind of spy only existed in fiction, and Forsyth led as mundane and unexciting a life as an official working for the Ministry of Pensions.

And yet, he reminded himself, Monika Paniatowski didn't see him like that – and Paniatowski should know, because she had clashed with Forsyth before.

A waiter appeared at Forsyth's side, stood there discreetly until the silver-haired man deigned to notice him, then escorted the guest from London into the hotel's Balmoral Restaurant and Grill.

'I hope you have a really nice meal, Mr Forsyth,' Crane said wistfully, under his breath. 'I might even grab a bar of chocolate myself, later.'

He was conscious that somebody had sat down in the chair to his left, but kept his eyes firmly focused on the entrance to the restaurant.

'Mistake Number One,' said a voice he recognized.

Crane turned. 'Mistake, Sarge?'

'If you were an ordinary member of the public, instead of a bobby involved in surveillance work, you would have at least given anybody who sat down beside you a quick glance.'

'Any more mistakes?' Crane asked, rattled.

'A couple,' Cousins replied easily. 'For a start, you've been focusing your attention exclusively on the target.'

'And what *should* I have been doing, instead?'

'You should have been on the lookout for anybody else watching him, or for anybody watching *you* watching *him*.'

'Do you think there *is* anybody doing that?'

'No, or I wouldn't be taking the risk talking to you now. But the only reason I can say that with any certainty is because I've been checking out this bar for the last ten minutes myself.'

'You said there were a couple of things.'

'So I did – and the second is the way you're turned out.'

'My suit, you mean?'

'Yes.'

'It's a good suit, this, Sarge,' Crane protested. 'It's as good as the ones that everybody else here is wearing.'

'Not quite – at least not to the trained eye,' Cousins said gently. 'But you're right – it *is* a good suit. What's wrong is the *way* that you're wearing it.'

'So how would you prefer me to wear it? Upside down? With the trousers wrapped around my head, and the jacket covering my legs?' Crane asked. And then he felt guilty, because what Cousins was offering him was not a rebuke but constructive criticism. 'Sorry, Sarge,' he added.

'Think no more about it,' Cousins said easily. 'The problem is, you see, you look as if you're on the way to a wedding.'

'And how should I look?'

'As if it's not a suit you reserve for special occasions, but your normal working clothes – the rising young executive's equivalent of a pair of overalls. You need to look at home in it, and you could start by loosening your tie a bit.'

Crane grinned, and loosened his tie. 'Thanks, Sarge.'

'I've got another piece of advice for you, lad, totally unrelated to this surveillance,' Cousins said. 'Well, maybe two pieces, if I'm being strictly accurate. But since they're *not* related to your duties, you don't have to hear them, if you don't want to.'

'Go right ahead, Sarge,' Crane said, though the words were edged with uncertainty.

'The first is that if you keep trying to cover your lies by pretending to be a babbling idiot, there's a real danger that people will start thinking that a babbling idiot is just what you are.'

'I don't know what you're talking about,' Crane said.

'Now *that's* better!' Cousins said, with approval. 'No babbling there – just a blatant straightforward lie. But you might like to consider the other possibility, *which is not lying at all.*'

'You're talking about the Latin thing this afternoon, aren't you?' Crane asked, miserably.

'I'm talking about the Latin thing,' Cousins agreed. 'Just how educated *are* you?'

'I've got a university degree.'

'A good degree – or a bare pass?'

'A good degree.'

Cousins nodded, as if there'd been no surprises so far.

'And you're keeping it quiet because . . .?' he wondered.

'Because most bobbies don't trust anybody who they think has had too much education.'

'*Somebody* on the Force must know.'

'Somebody *must*. But nobody who I come into regular contact with has any idea.'

'And that's where I think you're making your fundamental mistake,' Cousins said. 'You're keeping a secret from the boss, and if she finds out about it – and she may well do – how do you think she's going to feel?'

'I don't know.'

'She'll feel as if she doesn't really know you at all. She'll also think that you don't trust her – and if *you* don't trust *her*, how can *she* trust *you*.'

'But suppose I tell her and she . . . and she . . .'

'And she *what*?'

Crane shrugged awkwardly. 'I don't know.'

'She starts treating you differently – as if you were some kind of freak or something?' Cousins suggested.

'Well, yes.'

'Then she wouldn't deserve the loyalty of a smart lad like you.'

'But then . . .'

'So the best thing you could do, under those circumstances, is to put in for a transfer and hope that, next time, you get a boss who's worthy of you. But that's not going to happen – not if DCI Paniatowski is the woman I think she is. Tell her, lad! Don't blurt it out like it's a confession – just tell her in a matter-of-fact sort of way. And I promise you, you won't regret it.'

'Thanks, Sarge, I really appreciate you taking the trouble to talk to me like this,' Crane said.

Cousins shrugged. 'It's no trouble at all. Helping out junior officers is all part of being a sergeant. But let's not take it too far.'

'Too far?' Crane repeated.

'If I ever catch you looking at me like you think I've suddenly become your kindly Uncle Paul, I'll smash your teeth in.'

Crane grinned. 'Understood,' he said.

Colin Beresford looked around the lounge bar of the Red Lion. The people there were not like the regular drinkers he'd have found at the Drum and Monkey, he thought. For a start, they were all roughly the same age – early to late thirties – and unlike the customers in the Drum, they were either on their own, or with one friend of the same sex.

Other differences were becoming apparent, the longer he stood there. The customers at the Drum might run a comb quickly through their hair before they left home, but that was about as far it went. The people in the Red Lion's lounge, on the other hand, were decked out in all their finery, and looked as if they had spent a good fifteen or twenty minutes staring self-consciously into the mirror before they set out for the pub.

The atmosphere was different, too – and that wasn't just because of the dim lights and the syrupy romantic music which was being pumped out of the speaker system. People who went to the Drum did so because they wanted a drink, whereas the people who came to the Red Lion were on the prowl. The evidence was there for all to see – the way the men assessed every new woman who entered the room, the women's habit of glancing around casually, and then whispering earnest messages to their friends.

All in all, Beresford decided, the Red Lion had earned its reputation as the most infamous pick-up place in the whole of Whitebridge.

And wasn't that why he was there himself – to pick up women?

But it wasn't easy. It wasn't easy at all.

He didn't know how to behave.

He didn't know what to say.

He felt like a man who'd been anaesthetized for the last thirteen years. And, in a way, that was exactly what he was.

He'd *almost* become a non-virgin in his late teens. He'd had a steady girlfriend called Janet – so steady that she'd stopped saying 'Don't!' every time he'd tried to put his hand up her skirt. A few more weeks, he'd been convinced at the time, and he'd have had it cracked.

Then his mother had been diagnosed with Alzheimer's disease, and his life had been turned upside down.

At first, he'd spent more time with Mum because he wanted the two of them to share things, while she still could. Later, he'd spent time with her because he was frightened of leaving her alone.

So Janet had broken up with him. It hadn't been a bitter parting – full of screaming and recriminations. It was just that they had both seen the inevitability of the situation, and she had simply drifted away.

She was married now, with three kids. He often caught sight of her in the centre of Whitebridge, but somehow – though he wanted to – he could never quite bring himself to stop and speak.

There had been no more girls after Janet, and that had been his choice – for even if he'd found a girl willing to take on the challenge of his mother, he could never have inflicted Mavis Beresford on someone he cared about.

Now, finally, his mother was in a nursing home.

But where did that leave him?

It left him, he accepted sadly, with the body of a man in his early thirties, but with the experience – at least, as far as dealing with women was concerned – of a spotty teenager.

'You look a bit down in the mouth,' said a voice to his left.

He turned, and saw the woman leaning against the bar. She was about his age, he guessed. Her hair was blonde, and if it was dyed, it had been well done. She had nice eyes, a smooth complexion, and a body that had all the right contours in all the right places.

It would be wrong to call her a raving beauty, he thought, but she was not half bad.

'Would you like a drink?' he asked.

'Yes, I would,' the woman replied, as if the idea had never occurred to her until he mentioned it. 'A gin and tonic would be nice.'

He ordered her drink, then said, 'My name's Colin.'

'And I'm Yvonne,' the woman told him. 'So what's your story, Colin? Divorced?'

Beresford shook his head. 'No, I'm single. I never quite seemed to get around to marrying.'

Yvonne smiled at him. 'Wise man.'

'You?'

'Divorced, with two kids,' Yvonne said. 'But don't worry about them,' she added hastily. 'They're staying with my mother tonight.'

'So what do I say next?' Beresford asked himself, in a panic. 'What the *bloody hell* do I say next?'

'How old are your kids?' he found himself blurting out.

Yvonne gave him a slightly strange look. 'This is my one night out a week, love. I look forward to it, and when I *am* out, the last thing I want to talk about is my children.'

Of course it was, Beresford thought. Even an idiot – even a complete *moron* – would know that.

'I'm . . . I'm not very good at talking to women,' he admitted.

Yvonne laughed. 'Well, you've certainly made that obvious enough,' she said. 'But you shouldn't worry about it.'

'Shouldn't I?'

'No! Not at all! You make a nice change from the oily sods I usually end up chatting to.'

'Thanks,' Beresford said, feeling as if he were drowning in his own inadequacy.

'Tell you what,' Yvonne said softly, 'why don't we go back to my place for the next drink? It's not as noisy or as crowded as this pub, and you might find it easier to *talk* there.'

'Thank you, but not tonight,' Beresford heard himself say.

'You're sure?'

'Yes, I . . . I've got an early start in the morning.'

Yvonne shrugged. 'In that case, I suppose I might as well go back to my mate.'

'Yes,' Beresford agreed mournfully. 'I suppose you might as well.'

He watched her walk to the far end of the bar, her hips swinging in what was no doubt an attempt to reassure herself that it was his loss, not hers. He continued to watch as she bent over and whispered something in her mate's ear, but when the mate looked wonderingly in his direction, he had to turn away.

He'd wanted to go home with her. He really had. The problem was that it had been all too easy to picture how things would have gone once they'd got there.

They are in her bedroom, both of them stripping off.

'You're very well-muscled, aren't you?' she says.

It is an invitation to pay her a compliment in return, but he is too embarrassed to even look at her.

'There's something you should know,' he says – because better he should tell her than that she should find out for herself.

'Yes?'

'I've never done this before.'

'Done what?'

'Slept with a woman.'

He can feel her eyes penetrating him. 'You're not queer, are you?' she asks, a harsher edge entering her voice. 'Because if you are . . .'

'I'm not,' he assures her. 'I've never slept with a man, either.'

She laughs, more relaxed again. 'You're winding me up,' she says. 'You have to be.'

But that would be the problem, wouldn't it? He wouldn't be winding her up at all!

Would he ever be able to break the vicious circle, he wondered. And if so, how?

Make his situation into a film, and it would be bloody hilarious, he thought. But when it was your own life, it was a bit difficult seeing the funny side.

The man leaning heavily against the public bar in the Vulcan was in his mid-thirties, and looked the worse for drink.

Paniatowski sat on the stool next to his, ordered a vodka, and said, 'I'd like to talk to you.'

The man looked at her through bleary eyes. 'Not tonight, love,' he said. 'I'm not in the mood for that kind of thing.'

'Neither am I, Mr Quinn,' Paniatowski said, holding up her warrant card. 'It's serious matters that *I* want to talk about.'

Quinn shook his head, as if hoping to clear his brain a little.

'Thought you looked familiar,' he slurred. 'I saw you on the telly earlier, didn't I? You're the bobby who's investigating Andy Adair's murder.'

'That's right, I am,' Paniatowski agreed. 'And what can you tell me about Mr Adair?'

'He was the best mate a man ever had,' Quinn said mournfully, 'and now he's dead.' He made a sweeping gesture with his arm. 'End of story.'

'I'm afraid it isn't, not by a long chalk,' Paniatowski told him. 'You were mates in the army. You served together in Northern Ireland, didn't you?'

'That's right, we did.'

'And he was discharged a couple of months after you were.'

'You have been doing your homework.'

'And you came back to Whitebridge.'

'Yes.'

'And why wouldn't you? It's your home town, and besides, there was a job already waiting for you in Dixon's foundry. But Adair was from Oxfordshire, so what made *him* move here? Were you the one who suggested it?'

'I suppose so.'

'And what did you say, exactly?'

'I think I told him it was a nice place to live.'

'Whitebridge!' Paniatowski said incredulously. 'You told him *Whitebridge* was a nice place to live? And which part of it did you think a man brought up in the Thames Valley would find particularly enchanting? The factory chimneys – or the derelict mills?'

Quinn shrugged. 'There's some nice scenery around the town – the moors and that.'

'You don't look to me like a man who'd go in much for scenery,' Paniatowski said, sceptically. 'But we're not talking about you, are we? We're talking about Andy Adair – a man who moved here knowing nobody but you. It doesn't make any sense, unless, like you, he had a job to go to.'

'What do you mean?' Quinn asked, his tone hovering somewhere between aggression and suspicion.

'But he *didn't* have a job to go to, did he?' Paniatowski continued. 'At least, no job that we've got any record of – no job the *tax man* knows about.'

Quinn said nothing.

'But job or no job, he had his rent to pay every week,' Paniatowski continued. 'And there were his daily boozing costs to cover, even if he did most of that boozing with a generous mate. And yet he hadn't bothered to register as unemployed, which meant he couldn't even draw the dole. Don't you find that just a little bit strange, Mr Quinn?'

'Never thought about it,' Quinn said, unconvincingly.

'So where *did* his money come from?' Paniatowski asked.

'I had nothing to do with it. I wasn't involved at all,' Quinn told her – and the moment the words were out of his mouth, it was clear from the expression on his face that he regretted them.

'Nothing to do with *what*?' Paniatowski demanded. 'Not *involved* with what?'

'Listen, I've just lost my best mate, and I'm devastated,' Quinn said. 'All I want is a bit of peace and quiet.'

'So that you can reflect on his life and death?'

'Yes, if you like.'

'Fair enough,' Paniatowski agreed. 'You'll get lots of peace and quiet in a cell at the local nick.'

Quinn blinked, as if he was finding it hard to follow this new turn their conversation was taking.

'What are you . . . what are you talking about?' he asked.

'You've got a simple choice to make,' Paniatowski told him. 'You can either talk to me now, or I can arrest you for being drunk and disorderly – in which case you talk to me later.'

'You bloody bitch!' Quinn muttered, half-under his breath.

'Yes, you're right, that's just what I am,' Paniatowski agreed. 'A bloody bitch with a set of handcuffs in her pocket. So what's it to be?'

Quinn looked longingly at the door.

He wanted to make a dash for it, Paniatowski thought, but he wasn't yet *quite* drunk enough to persuade himself he'd be able to make it.

'What do you want to know?' Quinn asked, turning slightly so he was facing the bar again.

'I want to know about this job of Andy Adair's – the one that you had nothing to do with.'

'Look, don't ask me to talk about that,' Quinn pleaded. 'I promise you, I would if I could – but I just can't.'

'*Why* can't you?'

'Because it's not just about Andy. There's other people involved – and if I snitch on them, my life won't be worth living.'

Other people!

Paniatowski wondered whether it was Forsyth himself who'd put the frighteners on Quinn.

Probably not.

Forsyth's approach was too subtle – too nuanced. An ex-soldier like Quinn would likely respond better to the threat of physical force, delivered by one of the spy's henchmen.

'Once you come out in the open with what you know – once I've got it all down on record – neither the army nor the intelligence service will dare touch you,' she said.

'What are you talking about?'

Paniatowski sighed. 'Listen, why pretend, when you're not fooling anybody – least of all me? After Adair left the army – if, indeed, he actually *did* leave the army at all – he was recruited to do some kind of work for the intelligence service in the Whitebridge area.'

'Was he?' Quinn asked.

Paniatowski stamped her foot impatiently. 'For God's sake, Mr Quinn, you *know* he was. That's the little job of his that you had nothing to do with.'

And yet, even as she spoke the words, she was beginning to have her doubts. Quinn really *did* look as if he had no idea what she was talking about – and she was far from convinced that he was that good an actor.

'You've got it all wrong,' the ex-soldier said. 'Andy wasn't working for the intelligence service, he was working for . . .'

'For . . .?'

'I'm not saying.'

Maybe he *was* that good an actor after all, Paniatowski thought. But *if* he was, it was taking him a great deal of effort to maintain the front, and if she pushed a little harder it might just collapse.

'Have you ever considered the possibility that by keeping quiet you could be putting *yourself* in danger?' she said.

'How do you mean?' Quinn asked.

He looked so *genuinely* bewildered that Paniatowski was tempted to give it up then and there.

Then she remembered other interrogations she had conducted, and how, just as everything had looked hopeless, the suspect had suddenly caved in.

'How might *you* be in danger?' she ploughed on. 'Well, if it *was* the IRA who executed your mate Andy . . .'

'The IRA!' Quinn exclaimed. 'Yes, I suppose it *could have* been them, couldn't it!'

'Is this the first time that possibility's crossed your mind?'

'Well, yes,' Quinn admitted.

'Even though you were both paratroopers in Northern Ireland? Even though you were both involved in the Bloody Sunday massacre?'

'There was a sniper at Derry Corner,' Quinn said sullenly. 'We were fired on first. We were only defending ourselves.'

'Even so, there must have been times when you thought the IRA might try to get its revenge for what you'd done,' Paniatowski said. 'But not this time, you didn't,' she mused. 'Now why *was* that? Could it be because you already had other ideas about who might have done it?'

From the expression on Quinn's face, she knew she had hit the nail right on the head; knew both that the ex-soldier was no kind of actor *at all*, and that he *did* have his own theories about who had killed his best friend – and why they might have done it.

'Well?' she demanded.

Being backed into a corner seemed to have given Quinn renewed strength, and now he held out his hands, palm down, in front of him.

'If you're going to arrest me, do it now,' he growled like a wounded animal. 'And if you're *not* going to arrest me, you can piss off!'

ELEVEN

The Meteorological Office had warned of heavy rain overnight – and, for once, had almost got it right. There were thunderstorms on the Pennine Hills, with sheet lightning which could be clearly seen from both the Lancashire Moors and Yorkshire Dales. But though threatening clouds did mass over Whitebridge under the cover of darkness, they had still not decided whether to open up or not when a wandering wind took them in its grip and shunted them out to sea, leaving the sun to rise on a perfect late summer day.

From his suite in the Royal Victoria, Mr Forsyth looked up at the clear blue sky, and allowed himself a rare moment of reflection.

The problem with the general public's perception of the intelligence service, he thought, was that, one way or another, they invariably got it wrong. There were those who saw spies as incompetent bunglers, forever tripping over their own feet and achieving nothing, and those who saw them as evil men, with an almost superhuman cold-bloodedness and unlimited power.

The truth, as with most generalizations, lay somewhere in the middle. Agents *did* make mistakes – some of them monumental ones – but they were never the clowns they were portrayed as in the spoof movies. And though it was sometimes necessary to have impediments to national security liquidated, such a course of action was a last resort, and could sometimes rebound very badly on the career of the man who had initiated it.

This operation in Whitebridge was a case in point. It had been made necessary by a mistake – for which he partly blamed himself – but resolving the difficulty was by no means as simple as an uninformed outsider might assume.

The detective constable who Monika Paniatowski had assigned to watch him was just one example of the complexity involved. Having the young man removed was certainly an option – and one which he could probably, in the long term, justify to his masters in Whitehall – but once you decided to knock over one domino, you ran the real risk that the rest of them would tumble down as well. And anyway, knocking the dominoes over was not at all what the game was about – the trick was to move them to a different position without anyone even realizing they had been moved.

He found his thoughts turning to Monika Paniatowski. Though he was well aware that she loathed him, he was really quite fond of her. It was not so much her physical appearance he admired, as her spirit. It presented him with a challenge. It made the game a little more interesting. Of course, he might have to crush it in the end, but there would even be a guilty pleasure in doing that.

Forsyth wondered – briefly – if his own sexual impotence had anything to do with his attitude to Paniatowski.

Then he rang room service, and ordered himself a hearty breakfast.

Even in the later stages of her illness, his mother had loved a blue sky, Colin Beresford reminded himself, as he looked out of the window. Of course, he quite accepted she might not even have known it was a *sky* at all – might just have regarded it as a soothing shade of colour in a universe she could no longer come to grips with – but even that must have been *some* consolation to her.

He wondered how Yvonne, the woman he had met the previous evening, was feeling that morning.

Had she woken up depressed, weighed down by her complete failure to pull him?

Or had she, on the other hand, woken up next to a man – a beefy, self-assured man who had not worried for a second about what would happen once they'd got undressed?

'I have to do something about my life,' he said to the walls of his bedroom. 'I can't go on like this.'

When this case was over, he promised himself, he *would* do something about it. Once they had the killer safely in custody, he would make a determined effort to overcome his reticence.

Yet as he was brushing his teeth, it seemed to him that there was at least one small part of his brain which hoped that solving the murder would take a long, long time.

*   *   *

Sir William Langley strode through the gardens of Ashton Court, his home, with a squire-like swagger which he could not entirely carry off.

The Court, located a few miles outside Whitebridge, had begun life as a medieval manor house, though additions over the next few hundred years had quite obscured its origins. It stood in extensive grounds, tended by a small army of gardeners whose successful battle against the thin moorland soil had resulted in a series of linked gardens which *Lancashire Life* had once described as 'quite stunning'. There was a river running through the property with excellent fishing, and the grouse moor which abutted the estate could always be relied on to provide a rewarding day's shoot.

All in all, it was a stately pile, and if any of Sir William's weekend house guests went away with the impression that it had been owned by his family for countless generations, well, that was certainly not due to anything that *he* had explicitly said.

It was Sir William's habit to inspect his gardens early in the morning, while the dew still lay heavy underfoot, and that morning was no exception. Following the same route he always did, he first visited his rose garden. The glasshouses were next, but having no real feel for nature, he gave the fruit and flowers growing in them little more than a cursory inspection. That task completed, he strolled around the edge of the artificial lake, heading towards what was really his favourite part of the grounds – his collection of statues.

The statues Sir William owned could be roughly divided into three distinct groups.

The first group, bought on the recommendation of people who knew about these things, were very modern, and though there were times when they seemed to him to be no more than pieces of scrap metal randomly welded together, he wisely kept his opinion to himself.

The second group were very old, and had come from Greece, Italy and various other spots around the Mediterranean with a reputation for an antique past. When he'd seen his initial purchase in this group for the first time, Sir William had wondered aloud if the ravages of the centuries could be disguised by a little skilful repair work, but his 'experts' had positively blanched at the suggestion, and so the statues remained chipped and cracked, which, he supposed, at least proved they *were* old.

He'd taken advice from no one on the purchase of his third group of statues, and – perhaps for that reason – they were his favourites. They reminded him of the municipal statues he'd seen as a child – and indeed, many of them *were* those same statues. The one of John Bright, the great radical reformer, had dominated the space in front of Whitebridge Town Hall, until the council had decided it stood in the way of progress. The equestrian statue of the Duke of Wellington, raised as the result of a public subscription, had been a feature of the corporation park until a few years earlier. Peel, Gladstone, he had them all, and when he looked up at them, he liked to think that their firm, resolute jaws reminded him of his own.

It was as he approached his Queen Victoria that he noticed a new statue which he couldn't, for the life of him, remember buying. Nor could he think of what would have possessed him to purchase the sculpture of a naked man on his hands and knees – because, really, though avant-garde art was all very well in its place, there had to be *some* limits imposed by good taste. And even if *had* bought it, he would surely have ordered a plinth, too, instead of merely dumping it on the ground like that.

The closer he got to it, the more he thought about how horribly realistic it seemed to be. Then he saw the man's face – and the gash in his throat – and realized there was a *reason* it seemed so realistic.

And it was at that point that he came to a complete – very unsquirely – halt, and vomited.

Though he was sound asleep, there was a warm smile on DS Paul Cousins' face. He was dreaming of the past – a past in which his wife was still alive.

It was a vivid dream.

He could feel her lips press against his as she kissed him.

He could smell her breath brushing gently against his cheek.

It was a long time since he'd had such a dream. Dreams like that didn't come to men who paced the kitchen floor until they had worn out the linoleum. They didn't visit distraught police sergeants who banged their heads against the living-room wall until the pain became so intense that it stopped them thinking about anything else. Only recently – back at work, and with a purpose in life once more – had he rediscovered the level of sleep which had been eluding him for over two years and which now invited the dreams back in.

The dream continued.

It is springtime, and they are walking across a meadow, hand in hand. Small insects buzz noisily in the grass, and the buttercups' golden heads glisten in the sunlight.

'Do you think we'll always be as happy as we are now, Paul?' Mary asks.

Cousins realizes that the answer should come straight to his lips without any need for thought – but it doesn't.

Perhaps he already knows this is nothing but a dream, and that Mary is dead.

Or perhaps he is simply being the man he was back then – an inborn optimist who forces himself to put a brake on that optimism, an idealist who is nonetheless not blind to the harsh realities of the world in which he lives.

'Do you, Paul?' Mary asks worriedly.

'I think we'll always be happy,' he replies, 'but as we get older, that happiness might take a different form to the one it's in now.'

'But we'll still love each other as much as we do now, won't we?' Mary pleads.

And this time he experiences no feelings of hesitation at all. 'Yes,' he says, 'we'll still love each other as much as we do now. That will never change.'

And yet . . . and yet . . . something is already *changing. There is a harsh metallic sound – quite at odds with the peace of the countryside – ringing in his ear, and try as he might, he cannot make it go away.*

'What's the matter, Paul?' Mary asks.

'Nothing,' he says.

But it's not true. Her voice no longer seems as clear – as real – as it was. The ground beneath his feet, which was so substantial moments earlier, now feels as if it will open up and swallow him entirely. The sky is losing its colour, the flowers are losing their shape – and still the bloody ringing will not go away!

Even before he'd opened his eyes, he was groping for the bedside telephone.

'Yes?' he growled into the instrument.

'Is that you, Paul?' asked a voice on the other end of the line – a voice which sounded *worried*.

And with just those four words, the world that he'd been inhabiting a few moments earlier – and which was already fading from his memory – quite melted away.

'Ma'am?' he said, although there was no real need to ask. 'What's happened? Have we got a new lead?'

'No,' Paniatowski replied. 'Not a lead.'

'Then if it's not a lead,' Cousins said heavily, 'it must be another body.'

'That's right,' Paniatowski agreed. 'It's another body.'

'Well, shit!' Cousins said.

TWELVE

Paniatowski's gaze was directed at a wall lined with leather-bound first editions, but that wasn't really what she was *seeing* at all.

'Shit, shit, shit . . . shit!' she kept repeating, silently to herself.

She should have anticipated this, she thought. She should have been able to work out for herself that a killer who took so much care over the details of his first murder would probably not stop at one.

But she *hadn't* anticipated it. She'd been so wrapped up in the details of Adair's murder and the sudden – and unwelcome – arrival of Mr Forsyth that it hadn't even occurred to her that the murderer would strike again.

Would it have taken Charlie Woodend so much by surprise, she wondered. Or would Charlie have been prepared, and already have a contingency plan in place to follow up this new development in the investigation?

She didn't know – *could have* no way of knowing. But one thing she was certain of – when the press heard there'd been a second murder (and learned the details of both the killings) they would have a field day. And, once again, she'd find herself under the microscope, with her competence being questioned every single step of the way.

She turned her attention to Sir William Langley, who was huddled protectively in the wing armchair in front of her.

No one wants to find a naked, murdered man in his own back yard – even if the back yard in question *is* at least a couple of hundred yards from the back doorstep – she thought, but even allowing for that, Langley seemed to have taken it harder than *most* men in his situation would have.

'Who could have done such a thing?' Langley asked, speaking over the top of a brandy glass which had been nearly full a couple of minutes earlier, and now was almost empty. 'Who could have done such a thing *to me*?'

'Quite,' Paniatowski agreed silently. 'Let's not bother our

heads about who could have done it to the poor bugger out
there – we should concentrate on who could have done it to
you!'

'Did you get a close look at the victim, sir?' she asked.

'Sir William,' the man in the armchair replied. 'I would
appreciate it if you'd call me Sir *William*.'

So that was how it was going to be, was it? Paniatowski
wondered. Nerves shot to hell, but still clinging to his precious
title at all costs.

'Did you get a close look at the victim, *Sir William*?' she
said.

Langley shuddered. 'A closer look than I'd have liked. I
didn't know he was dead at first, you see. I didn't even know
he was *real*.'

'And did you recognize him?'

'How could I possibly have recognized him?' Langley
demanded, in what could have been anger, and could have
been fear – and just possibly was both. 'I'm a merchant banker,
my good woman.'

'So?'

'So I draw my circle of friends exclusively from other
merchant bankers and the top men in the professions. So I
simply don't come into any contact with that class of person.'

'Which class of person?' Paniatowski asked.

'People like him,' Langley said, amazed that she'd felt the
need to even ask such a stupid question. 'People . . . like . . .
the . . . dead . . . man,' he added, spacing out his words in case
she still hadn't got the point.

'Ah, I see,' Paniatowski said.

'I should damned well think you would,' Langley said. 'After
all, you are supposed to be a *chief inspector*.'

'But what I still *don't* see is how you know he *is*, in fact,
"that class of person".'

'I beg your pardon?'

'We tend to judge people by the clothes they're wearing
and the way they speak. But the dead man wasn't wearing any
clothes *at all* – and dead men are notoriously silent. So if you
don't know him, how do you know he isn't another merchant
banker?'

'He doesn't *look* like a merchant banker,' Langley said
peevishly.

'And how *do* merchant bankers look?' Paniatowski countered.

Langley considered the question for a second. 'I may have expressed myself badly,' he conceded, 'but that's perfectly understandable, after the ordeal I've been through.'

'So you forgive yourself,' Paniatowski said softly.

'What was that, Chief Inspector?'

'I said, yes, Sir William, it is understandable. So how did you *mean* to express yourself?'

'I suppose what I really meant to say was that the people with whom I rub shoulders are simply not the kind of people who get themselves murdered – and, especially, murdered in such a ghastly manner.'

'So, just to be quite clear on that matter, you're saying that you've definitely never seen the dead man before?'

Langley looked vague – and slightly troubled.

'I suppose I may possibly have *seen* him before,' he said finally. 'One sees all sorts of people – hundreds of them, every day – whether one wants to or not, doesn't one?'

One does, Paniatowski thought. But one isn't usually so bloody cagey about it.

'Sorry to be so persistent,' she said, 'but I really need you to spell it out for me. You're saying, if I understand you correctly, that even if you *have* seen him, you don't *recognize* him – and you certainly couldn't put a name to him?'

'Just so,' Langley agreed.

'Bloody liar!' Paniatowski thought.

The grounds outside the house had been transformed since Langley had taken his early morning stroll. A large section – from the artificial lake to the trees which ran around the boundary – had been cordoned off, and within this roped-in area more than a dozen policemen were already at work.

In the statue garden, several technicians were dusting the metal statutes for fingerprints.

On the lawn surrounding the statue garden, a line of uniformed officers were slowly advancing, carefully examining each blade of immaculately cut grass in front of them before taking a step forward.

There was no sign of either an ambulance or Dr Shastri's Land Rover, but tyre tracks at the edge of one of the flower beds were ample proof that they had both been there.

DS Cousins was standing just outside the cordon, from where he could observe all the other officers at the same time. He had his hands reflectively on his hips, and a cigarette dangled languidly from his mouth.

'I thought you'd given up smoking, Paul,' Paniatowski said.

Cousins smiled sheepishly. 'I *had*, ma'am,' he said, 'but there's nothing like a couple of nasty murders for driving you back to the weed.'

Paniatowski watched the technicians at work for a moment, then said, 'So what have you got for me, Sergeant?'

'In most respects, this murder seems to be almost identical to the previous killing, ma'am,' Cousins replied. 'For example, while Dr Shastri's not prepared to be definite about it until she's conducted a thorough examination, she *thinks* that the latest victim's been dead for about the same amount of time as the last victim was when we found him—'

'But we didn't really *find* him at all, did we?' Paniatowski interrupted. 'It's much more a case of us having been *led* to him. The killer dumped his first victim in a place he knew the kennel owner walked past every morning, and left his second where he knew Langley would be bound to come across it on his stroll. It's as if he doesn't just want them to be *found* – he wants them to be found *quickly*.'

'Maybe it's more a case of him wanting them found *before the rigor wears off*,' Cousins suggested.

'You may have a point,' Paniatowski agreed. 'Go on with what you were saying.'

'In each case, death was caused by the victim having his throat ripped out by some kind of steel claw,' Cousins said, 'and both victims were – I assume – posed on their hands and knees until rigor set in. The only difference between the first and second killings is that there's no evidence of pre-mortem torture this time.'

'And how do you explain the fact that the second victim wasn't tortured?' Paniatowski wondered.

'I can't explain it,' Cousins admitted. 'If we knew *why* the killer tortured the first one, we might be able to speculate on why he spared the second. But since we haven't got a clue what his motivation is . . .' He waved his hands helplessly in the air. 'Well, we're a bit stuck for the moment, aren't we?'

'We are indeed,' Paniatowski agreed. 'What about the driving licence that was left in front of the body?'

'That's another point of comparison for you,' Cousins said. 'It belonged to the victim, just like the first one belonged to Adair.'

'So who *is* the victim this time?'

'A feller called Simon Stockwell. He's thirty-two years old – or, at least, he *was* thirty-two years old until sometime last night.'

'Do we have any details, apart from name and age?'

'We do,' Cousins said. 'In fact, I'm amazed at the amount of stuff that Inspector Beresford's team has been able to come up with at this early stage in the investigation.' He took his notebook out of his pocket, and flicked it open. 'Stockwell lived on the Pinchbeck Estate with his wife and three kids, and he was a painter and decorator by trade.'

Paniatowski looked over Cousins' shoulder at Sir William Langley's home. 'Find out if Stockwell had ever done any work here,' she said.

'Here?' Cousins repeated, as if he suspected he might have misheard. 'At Ashton Court?'

'That's right.'

Cousins shrugged. 'I'll have it checked out since you've asked me to, ma'am, but I think it'll be a waste of time. Knowing how to slap on three coats of emulsion paint and hang wallpaper more or less straight isn't enough to get you work in a place like this.'

No, it probably wasn't, Paniatowski agreed silently. But if he'd done some work there, it would explain how Langley came to know him – and she was more convinced than ever that Langley *had* known him.

'What else have you got for me?' she asked.

'Our Simon seems to have been a bit of a thug, and had a criminal record, stretching back to the time he was a teenager.' Cousins said, consulted his notebook again. 'He was first arrested for being drunk and disorderly in 1957.'

'He would only have been sixteen then,' Paniatowski said, doing a quick mental calculation.

'That's right, he would,' Cousins agreed. 'He was arrested again, for assault and battery this time, when he was nineteen, and he was put on two years' probation. When he was twenty-three, he did a thirty-month stretch for grievous bodily harm.

Since then, he's not been charged with anything, so maybe he's
kept out of trouble – or maybe he's just got more careful.'

'Perhaps getting married calmed him down,' Paniatowski
speculated.

But even if he had calmed down, he still didn't sound like
the kind of person who Sir William Langley would invite
round for cocktails, she thought.

'Was he ever in the army?' she asked.

Cousins looked pained – or perhaps merely unwilling to
disappoint her.

'No, ma'am, I'm afraid he wasn't.'

So if he *did* know Andy Adair, it was not as a result of
them having served together.

'Does he have any *other* connection with Northern Ireland?'
Paniatowski asked, grasping for a straw – *any* straw. 'Did he,
for example, work there for any length of time?'

'If he did, Inspector Beresford's lads haven't found out
about it yet.'

If Stockwell hadn't been to Northern Ireland, then the IRA
connection to the murders was looking more tenuous,
Paniatowski thought.

But if there *wasn't* an IRA connection, then what the hell
was that bastard Forsyth doing here in Whitebridge?

Perhaps they were dealing with a *real* nutter, who selected
his victims at random.

But that didn't make any sense either, because the killer
had chosen to leave Stockwell's body in the grounds of Ashton
Court, which meant that he'd known Sir William Langley
would recognize him.

She was going round in circles, she thought. Maybe it was
time to go off on a different tack, and see if that led anywhere.

She looked around the sculptures. They might be called an
eclectic collection, she supposed, but *indiscriminate* definitely
had a more convincing ring to it as a description.

'Do you reckon these are valuable?' she asked.

Cousins grinned. 'I'm no expert on such matters, ma'am,
but *I* certainly wouldn't give them garden-space.'

'Me neither,' Paniatowski agreed, 'but then, as my daughter's
always telling me, I'm a bit of a philistine when it comes to
the fine arts.'

She realized that she no longer had Cousins' full attention, and the reason was that some of that attention was now focused on the uniformed men conducting the search on the lawn.

'Excuse me a minute, ma'am,' Cousins said. He raised his cupped hands to his mouth and called out loudly, 'Can you hear me, Constable Pickering?'

The constable in question, who was slightly ahead of the other officers in the line, turned around.

'Yes, Sarge,' he called back.

'You're involved in a search, lad, not a race,' Cousins told him. 'There's no prize for breasting the tape first. So stop getting ahead of yourself, and match your pace to that of your mates.'

Constable Pickering looked mortified. 'Yes, Sarge, I will,' he said. 'Sorry, Sarge.'

'Don't apologize,' Cousins told him. 'Just make sure it doesn't happen again.' He turned back to Paniatowski. 'Shouldn't have done that while you were here, should I, ma'am?'

'Why not?'

'Well, it's bad enough being told off by a sergeant, but it must be even worse when you know the boss is watching.' He paused. 'Don't hold it against the lad, ma'am. Keeping in line is more difficult than it looks.'

Paniatowski smiled. 'I do *remember*, you know. I wasn't *born* a chief inspector.'

Cousins smiled back. 'Course you weren't, ma'am, though there are *some* chief inspectors I could mention who act not only as if they descended straight from heaven into the job but also already had three pips on their shoulders when they did it.' He lit up a fresh cigarette from the stub of his old one. 'It's getting to be a habit this,' he said, grinning as he drew the smoke into his lungs. 'You were asking me about whether or not I thought the statues were valuable, ma'am.'

'Yes, I was,' Paniatowski agreed.

'As far as the municipal ones go, I think he'd be hard pushed to *give* them away.'

'What about the modern and classical ones?'

'That's a different matter altogether. I've not talked to Sir William myself, but from the general atmosphere of this place I get the distinct impression that if they *weren't* valuable, he would never have bothered putting most of them on display.'

That was the impression she'd got too, Paniatowski thought.

'So if they are valuable, what kind of security has he got protecting them?' she asked.

'You can't see it for the trees, but there's a ten-foot wall running around the entire property,' Cousins told her. 'That's enough to keep most people out, and anybody wanting to steal one of these monstrosities would have a bugger of a job getting it out over the wall.'

'And how about getting a body with full rigor mortis *in* over the wall?'

'I don't see that would be much of problem. Two fellers with ladders could manage it easily.'

'And what about *one* man with a ladder?'

Cousins was silent for a moment, then he said, 'So you think it's just one man, do you?'

'Yes.'

'Any particular reason – or is it just a feeling in your gut?'

'It's just a feeling in my gut,' Paniatowski admitted.

Cousins shook his head wonderingly 'And there I was thinking that it was just me.'

'So *you* think it was only one man, as well.'

'I do. I don't know how many men are involved in the actual killings – if I learned it was half a dozen, I wouldn't be too surprised – but when it comes to disposing of the bodies, I firmly believe it's down to one of them. The way I see it, it's his vision of how things *should* be done – and it's too *personal* a vision to share.' Cousins grinned self-consciously. 'Which, I suppose, is just a fancy way of saying it's my gut feeling as well,' he concluded.

'So *could* one man manage it?'

'It would be more difficult than if there were two of them, but by no means impossible. The thing is, you see, there are large sections of the wall facing nothing but open country-side. So even if he hit difficulties, he had all the time in the world to work out a solution to them.'

'We need to check the perimeter, to find out exactly where he *did* enter the grounds,' Paniatowski said.

'Good idea, ma'am,' Cousins replied.

Paniatowski smiled again. 'The way you said that, you made it sound as if *I* hadn't told you we should conduct the search, you'd never thought of it yourself,' she said. 'Why was that?'

Cousins looked guilty. 'It's what they call applied psychology, ma'am,' he admitted.

'Explain yourself.'

'With some DCIs, the very worst thing you can do is suggest we follow a particular course of action, because that pretty much guarantees that the *last thing* they'll do is follow it. So what I do, ma'am, is wait for *them* to make the right suggestion.'

'And if they don't?'

Cousins' guilty expression deepened. 'Well, you know . . .' he said, very vaguely.

'No,' Paniatowski replied, 'I'm not sure I do.'

'If they don't come up with the idea themselves, then I suppose I usually find a way to make them *think* they have.'

'But you won't be trying that trick on *me* again, will you, Sergeant?' Paniatowski asked.

'No, ma'am, I've learned my lesson, and I most certainly won't,' Cousins agreed.

'So when *were* you planning to conduct the perimeter search?' Paniatowski wondered.

'As soon as the lads have finished the grounds, ma'am.'

'Good.'

'Not that I've exactly got high hopes of finding anything useful. If it had rained last night – like it was supposed to – the ground would have been sodden and we might have got some decent footprints. But it didn't bloody rain, did it?' Cousins grumbled.

If it rained last night, the bastard would either not have left the body here at all, or would have some ingenious way to cover his tracks, thought Paniatowski, who was gained a grudging respect for the killer.

'I'm going to leave you in charge here,' she said. 'Is that all right?'

'Fine with me,' the sergeant said easily. 'Where will you be if I need to contact you?'

'From about half-past two, I'll probably be in the Drum, with Inspector Beresford,' Paniatowski said.

'And before then?'

'I could be anywhere, but one of things I'll definitely be doing is talking to Simon Stockwell's widow.'

'Oh aye,' Cousins replied, looking away.

, 'Is there something wrong with me doing that?' Paniatowski asked.

'No, ma'am, not *wrong*,' Cousins said carefully, as he turned towards her again.

'Spit it out,' Paniatowski told him.

'You're the boss, ma'am. You have been for a few weeks now.'

'Strangely enough, I *had* noticed that myself.'

'Maybe you had – on one level. But sometimes, I think it's still not quite all soaked in yet.'

'In what way?'

'Being the boss, you've got all kinds of extra responsibilities you didn't have before. So what that means is that you can leave unpleasant little jobs like talking to Mrs Stockwell to somebody who's a bit lower down in the pecking order, if that's what you want to.'

'And suppose I *don't* want to do that?' Paniatowski asked.

Cousins shrugged. 'Then you go and see her yourself, I suppose. Like I said, you're the boss – which means that you make the rules and the rest of us just follow them.'

THIRTEEN

The Pinchbeck Housing Estate had played a small role in Monika Paniatowski's first major case as a DCI, and it had been during that investigation that Sergeant Walker – *Inspector* Walker now – had told her, with arrogant certainty, that the people who inhabited the estate were 'the scum of the earth'.

Looking back on that particular encounter she felt ashamed that, even allowing for the fact that she was new to the job and still unsure of herself, she'd issued him with no more than a mild rebuke.

It wouldn't happen now.

Not with Walker.

Not with *anybody*.

If she could relive that moment, she'd tell the sergeant, in no uncertain terms, that his comment revealed more about his own pig ignorance and blind prejudice than it did about the people on the estate – because while there were undoubtedly some real rough buggers living there, the vast majority of the inhabitants were ordinary, decent, hard-working people.

Even so, as she approached the estate she felt her stomach knot into a tight and painful ball. But that was nothing to do with the people who lived there now – it was all tangled up with her own unhappy past.

When they first arrive in England, Captain Arthur Jones, who married Monika's mother amid the wreckage of war-torn Berlin, installs his family in a pleasant detached house on the other side of Whitebridge to the Pinchbeck Estate.

'And this is only the start,' he tells his new wife and new stepdaughter.

And so it is, though not in the way he means.

During the six years of the war, Jones has got used to giving orders. Back in civilian life, he simply cannot adjust to taking them instead. He drifts from job to job, each one a little meaner than the one which had preceded it.

As his wages grow ever smaller – and his savings trickle away – the family is forced to move from the house which was to be 'only a start' and settle in a more modest, semi-detached house on the Pinchbeck.

Monika doesn't really mind the change in their circumstances. After her horrific wartime experiences, she can live quite happily in any place where there is a roof over her head, regular food on the table and – most importantly of all – people aren't shooting at her.

Arthur Jones, on the other hand, takes it hard. He feels humiliated. He feels emasculated.

That is when he takes to visiting Monika's bedroom in the middle of the night.

At first he does no more than cuddle her, and while she doesn't exactly like it, she tells herself that her stepfather is only being affectionate. But soon his demands increase.

And she submits – because what else can she do? If she turns him down, she tells herself, he might throw his new family out on the street. And after all her mother has been through, Monika cannot bring herself to inflict new suffering on her.

So she lies there, night after night.

Suffering herself.

Waiting for it to end.

And eventually, it does.

'And eventually, it did,' Paniatowski reminded herself, as the MGA flashed past row after row of houses on the Pinchbeck Estate. 'And now it's all in the past. Now it's as if it had never happened.'

A small boy, chasing a ball, suddenly ran out on to the road ahead of her, and as Paniatowski slammed on her brakes, she realized she must have been driving at double the speed limit.

The brakes screamed, the wheels locked, the MGA slewed to the side, and the engine shut down in protest.

'Jesus!' she gasped, as she watched the boy – who had no idea how close he had come to death – pick up his ball and trot unconcernedly away.

With trembling hands, she lit up a cigarette.

'It wasn't your fault,' she told herself. 'None of it was your fault.'

But still the shame and humiliation of a much younger Monika clung to her like napalm.

'After seeing the way you conducted yourself on that search of the lawn, I've decided to adopt you as one of my special projects,' DS Cousins told Constable Pickering, as the two of them walked down the driveway, away from Ashton Court itself and towards the big double gates which opened on to the road.

'One of your special projects,' Pickering repeated.

'That's right,' Cousins agreed. 'But before you start feeling too pleased with yourself, I'd better explain what that means. You see, all uniformed constables are gormless – that's pretty much the definition of a Plod. But some are a bit more gormless than others, and when I find one who's championship-class gormless, I like to take him in hand and see if I can knock a bit of sense into him.'

'I see,' Pickering said, worriedly.

Cousins laughed. 'You shouldn't take me so seriously, lad,' he said. 'What I actually need is a second pair of eyes, and in this case, I'm borrowing yours.'

'I see,' Pickering said again – though he didn't really.

They had reached the gates, and when they'd stepped outside into the road, Cousins pointed to a large sign which had been mounted on the wall.

'Read that to me,' the sergeant said.

'These gates are protected by an Elite Security Company's Alarm and Surveillance System,' Pickering read obediently.

'And what do you make of that?' Cousins wondered.

'Well, I assume it means that the gates are wired,' Pickering said awkwardly.

'That's exactly what it means,' Cousins agreed. 'The wires are partly concealed, but if you look closely, you can see them. Now tell me, Constable Pickering, do you see any wires running from the gates to the walls?'

Pickering looked closely, assuming he was being tested in some way, and then said, 'No, Sarge, I don't.'

'That's because the wall *isn't* wired,' Cousins said. 'And by putting up that sign, the so-called security company has alerted any potential intruders to the only risk they might be running.' He sighed. 'They might as well have put up a second sign which said, "Don't break in here! Go round the back, where it's safer for you!" And it's my guess that that's just what the killer *will have* done.' He lit a cigarette, then continued, 'Let's go and see how the rest of the lads are getting on, shall we?'

They walked along the front wall. Every fifty yards or so, they passed a uniformed constable who was carefully examining the ground for any signs of the intruder.

'The lads on this stretch of the wall are probably wasting both my time and theirs,' Cousins said to Pickering in a low voice. 'Still, it has to be done, if only in the interest of thoroughness.'

'*Why* are they wasting time, Sarge?' Pickering asked.

'Think about it, lad,' Cousins said. 'If you were breaking into the place, would you do it from the front, where you might be spotted by a passing motorist, or would you go round the back?'

'I'd go round the back,' Pickering admitted.

'So would I – and I think we'll find that's just what the bastard did do,' Cousins said.

In Paniatowski's experience, WPCs fell into two basic categories. The first of these was lean and athletic, as she had been herself. The second was slightly overweight and tending towards being matronly – and it was one of these potential matrons who was standing – smoking – outside the Stockwells' front door.

The WPC saw the red sports car approaching, quickly removed the cigarette from her mouth, dropped it to the ground, and covered it with her foot, and by the time the DCI was walking up the path towards her, there was no evidence she had been doing anything but standing on alert guard duty.

'How's it going, Gloria?' Paniatowski asked.

'Could be worse, ma'am,' the WPC replied.

Paniatowski smiled. Could be worse was almost the official motto of the people who lived in Lancashire, she thought, and it covered everything from a football match being rained off to a leg being amputated.

'Tell me what you've done so far,' she said.

'First off, I asked the neighbours if they wouldn't mind looking after the kids for a bit,' the WPC replied. 'Then, once they were out of the way, I made a cup of tea for Mrs Stockwell, and asked if she'd like me to sit with her.'

'But she didn't want you to?'

'She said she'd rather be on her own for a while.'

Paniatowski nodded. 'Where is she now?'

'In the front room, ma'am.'

'And what sort of *state* is she in?'

The WPC shook her head slowly. 'Not good.'

Of course she wasn't good, Paniatowski thought. A death in the family was always a difficult thing to come to terms with, but learning that the death was not due to natural causes – that the life had been stolen, rather than just lost – was even worse. And it would be much, *much* harder yet, when the woman learned – as she must eventually – that her husband had been stripped not only of his existence, but also of his dignity.

'You were smoking when I drove up, weren't you, Gloria,' Paniatowski said accusingly.

The WPC looked guilty and shuffled the foot under which the offending cigarette was concealed.

'Yes, ma'am, I was,' she admitted. 'I know that I shouldn't have been, but . . .'

'What did you think I'd say if I caught you?' Paniatowski wondered.

Gloria shrugged. 'I'm not sure, exactly, ma'am, but we both know I'm not supposed to smoke when I'm on duty, so I thought it might be best . . .'

'Just to hope that I hadn't seen you?'

'Yes, ma'am.'

Paniatowski sighed exasperatedly, though whether her exasperation was aimed at herself, at Gloria, or at the police force's rules and regulations, she was not entirely certain.

'You've just spent over an hour dealing with a woman who's lost her husband, haven't you?' she asked.

'Yes, ma'am.'

'And you do know it's a job most of your male colleagues wouldn't have the stomach for, don't you?'

Despite herself, the WPC grinned. 'That's men for you, ma'am,' she said.

'So bearing in mind the emotional roller-coaster ride you've just been on, did you *really* think that I was going to haul you over the coals for a minor infringement of regulations?'

Gloria looked down at her feet. 'There's some as would, ma'am,' she mumbled.

'Yes, there are,' Paniatowski agreed. 'But I'm not one of them. Please remember that in future.'

'I will, ma'am,' the WPC promised.

Paniatowski nodded again. 'Right then, I suppose I'd better get this over with,' she said.

She pushed the front door open, stepped into the corridor, and tapped gently on the door to the left.

'Who . . . who is it?' asked a tremulous voice from inside.

'Police, madam. DCI Paniatowski. Can I come in?'

'All right.'

The front room offered no surprises. There was a fitted carpet (patterned in extravagant swirls), a three-piece suite in imitation leather (which would probably be clapped out by the time the final hire-purchase payment was made), and a brand-new colour television set in pride of place in front of the window.

The woman sitting on the sofa came as no surprise, either. She had mousy brown hair, which hung lankly over her shoulders and framed her pinched features. She was probably in her earlier thirties, but looked older. And though some of that could be put down to the shock she had just received, it was likely that considerably more of it could be ascribed to the life she had led – and probably, bearing in mind his criminal record, the husband she had led it with.

'I'm sorry to have to disturb you at such a distressing time,' Paniatowski said softly.

Mrs Stockwell looked up at her, and Paniatowski noticed the bruising just below her right eye.

'How will we manage?' the widow asked her plaintively. 'However will we cope, now that he's gone?'

'I'm sure all your friends and relatives will do what they can to help you,' Paniatowski said, aware of just how inadequate her response was, yet unable to offer anything more reassuring.

'There's all the bills to be dealt with, you see, miss,' the widow moaned softly. 'We're three weeks behind with the rent, an' then there's the payments on the telly . . .'

'Do you mind if I sit down?' Paniatowski asked.

'What?' Mrs Stockwell replied, as if the question had taken her completely by surprise.

'Do you mind if I sit down?'

'No. Sit down if you want to.'

Paniatowski sat on one of the easy chairs facing the sofa. 'Could I ask you a few questions?'

The widow did no more than nod – and even that seemed to have taken her a considerable effort.

'What do you know about your husband's movements last night?' Paniatowski asked.

'His movements?' Mrs Stockwell repeated.

'Was he at home?'

Mrs Stockwell laughed bitterly. 'At home? He was *never* at home – not as long as the pubs were open. He stayed out till midnight every night – an' it was even worse on Thursdays.'

'Thursdays?' Paniatowski repeated.

'Thursday nights – or Friday mornings, rather – he never came back until three or four o'clock.' Mrs Stockwell shuddered. 'I used to dread them early mornings.'

'Why?'

'Can't you guess?'

'Of course I can,' Paniatowski thought.

'I'd like to hear it in your own words,' she said aloud.

'There's no point in me pretendin' to you that he didn't knock me about, because everybody who lives round here *knows* he did,' Mrs Stockwell said. 'But sometimes he was better than others. Sometimes, he could be nice as pie. He'd buy presents for the kids, an' cuddle me just like he used to do in the early days. But that never happened on them early Friday mornings. Then, he was always lookin' for trouble. Sometimes, he'd even *wake me up* to give me a thumpin'.'

'So where did he go on Thursday nights?'

'I've no idea – an' I never dared ask him. But I *do* know that wherever it was, it wasn't in town.'

'*How* do you know that?'

'I've got this cocoa tin that I keep my money in,' Mrs Stockwell said dully. 'It's not much – a few quid – but it's there for emergencies. He knows about it . . .' The widow gulped. 'He *knew* about it, but he'd always left it alone – until a couple of Thursdays ago.'

'And what happened then?'

'He asked me where I'd put the tin. I told him I'd been

savin' up for a new pair of shoes for our Liz, an' he said, bugger that, he needed to buy for petrol for his van. I said, couldn't he wait a few days, an' he said no, he bloody couldn't. So I gave him a quid, an' he said that wasn't enough. Said he needed a full tank for where he was goin'. So I had to give it to him, didn't I?'

'Who were his friends?' Paniatowski asked.

Mrs Stockwell shrugged. 'The fellers he went out drinkin' with, I suppose. I didn't know any of them. He never brought them back here.'

'And which was his favourite pub?'

'Any of them that sold beer,' Mrs Stockwell said, increasingly bitter. 'But most lunch times you'd find him at the Clog and Billycock.'

Paniatowski stood up.

'I have to go,' she said, 'but I'll tell the WPC – her name's Gloria, by the way, in case she hasn't introduced herself properly – to stay around for a couple of hours more, in case you need anything.'

Or in case you remember something that might help the investigation, she added silently – not that there's much chance of that.

'If the bastard was goin' to get himself killed, why didn't he get himself killed at work?' Mrs Stockwell asked. 'At least that way we might have got some compensation.'

When a murder inquiry was underway, the incident room in Whitebridge Police HQ looked much as it had done in the days when he'd been a humble detective constable, Beresford thought.

There was still a large old-fashioned blackboard at the front of the room. There were still a series of desks – laid out in a horseshoe pattern for easier communication – with a newly drafted-in DC sitting at every desk and talking earnestly on the telephone. The only thing which *had* changed, he supposed, was him. He was no longer a fresh-faced bobby looking up to the inspector for guidance – he *was* that inspector.

And he liked his new role. He really did. But there were times when – looking back on those still recent days when he'd been a sergeant, Monika had been an inspector, and they'd been out in the field together – he felt a great sense of loss.

But this wasn't the moment for nostalgia, he told himself. The boss had given him a job to do, and it was up to him to bloody well do it.

He walked the length of the room, listening at random to some of the constables' telephone conversations in their entirety and catching just a phrase or two of others.

'So, apart from that one time he defaulted, Mr Stockwell's been keeping up on the regular payments on his decorator's van, has he?' one of the constables was asking a clerk at the finance company.

'And Sir William Langley left the school in which year?' another was saying. 'Yes, I do realize that would make you the oldest school secretary in the business if you'd actually been there at the time, but I assume there are records you can check . . . Yes, thank you. Did he apply to go to university? . . . Oh, you wouldn't have a record of that, even if he did.'

'Did Stockwell ever come into your pub with a big man who walked like he might have been a soldier? . . . No, I didn't specifically say Andy Adair! Will you answer the question as I phrased it, Mr Simpson.'

'I can assure you, sir, we are not conducting an investigation into your friend Sir William. It's merely that his name came up in the investigation we *are* conducting . . . No, I'm afraid I can't give you any details of that investigation.'

Beresford returned to his desk. The brief the boss had given him had been to try and establish a link between Simon Stockwell and Sir William Langley, and so far he'd been singularly unsuccessful. In fact, he admitted to himself, the more his team discovered about the two men, the wider the gap between them grew.

He glanced down at the team's findings so far:

Langley and Stockwell had been born at different ends of the town, twenty years apart.

Langley had gone to the local grammar school, Stockwell had attended a secondary modern.

Young Langley had been a Cub, and then a Boy Scout, the Scouting Association had confirmed. Young Stockwell had belonged to several gangs of tearaways, his probation officer had noted in his record.

Stockwell never bought a car from the other man in Langley's motor-business days, and it went without saying that now Langley had moved on to bigger and better things, Simon Stockwell was most definitely not one of the investors in his merchant bank.

Langley was a big wheel in the Whitebridge Golf and Country Club, Stockwell spent most of his free time in the Clog and Billycock.

Langley usually went to Italy for a month in the summer, Stockwell's family were lucky if they got the occasional day trip to Blackpool.

Langley was a staunch Conservative, Stockwell voted Labour when he could be bothered.

Neither of them seemed to have ever been to Northern Ireland, or to have had any significant connection with anybody Irish.

And last – but not bloody least – the Inland Revenue was adamant that Stockwell had never done any paid work for Langley as a decorator, or in any other capacity.

Beresford ran his glance over the horseshoe of desks, and once again felt the yearning to be back out pounding the streets.

He wouldn't be missed in headquarters if he slipped away for an hour or so, he managed to persuade himself, so perhaps he'd go and see how DS Cousins was getting on at Ashton Court.

FOURTEEN

'I think we've found what you were looking for, Sarge,' one of the uniformed constables said, pointing to the foot of the wall which surrounded Sir William Langley's estate.

Cousins bent down and examined the two rectangular indentations – both four inches long and two inches broad – which had been made in the earth.

'What would you say they indicate, Constable Pickering?' he asked.

'A ladder,' Pickering said dutifully.

'Couldn't be anything else, could it?' Cousins agreed. 'So this is where the bastard gained access.'

Pickering knelt and ran his finger across the dip. 'Do you think so, Sarge?' he asked dubiously.

'Don't you?' Cousins replied.

'Well, I don't know,' Pickering admitted. 'There's no chance he could have brought the body in some time *before* last night, is there?'

'No, there isn't,' Cousins said. 'Stockwell was seen alive as late as yesterday afternoon. What makes you ask that?'

'Well, I do a bit of gardening, you see – on an allotment,' Pickering said, in a low voice, as if he didn't want the other constable to hear him.

'So?'

'So you can tell when earth's been turned over by the state it's in. Its texture, and that. I think it's something to do with oxidation.'

'Possibly it is,' Cousins said, impatiently, 'but what's your point, lad?'

'I think these indentations are more than a few hours old.'

'Do you, by God?' Cousins asked. 'Then let's go and see if we can find any more.'

They found a second set of indentations half a dozen yards further along the wall.

'*Now* do you see why I thought it would be useful to bring a second pair of eyes along?' Cousins said.

The constable nodded. 'Yes, Sarge.'

'And are these indentations more recent than the others?'

'Definitely.'

'They're deeper, too,' Cousins mused. 'What does that tell us?'

'That there was more pressure on the ladder.'

'And why was that?'

'Because a different man – a heavier one climbed up it. Or maybe . . . maybe it was the same man, but he was carrying something!'

'Like *a corpse*,' Cousins said grimly. 'God, he's a cold-blooded bastard, this killer.'

'You can say that again,' Pickering agreed. 'To have ripped somebody's throat out like he did, and then take the body and—'

'That's not what I meant,' Cousins interrupted. 'I'm talking about the fact that there are *two* sets of ladder impressions, instead of just *one* – and that according to you, the first one's older.'

'So . . . so he didn't *just* dump the body last night . . .' Pickering gasped.

'That's right,' Cousins agreed. 'He'd been here before, to do a dry run.'

When Colin Beresford saw the two men kneeling at the base of the wall – and examining something they obviously regarded as significant – he felt a twinge of envy which he recognized as both unworthy of him and as almost inevitable.

He coughed, partly through embarrassment, partly to let them know he was there.

Cousins looked up. 'Something wrong, sir?'

'No,' Beresford replied, realizing he was sounding defensive. 'Why should there be?'

'No reason at all,' Cousins replied reasonably. 'I just didn't expect to see you here, that's all.'

'Meaning I should be back at HQ,' Beresford thought. 'Meaning I have no business abandoning my post and galli-vanting about the countryside!'

'So what have you found?' he asked aloud.

'We think this is where he got in, sir – and that's mainly down to Constable Pickering's smart thinking, because if it had been left up to me, I'd still have been looking somewhere else.'

'How did he manage it?' Beresford asked, trying to sound inspectorial.

'The way we have it figured, he rested the first ladder against the wall, then climbed up it, carrying the second ladder. When he reached the top of the wall, he lowered the second ladder down on to the other side. Once he'd done that, he climbed back down again to pick up the body.'

'Why would he have done it that way,' Beresford wondered. 'Why not just use one ladder and drop the body over the wall?'

'We think he didn't want to run the risk of damaging it, sir. We think he wanted it to look exactly as it *did* look when Langley found it.'

That made sense, Beresford thought.

'Have you checked for ladder impressions on the other side of the wall?' he asked.

'Not yet, sir, but it's our next step. I'll also have the lads look for tyre tracks on *this* side of the wall, and for anything the killer might have inadvertently dropped while he was carrying the body.'

'He's got it all under control,' Beresford thought, disappointedly. 'There's absolutely nothing here for me to do.'

'Have you questioned the staff?' he asked.

'Not yet,' Cousins said. 'But it's down on what my wife used to call my "to do" list.'

'*I* might as well question them, since I'm here,' Beresford said, and when he saw the puzzled look come to Cousins' face, he said, 'It'll save you a job.'

'I suppose it will, sir,' Cousins agreed.

The public bar of the Drum and Monkey was the haunt of men who made their living with their sheer muscle power – men who dug ditches and carried builder's hods weighed down with bricks. The Clog and Billycock, on the other hand, seemed to cater for men who were one step up the job ladder, and surveying the car park, Paniatowski counted eight tradesman's vans.

She entered the pub and went straight over to the bar, where she found the landlord half-heartedly polishing a pint glass.

'Yes?' he said, the tone of his voice suggesting that he regarded customers as an unnecessary intrusion on his privacy.

Paniatowski showed him her warrant card. 'I'm looking for anyone who might know Simon Stockwell.'

The landlord sniffed. 'Then you'll want to talk to that lot over there,' he said, pointing.

There were four men sitting around the table that he'd indicated. Two of them were wearing blue overalls, which said on them that they worked for Speedy Plumbers. The other two, in brown, were employed by Hanson Electrical.

'Just look at them,' the landlord said sourly. 'God's gift to home improvements.'

'He drinks with them regularly, does he?'

'Regular enough. Most dinnertimes *and* most evenings.' the landlord said. 'Can I get you a drink?' he asked, belatedly remembering what he was there for.

'What brands of vodka do you stock?' Paniatowski asked.

'Vodka?' the landlord repeated, as if the word were as alien to him as it would be to a Himalayan goat herder. 'I don't think we stock *any*. There's no call for it.'

'That's what I thought,' Paniatowski said. 'Thank you for your time.'

The four men were already deep in conversation as Paniatowski crossed the room, and it was the elder of the plumbers who was holding the floor.

'So I says to her,' he was telling the others, 'I says, "Look, lady, I can do it cheap if you like, but cheap can work out very expensive in the long run." An' she says to me, "Well, if you're convinced that these copper-cryptic pipes are the best, I'd better have them, hadn't I?" So copper-cryptic pipes it was.'

'I don't think I've ever heard of copper-cryptic pipes,' one of the electricians said.

The plumber chuckled. 'That's hardly surprisin', considerin' I'd just made the name up.'

The four men became aware of Paniatowski's arrival simultaneously, though their reactions to her were all different. The better-looking of the electricians gave her a broad smile, suggesting that, if she played her cards right, she could have him. His spotty partner, on the other hand, was already reconciled to failure, and contented himself with staring at her breasts. The younger plumber looked to his mate for guidance about the nature of the fun which was bound to follow. And the older plumber sucked in his gut – as if he thought that by this one act he could hide all the evidence of twenty years' over-indulgence in ale and fry-ups.

She knew them all, Paniatowski thought. They were the lads who had hung around on street corners and shouted obscenities after the twelve-year-old Monika. They were the callow – and callous – police cadets, who had covered their own feelings of inadequacy by picking on another cadet, simply because she had the nerve to be a woman.

On their own, they were nothing. But put them in a group, and it wouldn't take them long to persuade each other that the girl who had drunk too much – and passed out in the corner of the bar – really *wanted* all of them to have sex with her.

It was the older plumber who fired the opening salvo, just as she'd expected it would be.

'Well, well, well,' he said, with a lasciviousness which would have been insulting if he hadn't been pathetic. 'Just look what we've got here. And what can we do for *you*, Sweetie?'

'I'd like to ask you a few questions about Simon Stockwell,' Paniatowski said.

'Got you up the duff, has he?' the older plumber chortled. 'I didn't know he had it in him.'

'Must have had it in *her*, though, hey, Brian?' asked the younger plumber, nudging his partner in the ribs.

'Bit of a ladies' man, was he?' Paniatowski asked.

'Well, you know what us lads are like when we're offered the chance of a bit of loose,' the older plumber replied. Then, as the last two words that Paniatowski had spoken began to sink into his underemployed brain, he frowned. 'Did you just say, "Bit of a ladies' man, *was* he"?'

'That's right,' Paniatowski agreed. 'He didn't look like much of a ladies' man the last time *I* saw him, but then most men don't when they've had their throats ripped out.'

'Was he . . . was he dead?' the older plumber asked, incredulously.

'Either that, or he was doing the best bloody impression I've ever seen in my life,' Paniatowski replied.

'But he was only in here last night,' the good-looking electrician said.

'No, he wasn't,' the spotty one disagreed. 'I remember you sayin' that you wondered what had happened to him.'

'And now you know,' Paniatowski said.

'Was he . . . I mean, do you know if . . .?' the older plumber began.

'If you can remember back as far as two minutes ago, you'll recall that I told you *I'd* be the one who'd be asking the questions,' Paniatowski said sharply, producing her warrant card.

'Of course, Sergeant,' the older plumber said shakily.

'That's *Chief Inspector*!' Paniatowski barked.

'Of course, Chief Inspector,' the older plumber said.

Well, that was the softening-up process over and done with, Paniatowski thought.

'The man who you all spent so much time boozing with used to go home and knock his wife about,' she said. 'You were aware of that, weren't you?'

The four tradesmen bowed their heads like guilty schoolboys.

'We knew they didn't always get on well together, but we never really talked about what went on at home,' the spotty electrician said.

Which was about as close to an admission that they *did* know about it as any of them was likely to make.

'You hinted that he had an eye for the ladies,' Paniatowski said.

'That was just our bit of fun,' the older plumber replied, back-tracking furiously. 'Fellers like us don't go chasin' skirt. All we want after a hard day's work is a few pints.'

'So no girlfriends?'

'None he ever told us about.'

'What about enemies?'

'Enemies? Simon didn't have any of them. Everybody thought he was a good lad.'

'Really?' Paniatowski asked sceptically. 'Well, let me tell you, I've just been talking to his wife, and she's not exactly his biggest fan.'

'Ah, but she's a woman, you see,' the older plumber explained. 'Simon was more of a man's man.'

'So he wasn't in here last night,' Paniatowski said. 'But he was *never* in here on Thursday nights, was he?'

'No, he wasn't,' the spotty electrician said. 'We all miss the occasional night, but now I come to think about it, it was *always* Thursday that Simon missed.'

'So maybe he *did* have a bit on the side, after all,' the younger plumber suggested. 'Maybe a married lass, whose husband was always away on Thursday nights.'

'Do you really think that if Simon had been getting a bit of married nooky he'd have been able to keep quiet about it – especially after a few pints?' the older plumber asked scornfully.

'No, I don't suppose he would,' the younger plumber admitted.

'And I'm bloody sure he wouldn't,' Paniatowski thought.

The butler had announced that his name was Mr Lennox.

Not *Sam* Lennox or *Jack* Lennox, but *Mr* Lennox.

Beresford considered that affectation ridiculous. After all, this was the 1970s, for God's sake. The Beatles, with their mould-breaking informality, had been and gone. Now, kids who would once have called their parents' adult friends Uncle Sid and Auntie Elsie referred to them quite openly as just Sid and Elsie. And yet, as far as this man was concerned, nothing seemed to have changed.

There were other things about the butler which were anachronisms, too. Though it was a warm summer day, he was wearing both a jacket and a waistcoat. And though Beresford was a police inspector, and he was – when all was said and done – no more than a domestic servant – he gave the impression that in deigning to grant the other man an interview *at all*, he was being gracious well beyond the bounds of necessity.

'How many people work at Ashton Court?' Beresford asked.

'Sir William has a staff of twelve in his service,' the butler replied.

'And do they all live here?'

Lennox wrinkled his nose in what might have been contempt at the question or merely contempt at the situation.

'Oh, dear me, no,' he said. 'With the exception of myself and my lady wife, who is the housekeeper, all the staff are provided by an agency, and come in on a daily basis.'

'Why does Langley use agency staff?' Beresford wondered.

'Sir William has no choice in the matter,' the butler told him. 'There was a belief in service in this country before the War, but that is now quite gone, and I shall never forgive Adolf Hitler for destroying it.'

'I'm sure he'd be mortified to hear that, if he was still alive,' Beresford thought.

'So what hours do the agency staff work?' he asked aloud.

'That depends on the circumstances. If Sir William has a dinner party – and is prepared to pay out ruinous amounts of money in overtime – they will condescend to stay quite late. Otherwise, the agency minibus picks them up at six o'clock in the evening, leaving myself and Mrs Lennox to run the whole establishment alone.'

'What about last night?'

'Last night, they left at six, as usual,'

'Leaving who, exactly, in the house?'

'Just myself and my wife.'

'Not Langley and his wife?'

'Sir William was out attending one of the numerous functions to which he is invited. Lady Langley is away on a cruise.'

'So what time *did* Langley get home?'

'That, I cannot say. My wife and I, as is our custom, went to bed at around nine o'clock.'

'That's rather early, isn't it?' Beresford asked.

The butler sniffed. 'For you, perhaps. But we have a household to run, and that necessitates being up very early in the morning.'

'Very commendable, I'm sure,' Beresford said.

But having seen the butler's bloodshot eyes and the broken veins in his cheeks, he did not really think it was just tiredness which drove the couple to bed so early.

It was two young boys who found the van parked in front of the loading bay of one of the derelict mills in Whitebridge's industrial wasteland.

They had not been expecting to find it. They had not been expecting excitement of any kind as they took a short-cut from their school to the games field. And – as they raced each other on their bicycles – perhaps they wouldn't even have noticed it at all, but for the fact that it was on fire.

The boys dropped their bikes, and cautiously approached

the burning vehicle. It was a yellow van, with two ladders strapped to the roof. Flames were licking the paintwork on the side, making the stencilled sign which said 'Simon Stockwell, Painter and Decorator' bubble and blister.

'We shouldn't get any closer,' the older boy said worriedly.

'It'll be all right,' the other assured him.

The first boy was not convinced. 'When a car's on fire, it can blow up,' he said. 'I've seen it on the telly.'

'This isn't a car, it's a van,' his friend said contemptuously.

But even so, he had come to a halt.

The flames had reached the roof by now, and were greedily devouring the wooden ladders, which were encrusted at their bases with earth from Sir William Langley's estate, and would have been of great interest to Whitebridge Police's forensic department.

There were other things about the van which would have been of interest to the department, too – in fact, it would have had a field day with the vehicle – but the fire was rapidly destroying them all.

The older boy checked his watch – which he had been given for his birthday – and saw that it was twelve-forty-seven. He must remember that, he thought. Somebody, he was convinced, had deliberately set fire to the van, and the police would surely want to know all the details.

He was already starting to see himself as the star witness, who would help to solve this serious – this very *important* – crime.

The bobbies would be *very* impressed with him, he thought. They might even give him a medal.

He looked around for any signs of the master criminal who had started the fire, but the arsonist seemed to be long gone.

It was the tins of paint thinner which finally brought the process to its spectacular end. As the van had got hotter and hotter, they had begun bubbling uncomfortably, and now they could bear the strain no longer. They exploded, and in the process ignited all other flammable liquids which surrounded them.

There was a terrific boom, and the van was lifted several feet into the air, before crashing down again.

The two boys were knocked over by the blast, but were otherwise unhurt.

'Better than the pictures, this, isn't it?' asked the elder boy, as he scrambled to his feet.

And his younger companion could do no more than agree with him.

FIFTEEN

George Baxter was not, by nature, a corporate animal, but since he was the chief constable of Central Lancs – and since chief constables were expected to put in an appearance at all kinds of functions and events – he forced himself to go through the motions, and even did his best to look as if he was more or less enjoying himself.

Even so, these events never got any easier for him to take, and he often found himself wondering – usually about halfway through the proceedings – if he should jack in his current post, and go back to being a simple street-level bobby whose only job was to hunt down criminals.

Yet even as he toyed around with the idea, he knew it was never going to happen. There *was* no going back, because there wasn't a chief constable in the entire country who would have been happy about having an *ex*-chief constable under his command.

Today, he was attending a Rotary lunch at the Whitebridge Golf and Country Club, and in order to make the whole thing as painless as possible, he had planned to arrive just as the pre-lunch drinks were coming to an end and the Rotarians were slowly making their way into the restaurant.

The moment he walked through the bar door, however, he saw that the expected exodus was far from happening, and realized that either he had got his calculations wrong or there had been some unforeseen delay.

'What's the problem, Terry?' he asked one of the waiters who was standing near the door to the restaurant. 'Shouldn't we be getting stuck into the grub by now?'

'You certainly should, sir,' the waiter agreed. 'But there's been a power cut, you see, and it's thrown everything out of kilter. You won't be sitting down for at least another fifteen minutes.'

'Well, bollocks!' Baxter said, *almost* under his breath.

It wasn't that he disliked the Rotarians as a whole, he thought, as he headed for the bar.

Some of them were great fellers, and the work they did for charity was outstanding.

But there were *others* who were so impressed with themselves that they were almost insufferable – and it was with one of these complacent, self-congratulatory toads that he invariably found himself stuck in a corner.

He looked around the room, and his eye fell on a red-faced man who looked so much like a country squire that the effect was to turn him into a grotesque parody of one.

'A case in point,' he thought.

Sir William Langley, investment banker and property magnate, was just the kind of Rotarian he most disliked.

Baxter knew quite a lot – more than he would ever have cared to – about the other man, including the facts that he hadn't always been either *Sir* William *or* a banker.

Langley, he'd been told, had first gone into business in the fifties, just at the time when working-class aspirations had expanded to include ownership of their own vehicles. And he had, by all accounts, been brilliant at catering for that need, buying clapped-out cars from their middle-class owners for cash, and selling them on again at credit terms which would have made the Mafia blush with embarrassment.

But that was all behind the man now – or so he thought. He saw himself, as was obvious whenever he opened his mouth, as someone who had earned the right to be admired.

And maybe some people *did* admire him, Baxter thought, but that certainly didn't include the older members of the Golf and Country Club. *They* still remembered being summoned to their doors by a knock – sometimes quite late in the evening – and opening it to find Langley standing there, with a roll of banknotes in his hand and an avaricious look on his face. Oh yes, they remembered all right, and sometimes – when he was not present himself, they would refer to him as 'Bumptious Bill the Banger Buyer'.

Given that Langley had had a nasty shock that morning – and then been dragged reluctantly into the middle of a major investigation – Baxter supposed he'd better go and have a word with the man. But, as it happened, that proved unnecessary, since the moment Langley noticed the chief constable standing there, he made a bee-line for him.

'Terrible business at my place this morning, George,' Langley said, without preamble.

'So I've heard,' Baxter replied. 'But you can rest assured that my officers are doing all they possibly can to get to the bottom of it.'

'Not the sort of thing a chap expects to find on his morning constitutional,' Langley persisted.

'I'm sure it isn't.'

'And the thing is, George, it's slightly unnerved me.'

He *looked* unnerved, Baxter thought. More than that – he looked as if there was something more he wanted to say, but didn't know quite how to say it.

'Yes, it's rather unnerved me,' Langley repeated. 'So I was wondering whether it might be possible to give me some police protection for a while.'

'Police protection?' Baxter said.

'I've heard a whisper that I might be appointed to the Police Authority next year,' Langley ploughed on. 'And it certainly wouldn't do *you* any harm to have a friend on that august body, now would it?'

'I'm still not quite clear what you mean by "police protection",' Baxter said, with a cautious edge to his voice.

'Oh, nothing excessive, old chap,' Langley said, attempting to sound airy and casual – and failing on both counts. 'Nothing excessive at all. Three or four officers should do the trick.'

'Three or four officers!' Baxter gasped.

'They'd have to be on duty round the clock, of course,' Langley added hastily, in order to avoid any misunderstanding.

'You do realize that my force is running a major murder investigation, don't you?' Baxter asked.

'Yes, I *do* realize that,' Langley said archly. 'It was finding a corpse in my garden that really alerted me to the fact.'

'And *because* we're running that investigation, we're already stretched to the limit?'

'I appreciate you've got a lot of demands on your manpower,' Langley said, in a more conciliatory tone of voice. 'But it certainly wouldn't help matters, from your point of view, if there was a third victim – especially if that third victim was someone of significance, like me.'

And then he laughed, to show that he was only joking.

'Do you have any reason to think you might be the killer's next target?' Baxter asked, seriously.

Langley waved his right hand in a deprecating gesture.

'No, of course not! That's a ridiculous idea.'

'Then I don't see . . .'

'Although, when you think about it, the body *was* left on my estate, wasn't it? And so you certainly couldn't blame me for thinking that the killer might have it in for me, could you?'

'Couldn't I?'

'Well, no.'

'I'm afraid I don't see the connection,' Baxter said. 'Unless, of course, that connection comes through *the victim*. He wasn't a close friend of yours, by any chance, was he?'

'Of course not. He was a complete stranger to me, as I've already made quite clear to that dishy little policewoman of yours.'

'I take it that you're referring to Detective Chief Inspector Paniatowski,' Baxter said coldly.

'Yes, I . . . sorry, I should have shown her more respect, shouldn't I?'

'It would have been nice,' Baxter agreed. 'Did you know the other victim? Andy Adair?'

'Is it likely I'd have known a common soldier?'

'No, but then it's not likely you'd end up with a naked dead man in your garden, either.'

'I demand police protection!' Langley blustered. 'It's my right as a citizen.'

'If you take that argument to its logical conclusion, I should be assigning three or four of my bobbies to each and every person in Whitebridge,' Baxter pointed out, reasonably.

'Do I get the protection I need?' Langley demanded. 'Yes or no?'

'Yes,' Baxter replied.

'Good!' Langley said, with obvious relief.

'Or, at least, you'll get it the moment you can give me a good reason why you *should* have it.'

'You'll rue the day you crossed me,' Langley said angrily. 'I have considerable influence in this town, and I'll pay you back for this if it's the last thing I do.'

Baxter smiled, though he knew he shouldn't have. 'Then you'd better get a move on, hadn't you?' he said.

'I beg your pardon?'

'You said you'd pay me back if it was the last thing you did?'

'Yes?'

'And if your fears for your own safety are in any way justified, the last thing you do could be just around the corner, couldn't it?'

SIXTEEN

I t was a quarter past two, and the team had gathered around their usual table in the Drum and Monkey. Paniatowski had already outlined what she had discovered that morning, and now it was her inspector's turn to present his report.

'Thanks to the work done by Sergeant Cousins' lads, we've got some excellent tyre prints from the van that took Stockwell's body to Ashton Court,' Beresford was saying. 'Unfortunately, they're unlikely to do us much good, because I firmly believe it was Stockwell's own van that was used, and while the sergeant and I were out at Ashton Court, somebody else – most probably the killer himself – was torching that van. All of which means that that particular line of inquiry—'

'Hang on a minute!' Paniatowski interrupted. 'Did you say *you* were out at Ashton Court, Colin?'

'Err . . . yes, boss.'

'But I put you in charge of the incident room! What were you doing at Langley's place?'

Beresford shrugged awkwardly. 'There wasn't much happening back at headquarters, and I thought DS Cousins might need some help.'

'And *did* you need help, Paul?' Paniatowski asked icily.

'I didn't exactly *need* it, ma'am, but the inspector's help was certainly *appreciated*,' Cousins said, diplomatically.

'So just what *kind* of help were you able to offer the sergeant, Inspector Beresford?' Paniatowski asked.

'I made a mistake,' Colin Beresford thought miserably. 'I made a big mistake. I'm sorry, Monika.'

'I questioned the butler,' he said aloud.

'Really? And was that useful?' Paniatowski asked, unforgiving.

'He said that after the contract staff left at six o'clock, he and his wife were the only people in the house. He claims they went to bed early, and didn't hear anything during the night, but it's my guess that they were already drunk by the time they turned in, and wouldn't have noticed if a Panzer division had driven through the house.'

'Would the killer have known they'd be the only people left in the house?' Paniatowski asked Cousins.

'It's more than likely, if he'd done his homework – and I'm sure he always does,' the sergeant replied. 'The contract staff are driven to and from the house in a company van, so it wouldn't take a rocket scientist to work out when they weren't there.'

Paniatowski turned her attention to Beresford again. 'What have your team found out about Stockwell's movements yesterday?' she said. 'Or have you been so busy with other things that you've not had time to ask them yet?'

'He was painting a living room in a house up on Hill Rise yesterday afternoon,' Beresford said, ignoring the implied criticism because he didn't know what else to do. 'The woman he was working for was expecting him to be there until five o'clock, by which time the job should have been completed. But at around about three, Stockwell told her that he had to leave, because he had an important business meeting to attend. She wasn't best pleased, as you'd imagine, but he promised her he'd turn up early this morning and get the job finished.'

'Did he say who this meeting was with?'

'No, he didn't. She pressed him to tell her, of course, because she wanted the work finished, but he refused to go into any more detail, and just kept repeating that it was an important business meeting, and he had to leave. I think that was what the killer *told* him to say.'

'You think it was the killer he was meeting?'

'Yes, boss, I do.'

'Why?'

'Because to have reached the stage of rigor mortis he was in when he was found, he must have been killed within a maximum of two or three hours of leaving Hill Rise.'

'Good thinking,' Paniatowski said, but she was not quite prepared to let up on him yet, and added, 'Now if you've managed to find a connection between Stockwell and Langley, I'll be really impressed.'

'I haven't,' Beresford admitted.

'I wonder what Langley does on the Thursday nights,' DC Crane said, almost to himself.

'What was that, Constable?' Paniatowski asked.

'Well, ma'am, we know that Stockwell went missing on Thursday nights, and we also know, because the Sarge talked to his neighbours, that there were nights when Andy Adair didn't get home until three o'clock in the morning . . .'

'Were *they* Thursday nights, as well?' Paniatowski asked Cousins.

'The woman I talked to was a bit vague about what nights they were,' Cousins admitted. 'But I could try and pin her down.'

'You do that,' Paniatowski said. She turned to Crane again. 'Carry on with what you were saying, Jack.'

'Well, if it *was* Thursdays that Adair got home late,' Crane continued uncertainly, 'and if Langley *also* went missing on Thursdays . . .'

'That just might be the link we're looking for,' Paniatowski agreed. 'Check on that as well, will you, Paul.'

'Yes, ma'am, I'll do that,' Cousins agreed, but with a notable lack of enthusiasm.

'You don't think it will lead anywhere, do you?' Paniatowski asked.

Cousins shrugged. 'I think it was very clever of young Jack to come up with the idea, but I find it hard to picture Stockwell and Langley out on the batter together. I mean, can you really see Langley taking Stockwell clay-pigeon shooting, or Stockwell persuading Langley to join his darts team?'

'No, I can't,' Paniatowski admitted. 'Do you have a theory of your own, Sergeant?'

'I have an *idea*, but it's not as ingenious as DC Crane's, and it's certainly not grand enough to be called a theory,' Cousins said, with some reluctance.

'Let's hear it, anyway.'

'I think it's possible the connection between the victims only exists in the killer's own mind.'

'Go on.'

'He sees them both – and possibly Langley as well – as *bad* people. In Adair's case, that could be as a result of some-thing he did in Northern Ireland. In Stockwell's, it could be simply be that he used to beat the hell out of his missus.'

'So you're suggesting that, in his own mind, he sees himself as some kind of vigilante, who's simply punishing people for their wrongdoings?' Monika Paniatowski asked.

'Essentially, yes,' Cousins agreed.

'If that's the way he looks at life, he'll have to be a *real* nutter,' Beresford said.

And the moment he spoken the words, he cursed himself – because that just wasn't the kind of thing you should say to a man who'd recently been discharged from a mental institution.

'It's all right, sir,' Cousins said, reading the inspector's expression. 'If you all go around walking on egg shells when it comes to my medical history, we'll never get anything done. And I agree with you, he probably *is* a nutter. But that's no serious impediment to being a killer as well. In fact, it might even be a help.'

'Let's assume you're right,' Beresford said thoughtfully. 'Why did he leave the bodies where Toynbee and Langley were virtually certain to find them?'

Cousins shrugged again. 'Maybe he did it as a warning to them. Maybe the message he intended to leave was, "Mend your ways or you could end up like this, too." '

'You're forgetting our very good friend Mr Forsyth,' Paniatowski pointed out. 'He's not here because of some nutter – he's here because he thinks he's protecting our national security.' She turned to Crane again. 'What's Forsyth been doing this morning, Jack?'

'He had a leisurely breakfast in his room, and then he went for a stroll,' Crane said.

'A stroll?'

'That's what I'd call it, ma'am. He was ambling along as if he had all the time in the world. Then he went into St Martin's Church, which is one of the best examples of Victorian Gothic ... I mean, which some people say is a very interesting church. And Mr Forsyth really *did* seem interested in it. After that, he went to the museum. And now he's having lunch in the Royal Victoria.'

'Do you think he knew he was being followed?'

'I'm no expert on these kinds of things, ma'am.'

'Take a guess.'

'In spy films, when somebody thinks they're being followed, they look over their shoulders to catch a sight of their tail, or else come to an unexpected stop to see what the tail will do. But there was none of that with Mr Forsyth.'

'So just what bloody game *is* the bastard playing?' Paniatowski asked, exasperatedly.

'You could always ask him, boss,' Beresford suggested.

'Oh, don't you worry about that, I'm going to, right after the press conference,' Paniatowski told him. 'But whether he'll give me a straight answer to a straight question is another matter entirely.'

'What exactly are you going to say at the press conference?' Beresford wondered.

'I don't know yet – I still haven't talked it over with the chief constable. But whatever I say, it can't be anything like as vague as what I said yesterday. At the moment, I'm thinking of revealing the fact that both victims were naked, but holding back any information on the position they were found in.'

'Even that will whip the hacks up into a real frenzy,' Beresford warned her.

'I know it will,' Paniatowski agreed. 'But what choice do I have, now there's been a second killing?'

'If I was in your position, ma'am, I wouldn't hold *any* of the details back,' Cousins said.

'Are you mad?' Beresford asked, then, realizing he'd done it again, he continued, 'Listen, Paul, if we *do* release all the details, there'll be complete pandemonium.'

'I know,' Cousins agreed, levelly.

'And what, exactly, would that achieve in terms of the investigation?' Beresford asked.

'Nothing,' Sergeant Cousins conceded. 'In fact, it would bring all kinds of cranks crawling out of the woodwork, and make our job a lot harder.'

'Well, then?'

'But it would also scare the shit out of people.'

'And that's a *good* thing, is it?'

'I think so. Because, as well as scaring them, it would also put them on their guard. And they *need* to be put on their guard – because whatever the killer's motive, I don't think this will be his last murder. In fact, I think he's just getting started.'

Beresford had gone back to the incident room, Crane had returned to his surveillance of Mr Forsyth, and now the only two people left at the team's table were the chief inspector and her bagman

'How did I handle that, Paul?' Paniatowski asked.

'Handle what, ma'am?' Cousins asked innocently.

'Handle finding out that Inspector Beresford had deliberately disobeyed my instructions.'

'Well, you certainly made it plain you were displeased with him,' Cousins said cautiously.

'For God's sake, I know that. What I *don't* know is if I handled it *well*!'

'That's not for me to say,' Cousins demurred.

'It is if I order you to say it!'

The sergeant sighed. 'All right, ma'am. Inspector Beresford certainly deserved a bollocking for what he did, but you should have saved it for later, when me and young Crane weren't there.'

He was right, Paniatowski admitted to herself. She should have seen Beresford's behaviour as a breach of discipline committed by one of her subordinates, and dealt with it in a proper, official manner. Instead, she'd reacted emotionally, because she'd been hurt that her old friend Colin had let her down.

'Anything else you'd like to add?' she asked Cousins.

'Even while you're bollocking him, I think you could show a little more sympathy for his situation, ma'am.'

'What situation?'

'He's in mourning.'

'For who?'

'Not for *who*, for *what*. He's in mourning for his past – for the days when you and him were mates, and somebody else was in charge. He's suddenly realized that things have changed forever, and there's no going back.' Cousins paused for a moment. 'I'm going to tell you something now that, with my medical history, I probably shouldn't tell anybody. All right?'

'All right,' Paniatowski agreed.

'Sometimes, when I'm just opening my front door, I like to pretend that my wife's inside the house, waiting for me to come home. I don't really believe it, of course – not at any deep level – but I find it gives me comfort, if only for a moment. And DI Beresford was doing something like that this morning – just for a moment, he was pretending he was *DS* Beresford.'

'Will he do it again?' Paniatowski wondered.

'Probably,' Cousins conceded. 'But as time goes by, he'll do it less and less. Because however hard you try to prevent it, the memories start to fade. However much you try to convince yourself the past is still real, it's somehow not quite *that* real any more.'

'You're finding it harder to imagine your wife waiting for you, aren't you?' Paniatowski asked, softly.

A single tear rolled down Cousins' cheek. 'I am, ma'am,' he admitted. 'And that's my loss.'

From the moment they'd met – or, at least, from the moment they'd had their first serious talk – Paniatowski had been trying to work out who Paul Cousins reminded her of. Now, thinking about the way he'd dealt with PC Pickering earlier, the way he'd conducted himself in the meeting they'd just had, and the way he'd just been giving her advice, she thought she'd managed to pin it down.

'In some ways, you're a bit like Charlie Woodend, aren't you, Paul?' she asked.

Cousins brushed the tear off his cheek with the back of his hand, and grinned. 'There's some people who wouldn't take kindly to being compared to Cloggin'-it Charlie,' he said.

'I know there are,' Paniatowski agreed.

'But I'm not one of them,' Cousins said, as his face grew serious again. 'I regard it as one of the greatest compliments a bobby could ever be paid. Thank you, ma'am.'

'No,' Paniatowski said, 'thank *you*, Paul.'

SEVENTEEN

Edward Dunston was sitting at his desk – in an office remarkable for its absolute absence of any personal touches – and was fighting the urge to look up at the clock on the wall yet again.

Dunston was in his late forties, a tall, spare man who wore conservative suits and thin wire spectacles. His head was large and dome-shaped, and now he had lost most of the hair from his pate, a number of people had commented – usually behind his back – that he looked a little like one of the super-intelligent aliens so beloved by illustrators of science-fiction comics. He was generally regarded as being cold and humour-less – qualities he himself found admirable in a chartered accountant – and his staff were well aware that while they were expected to apply themselves with extreme diligence, they should give no sign that they were actually *enjoying* their work.

Despite his best intentions, Dunston felt his head move – and his eyes fix on the clock face.

A quarter to three!

In five more minutes, the pubs would be calling last orders.

He knew that some accountants of his acquaintance kept a bottle of booze secreted in their desk drawers, but he had always looked down on the habit. As far as he was concerned, working time was working time and drinking time was drinking time – and never the twain should meet.

'But Jesus, I could use a drink right now!' he thought.

He looked up at the clock again. Another few minutes and he would have no choice in the matter – another few minutes and it would be out of his hands.

'You can do this,' he urged himself. 'You can sit it out.'

But even as the thought flashed across his mind, he was already rising to his feet and beginning to make excuses for himself.

This was an emergency, he argued, as he reached for his hat. His nerves had been on a knife-edge for the last twenty-four hours, and if a whisky would help to settle them, then he was quite prepared to break his own rules for once.

He opened the door and stepped into his outer office, where his secretary was busy pretending to be so absorbed in her tasks that she hadn't even heard him.

'I'm going out for a few minutes, Janice,' he said.

His secretary looked up.

'Going out, Mr Dunston?' she repeated incredulously. 'But you've got an appointment at three o'clock.'

Damn it, so he had, Dunston thought – and not just *any* old appointment, a very important one!

'Make my apologies, will you?' he said over his shoulder, as he crossed the office. 'Ask the client if he wouldn't mind waiting.'

'But . . . but it's Mr Hoskins,' the secretary stuttered. 'He's never been known to wait for . . .'

'I shouldn't be more than half an hour,' Dunston said, opening the outer door and fleeing into the corridor.

He made it to the empty lounge bar of the Black Horse just as the barman was flashing the lights for last orders.

'Well, this is a surprise,' the fat landlord said, jovially. 'It's not often we see you in here at this time of day, Mr Dunston.'

'I need a drink,' the accountant gasped.

'Course you do,' the landlord agreed. 'What can I get you? The usual?'

'Yes, but make it a double,' Dunston said. 'No, on second thoughts, make it *two* doubles.'

'Coming up, sir,' the landlord said.

And it was not until he had turned his back on his customer that he allowed his eyebrows to arch in surprise.

Dunston sat down on one of the bar stools, and took his cigarettes out of his jacket pocket. As he struck a match, he noticed that his hands were trembling.

'You're blowing the whole thing out of proportion,' he told himself. 'So Andy Adair has been murdered. Well, people *do* get murdered.'

And Adair, being the rough sort of man he was, had probably been more likely to get murdered than most, his argument continued.

But his death didn't have to mean anything, in terms of the

people who knew him, even if they knew him through the . . .
through the . . .

'I said your two double whiskies are on the bar, Mr Dunston,'
he heard the landlord say.

'Oh, thank you very much, Tony,' Dunston mumbled.

The landlord grinned. 'You really are wrapped up in your
own thoughts today, aren't you?'

'I beg your pardon?'

'Not only didn't you notice your drink had arrived, but you
never heard me ask you if you'd mind if I turned the telly
on.'

'The telly?'

'Detective Chief Inspector Paniatowski's giving a conference on the latest developments in that murder investigation,
and if it wouldn't bother you, I'm quite keen to watch it.'

'I don't mind at all,' Dunston said.

'You're sure?'

'I'm sure.'

But it wasn't quite as simple as that – because while, in
some ways, he was *desperate* to hear what the chief inspector
had to say, the thought of listening to her also filled him with
dread.

If Paniatowski announced that the murderer had been
arrested – and especially if that murderer turned out to be
someone from Adair's army days who held a grudge against
him – then the sense of relief would be wonderful. But if
instead she said that the police were no further on in their
investigation, then the knot in his stomach would grow even
tighter than it was already.

The landlord switched on the set just as Paniatowski was
mounting the podium, and as Dunston watched her turn to
face the camera, he realized he was praying softly to himself.

'*There have been further tragic developments in the investigation we are currently conducting,*' Paniatowski said gravely.

'No!' Dunston thought, reaching for the first of his whiskies.
'It can't have got any *worse*!'

'*There has been a second murder, and we strongly suspect
that it was carried out by the same man who killed Andrew
Adair.*'

'Let it be someone I don't know,' Dunston pleaded silently.
'Let it be someone I've never even *heard* of.'

'*The second victim has been named as Simon Stockwell. He was thirty-two years old, and worked as a self-employed painter and decorator.*'

'No!' Dunston moaned.

'Are you all right?' the landlord asked, worriedly.

'*His body was discovered this morning at Ashton Croft, the home of Sir William Langley, a well-known and highly respected local businessman.*'

Langley!

As well!

'Me next,' Dunston sobbed. 'Me next. It could be *me* next.'

'Shall I call a doctor?' the landlord asked.

Dunston shook his head, and knocked back the second double whisky in a single gulp.

It would take more than a doctor to save him now, he thought.

Sitting in a comfortable armchair in his suite at the Royal Victoria, Mr Forsyth watched Monika Paniatowski's television performance with great interest.

So far, he thought, she had been doing rather well.

She had revealed that the two victims had both been found naked – which would have brought forth no more than an indifferent shrug if the journalists had been French, but had the English hacks almost jumping from their seats in excitement – yet had held back the information that they had been posed on all fours. That was sensible. In her situation, he would probably have done the same thing.

She had managed to field all the questions she didn't want to answer in a way which suggested she wasn't fielding them at all. Again, top marks.

But she was not entirely out of danger yet, and as the end of the press conference approached, she was starting to look more relaxed – which Forsyth considered was a bad sign.

'*I'll take one more question,*' she said, pointing to a journalist who already had his hand raised.

The reporter stood up. '*Tom Jenkins,* Daily Chronicle,' he announced. '*It's true, isn't it, Chief Inspector, that the first victim, Andy Adair, served as a soldier in Northern Ireland?*'

'Careful, Monika,' Forsyth urged.

'*Yes, it is true,*' Paniatowski agreed. '*But he also served in various other places around the world during his fairly long career.*'

'Good,' Forsyth nodded approvingly. 'Very good.'

'*But, as far as I know, he didn't shoot into a crowd of unarmed civilians in any of these other places,*' Jenkins said.

'*The Widgery Inquiry found there was no wrong-doing on the part of the Parachute Regiment,*' Paniatowski pointed out.

'*It certainly did,*' Jenkins agreed. '*But I doubt that was a finding which the Irish Republican Army was willing to accept.*'

'*Do you actually have a question, Mr Jenkins?*' Paniatowski asked, her patience starting to wear thin.

'*Yes, I do,*' Jenkins told her. '*And it's this – do you think that Andy Adair could have been killed by the IRA, in revenge for Bloody Sunday?*'

'It matters how you answer this, Monika,' Forsyth said, almost in a whisper. 'It's really important.'

'*As far as we've been able to establish, the second victim, Simon Stockwell, had no connections with Ireland at all,*' Paniatowski said.

'*I didn't ask you about Simon Stockwell,*' the journalist pointed out. '*My question was about Andy Adair's death. So I'll ask it again. Do you think that Adair's death had anything to do with the IRA?*'

Paniatowski hesitated. '*At this stage in the investigation, we're not prepared to rule* anything *out,*' she said finally.

'Oh dear, oh dear, oh dear,' Forsyth said, disappointedly.

'*Thank you all for coming,*' Paniatowski said to the journalists. '*You will be informed when the next press conference is to be held.*'

'You *are* a silly girl, Monika,' he said. 'And *because* you're a silly girl, I'm going to have to do something I was really hoping to avoid.'

He picked up the telephone, and dialled a number he had only recently memorized.

'Whitebridge Police Headquarters,' said the switchboard operator. 'Can I help you?'

'What a pleasant manner you have about you, young lady,' Forsyth replied. 'It's almost worth ringing up just to hear your voice.'

'Why, thank you,' the switchboard operator said, obviously

delighted. Then she remembered what she was there for, and continued, 'What is the nature of your business, sir?'

'I'd like to speak to Detective Inspector Walker, if that's possible,' Forsyth said.

'Is it urgent?' the operator asked.

'Well, no, it's not exactly urgent,' Forsyth admitted. 'But it *is* quite important.'

Looking out of the picture window of her well-appointed detached home in one of the most salubrious areas of Whitebridge, Mary Dunston was amazed to see her husband's car pulling into the driveway.

Edward *never* came home in the middle of the afternoon.

'It's the best time of the day to do business,' he always told her. 'When the clients come to see me, they've already had a heavy lunch and probably the best part of a bottle of wine. The food's making them sleepy, and the alcohol's convinced them they're the sharpest operator in the whole of Whitebridge. So I can run rings round them, and they don't even know it's happening.'

Yet there he was, getting out of his car, *in the middle of the afternoon.*

And didn't he look pale?

She went out to the hallway to meet him.

'Is something wrong, Edward?' she asked, worriedly. 'Has your mother been taken ill?'

Dunston brushed past as if she wasn't even there, and started to climb the stairs.

'Edward!' she called after him.

'I have to go away,' he said, over his shoulder. 'It's business – urgent business.'

She followed him up the stairs, and by the time she reached the bedroom he was already throwing clothes haphazardly into a suitcase.

'What's happened?' she asked, almost in tears by now.

'For God's sake, woman, have you gone deaf?' Dunston asked, harshly. 'I said, I have to go away.'

The phone on the bedside cabinet rang, making them both jump.

'Well, answer it,' Dunston said, continuing to cram the suitcase with his clothes.

Mary picked up the phone. 'Yes?' she asked in a sniffly voice. 'Yes, he is. I'll tell him.' She held the phone to her husband. 'It's for you.'

'I can't talk to anybody at the moment,' Dunston said dismissively. 'Take his number and say I'll call him back.'

'But he says it's very important. He says to tell you that it's about Moors' End Farm.'

Dunston snatched the phone from his wife's hand.

'Out!' he said to her.

Mary Dunston gasped with amazement.

'I'm sorry, Edward,' she said, in as dignified a tone as she could muster, 'but I'm not sure that I quite see what you expect me to—'

'Can't you understand plain simple English, you stupid bitch?' Dunston asked viciously. 'I told you to get out! Now bloody *do it!*'

With a sob, Mary Dunston fled from the room.

The man on the other end of the line chuckled. 'Have I just been inadvertently eavesdroppin' on a bit of a domestic disturbance, Edward?' he asked.

'I—' Dunston began.

'Plannin' to do a runner, are you?' the caller interrupted him. 'Now that really wouldn't be too clever at all – not when they're watchin' the house.'

'Who's . . . who's watching the house?' Dunston asked, with a tremor in his voice.

'The people who did for Andy Adair an' Simon Stockwell, o' course. See, Eddie, if you do a runner, they'll just follow you, an' as soon as they get their opportunity, they'll slit your throat. So your best move is to stay where you are, 'cos they can't snatch you without your missus seein' them – an' since they've got nothin' against her, they don't want to hurt her unless they absolutely have to. Course, if you stay there *too* long, they might decide they'll just have to pop her as well. That's why you need a Plan B.'

'Who are you?' Dunston gasped.

'Who am I? I'm the bloke who's goin' to save your bacon. Only it's goin' to cost you. How much cash have you got in the house?'

'I don't know. I have to think. There's probably around two hundred pounds in the safe.'

'Not enough,' the caller said dismissively. 'What's your wife's jewellery like? Good stuff?'

'Well, yes, it's . . .'

'I'll need that as well.'

'How do I know I can trust you?' Dunston whined.

The man at the other end of the line sighed heavily.

'Look,' he said, 'I can only get away with doin' this once, then for my own safety I'll have to make *myself* scarce. So if you don't want my help, I'll call somebody else on their list. I could try Len Gutterridge, for example. Course, he probably couldn't pay me as much as you could, but since you're clearly not interested . . .'

'Don't hang up!' Dunston pleaded. 'I *am* interested. I *do* want your help.'

'In that case, get all the valuables that you can together, and wait for my next call.'

'*When* will you call?' Dunston asked desperately.

'I can't say for certain, Eddie. But it will have to be within the next few hours, won't it? Because if I leave it any longer than that, you'll already be dead when I get there!'

Mr Forsyth had only been in possession of the office he'd commandeered for himself in Whitebridge Police Headquarters for a few hours, but it had already undergone some small – but significant – changes.

The desk had been moved, Paniatowski noted, so that now the person behind it sat with his back to the wall, rather than to the window.

An expensive-looking map of the British Empire in the nineteenth century had been mounted on the wall.

And then, of course, there was the photograph in the silver frame!

In the centre of the picture stood a tall white-haired woman, dressed in a sensible tweed suit, and with a string of pearls slung casually around her neck. She looked perfectly content with life, and the source of that contentment was clearly the two children – a dark-haired boy and a blonde girl – who were standing just in front of her, and had her hands resting comfortably on their young heads. In the foreground was a short stretch of immaculate lawn, and behind the woman's head was a mature oak tree.

It was the positioning of the picture which gave the game away, Paniatowski thought. It had been placed so the visitor could see it as clearly as the man behind the desk could – and what that visitor was meant to think was that this was a photograph of Forsyth's wife and grandchildren.

But it wasn't. She was sure of that.

So why was Forsyth making such a display of these people he had possibly never even met?

She didn't know.

She would perhaps *never* know.

But she still recognized the picture as nothing more than a prop in the elaborate game he was playing – a game whose rules she didn't understand and had no desire to learn.

Forsyth smiled up at her. 'The reason I summoned you here this afternoon, Monika—' he began.

'You *didn't* summon me,' Paniatowski interrupted. 'I can only be *summoned* by people I work for – and I don't work for you.'

'No, you don't,' Forsyth agreed easily. 'But you *do* work for people who are prepared to sub-contract you to me – with all that entails.'

'Just who are we talking about here?' Paniatowski demanded. 'The chief constable?'

Forsyth laughed lightly. 'Oh no, my dear. It goes *much* higher up the ladder than Mr Baxter.'

'So I'm to be your errand girl?'

'If you choose to see yourself in that light, it's entirely up to you. I would prefer to think of us as two people who are collaborating in the interest of the common good.'

'Yeah, right,' Paniatowski said wearily. 'So what is it you want?'

'I thought I'd already explained that adequately enough. I want you to give me a detailed report on the progress of your investigation into the murder of Andrew Adair.'

'And on my progress in the investigation into the murder of Simon Stockwell?'

'Yes, that too, I suppose – but only in so far as it overlaps with the Adair investigation.'

'In other words, you're not really at all interested in who killed Simon Stockwell?'

'You could say that.'

'Which means, by logical extension, that you're not really interested in finding out who killed *Adair*, either.'

'Andy Adair was a soldier who served his country faithfully and honourably, so naturally I wish to see his killer brought to justice,' Forsyth said, with a hint of rebuke in his tone.

Paniatowski shook her head. 'Faithfully and honourably,' she repeated. 'That's just *words*. The truth is that you don't *really* give a shit whether I find the killer or not.'

'I think you're being rather harsh again,' Forsyth said.

'Let's cut through all the crap,' Paniatowski suggested. 'You want a briefing on the investigation, and I'm prepared to give it to you – but I want something in return.'

Forsyth frowned. 'What you fail to grasp is that you're in no position to make conditions, my dear,' he said.

'And what *you* fail to grasp is that you can only push me so far, and then I'll dig my heels in and will not be moved another inch – whatever it costs me.'

'How like your old boss, Charlie Woodend, you're starting to sound,' Forsyth said.

'Yes, I've been working on it,' Paniatowski countered. 'And before we go any further, there's one other matter we should get cleared up.'

'Yes?'

'I'd prefer it if you addressed me by my official title, which is Detective Chief Inspector Paniatowski, but I'm prepared to tolerate you calling me Monika, if you must. What I will *not* tolerate is being addressed as "my dear". That's the way creepy old men with bags of sweets in their sweaty hands address gym-slipped schoolgirls in the park – and I'm no gym-slipped schoolgirl.'

'But I'm a creepy old man with a bag of sweets?' Forsyth asked, with the slightest hint of anger in his voice.

'If you choose to see yourself in that light, it's entirely up to you,' Paniatowski said, mockingly flinging his own words back at him.

Forsyth sighed. 'What is it that you want in return for graciously agreeing to brief me?'

'I want you to get your people to do a comprehensive background check on Sir William Langley. And I mean *comprehensive*. I want information I couldn't get myself, even with a search warrant.'

'I see,' Forsyth said. 'And in return for my doing that, I'll get your full cooperation?'

'Yes,' Paniatowski agreed, perhaps a little too readily.

'I want to be quite clear on this – I'll get your full and *unqualified* cooperation?' Forsyth pressed.

'As far as is possible,' Paniatowski said.

'And what does that neat little twisting of "full and unqualified" mean, exactly?' Forsyth wondered.

'It means that if I find out that you're attempting to pervert the course of justice, then all bets are off.'

'That seems more than reasonable, my dear Chief Inspector,' Forsyth said, taking his defeat gracefully.

Mike Traynor stood under the bridge, looking down at the brackish water. If he'd had any real empathy with history, he could have been thinking that this was, in many ways, one of the most poignant spots in the whole of Whitebridge. For it was along this now-lonely canal that scores of barges had once travelled, bringing bales of cotton to the mills and taking away the cloth that the mill workers had produced from it. If he'd had an ounce of poetry in his soul, he might have seen the stagnation of the canal as a symbol of the wider stagnation which had overtaken the whole town. But he had no interest in either history or poetry. And instead of *thinking* at all, he was busy *nursing* a sense of grievance over the fact that, instead of meeting in a cosy pub, Ted Walker had selected this grim spot for their rendezvous.

He saw Detective Inspector Walker coming along the towpath with a folder under his arm.

'And about time!' he thought.

'Evening, Mike,' Walker said, as he drew level.

'You sound bloody cheerful,' Traynor complained.

'You will, as well, in a minute or two,' Walker told him. He held up the folder for the journalist to see. 'What I have in here, Michael, is a nice little earner for me, and a nice little scoop for you.'

'A nice little scoop for me,' Traynor repeated sceptically. 'Do you know how many *real* scoops there are around?'

'Very few, I should imagine, or they wouldn't be scoops at all. But they do exist – this is undoubtedly one of them.'

'Anyway, however good it is, we're *already* too late to catch tonight's edition,' Traynor said peevishly.

'Indeed we are,' Walker agreed, his good humour unabated. 'But then this story would be wasted on a nasty little provincial rag like the *Lancashire Chronicle*. This, my friend, is a story for the nationals.'

Traynor felt his hands start to itch.

'Let me see it,' he said, reaching out.

Walker jerked the folder away. 'Before I show it to you, we should talk about how much you're going to have to pay for it,' he said.

'How can we possibly do that before I even know what the bloody story's about?'

'I've been thinking about what it's worth,' Walker continued, as if the other man hadn't spoken, 'and I've decided I'd like two hundred quid for it.'

'Two hundred quid?' Traynor repeated. 'Are you mad? Have you gone completely off your head?'

'No, I leave that sort of thing to DS Cousins, who's much better suited to it,' Walker said. 'The reason I fixed on that amount is that I reckon you can sell the story to the nationals for at least twice that – or maybe even more. But I'm not a greedy man by nature, so I'll settle for the two hundred smackers.'

Traynor licked his lips, and discovered that they'd suddenly gone very dry. 'It must be one hell of a story,' he said.

'It *is* one hell of a story,' Walker agreed.

The policeman wouldn't try to con him, Traynor thought.

Not for two hundred quid.

Not when they had an ongoing business relationship.

'All right, you'll get your money,' he agreed. 'But if the story's not as good as you say it is, I'll expect a discount on the next one you give me.'

Walker smiled complacently.

'Read the story and tell me what you think,' he said, handing the journalist the folder.

Traynor opened it, and flicked through the contents. Then he read it again, much more slowly, this time.

'Bloody hell, if this is true, it's a dynamite story,' he said when he'd finished. Then a concerned look came to his face. 'But *is* it true?' he continued.

Walker's smile widened.

'No,' he said.

'Then what the bloody hell do you think you're doing wasting my time with this piece of crap?' Traynor asked angrily.

'It's not true *now*,' Walker said, 'but by the time the story's published it *will be* true.'

EIGHTEEN

When it happened, it happened so quickly that if DC Jack Crane had blinked, he might well have missed it.

One moment, Crane was sitting in the lobby of the Royal Victoria – pretending to read the newspaper and deciding that since Forsyth had gone straight up to his suite after consuming his large and expensive meal in the Balmoral Restaurant, the spy was probably bedded down for the night.

The next moment Forsyth himself appeared, crossed the lobby, and stepped out on to the street.

Crane glanced down at the sweeping second hand of his watch. He'd give it a minute before he set off in pursuit, he told himself. For caution's sake, a minute was the least he should allow.

But how long that minute seemed to be lasting!

How listlessly that hand on his watch seemed to be performing its duty!

His resolution broke down after forty-five seconds, and as the hand reached fifty, he was at the exit.

Even with the broken resolution, he had almost left it too late – because the doorman had the door of a Rover 2000 held open, and Forsyth was already climbing into the driver's seat.

'I didn't even know he *had* a bloody car,' Crane thought.

'No, you didn't, did you?' sneered a malevolent voice from another part of his brain. 'But you should have made it your business to bloody *find out.*'

The doorman closed the car door, Forsyth started the engine, and the Rover pulled away from the kerb.

Crane – forcing himself to walk at a leisurely pace – made his way towards his Vauxhall Victor, which was parked a little way further down the road.

'Thank God that I at least had it pointing in the right direc-tion,' he thought, as he slipped behind the wheel and fired up the ignition.

He joined a stream of vehicles which was moving with typical downtown sluggishness. Looking ahead of him, he saw, with increasing panic, that there was no sign of Forsyth.

This was the first really *independent* assignment that the boss had given him, he reminded himself – and he'd fallen before he'd even reached the first post.

How would he explain that to her?

Would she blame him?

And what were the chances of her ever allowing him to work on his own again?

When he caught sight of the Rover, held up by a red traffic light on Market Street, he let out a huge sigh of relief.

It was going to be all right!

He hadn't blown it!

Yet!

What was important now was to let the boss know exactly what was going on. He picked up his radio, pressed the right button, and waited for the reassuringly competent voice of someone in Whitebridge Police Headquarters.

There *was* no reassuringly competent voice.

There wasn't even a static crackle to offer him a little hope that there might be one eventually.

'You bastard!' he shouted at the radio. 'You bloody useless bastard!'

But so what if he was on his own, he asked himself, calming down a little.

Did that really matter?

It was now ten thirty-seven and Forsyth couldn't possibly be going *too* far at this time of night.

It did not take long for him to realize how wrong that supposition had been. Forsyth was not heading for the centre of the town – as a man in search of a late-night drink, or a late-night prostitute, might have been. Instead he was driving towards the ring road.

It was a quarter to eleven by the time the Rover 2000 and its tail reached the A677.

The road was still busy at that hour. Carloads of middle-aged drinkers were returning from expeditions to isolated country pubs. Married couples were heading home, after spending the evening with one of their families. Heavy-goods lorries were setting out on overnight runs, and an ambulance

– having completed a mad dash to the hospital – tootled sedately along on the journey back to its base.

Crane slid his Vauxhall Victor into the space between a Mini and a blue builder's van. He was perhaps a hundred yards behind Forsyth's Rover, and as long as the traffic remained as thick as it was now, he was reasonably sure he could stay undetected.

'But what happens if the bloody traffic starts to thin out?' he worried, as the A677 joined the A59 at Whalley. 'And, even worse, what happens if Forsyth decides to turn off the main road and go down a minor one instead?'

If Forsyth did do that, there'd be no choice but to follow him, the detective constable decided.

But it wouldn't be easy – without the protective covering of other vehicles – to remain unnoticed. In fact, on the scale of suspicious behaviour, driving along a country lane – late at night, and in an area you probably weren't familiar with – ranked quite highly.

What was it the boss had said?

Something like, '*Forsyth's not that kind of spy. He's never been one of the pieces on the chessboard of espionage. He's the bastard who moves the pieces around. He wouldn't spot a KGB agent if he had his rank tattooed on his forehead – and I doubt he'll spot a fresh-faced young detective constable, either.*'

Yes, that sounded all very well – *in theory*.

But how good a spy did Forsyth have to be in order to spot the fact that a car was following him up a road to the arse-end of nowhere?

Crane tried the radio again – pressing down on the button so hard that his thumb hurt – but the sodding machine was still refusing to cooperate.

As they were approaching the boundary of Clitheroe, Forsyth indicated that he was intending to turn off the main road, just as Crane had feared he might.

He had no option but to increase the distance between them, Crane decided, as he flickered the intention to turn himself. That meant, of course, that he was running the risk of losing his quarry – but at least it was dark now, and Forsyth's lights would provide some help in keeping track of him.

The road Forsyth had chosen to take was indeed a country

lane – quite a narrow one, with high hedgerows either side, and drainage ditches running along its edges. Crane didn't know where it went, though from its general direction he supposed it must be leading towards the moors.

But why the hell would Forsyth want to go anywhere near the moors at that time of night?

Well, there was only way to find out.

Forsyth was driving slowly – almost as if he wished to make the detective constable's job easier for him – and there was a real danger they would soon be bumper to bumper.

Crane slowed down to a halt. He reached into the Victor's glove compartment and took out a map.

As he studied it, he began to count, 'One . . . two . . . three . . . four . . .'

By the time he had reached 'thirty', he had both familiarized himself with the map and given Forsyth time to get well ahead of him. He could no longer see the Rover's back lights, but he was not unduly worried by that. All it meant was the car had turned a bend. On this road, the man couldn't lose him by making an unexpected turn – because, as the map clearly showed, there was nothing for him to turn into.

It was growing dark outside, and Edward Dunston – who had been nervously gazing through his lounge window for over two hours – fretted about what that might mean in terms of his own survival.

Would the man who had rung him up with the rescue plan see the onset of darkness as an opportunity to put that plan into action, he wondered desperately.

Or would the men who the would-be rescuer said were watching the house choose that moment to swoop down on him?

'I wish you'd tell me what's worrying you, Edward,' said Mary Dunston, from the other side of the room.

She sounded very calm – eerily calm – at that moment, but he knew it wouldn't last. In the hours which had passed since the phone call, her mood had swung from the hysterical to the numb, and then back again.

She had begged him to allow her to call the doctor, or the police – or *anybody*. He had refused each time. He was putting his faith in the man who had called him – because he didn't see he had any choice.

'We are married, you know,' Mary said. 'And a problem shared is a problem halved.'

'For God's sake, can't you just shut up, you stupid bitch!' Dunston said angrily.

Mary started to sob softly to herself.

He wanted to turn round and comfort her, but he couldn't quite bring himself to do it. The only suffering he could handle at that moment was his own, he told himself – and he was not even making a particularly good job of that.

How had he allowed this to happen, he wondered.

Whatever had possessed him to put himself in a position in which, after over twenty years of happy – if unexciting – marriage, he could find it so easy to be brutal to his wife?

It wasn't his fault, he argued.

What he'd done would have passed without comment a hundred years earlier.

Jesus, a hundred years earlier, he'd have been rubbing shoulders with lords and clergymen while he did it!

But perhaps he wouldn't have found it so enticing back then. Perhaps it was the very illegality of the act – and the frisson of danger which accompanied it – which had so attracted him in the first place.

'Whatever it is you've done, Edward, tell me about it,' Mary said, in a choked voice. 'Tell me about it, and we'll face it together.'

He felt himself weaken. He *would* tell her about it, even though he could already picture the look of total disgust which would come to her face as he described what had gone on – even though he knew that when he had finished telling her, she would despise him. He would come clean whatever the cost, and maybe, that way, he could find a little redemption.

The phone rang, and he grabbed at it.

'Yes?' he gasped into the receiver.

'Have you got the money and the jewellery together?' asked a calm voice at the other end of the line.

'Yes . . . yes, I have.'

'How much is it worth?'

'I don't know. How *could* I know? I'm an accountant, for God's sake, not a jeweller.'

'You'll get nowhere with that attitude,' the other man said sternly.

'I'm sorry,' Dunston grovelled. 'I didn't mean to . . . I only wanted to . . .'

'You must know how much you paid for the jewellery in the first place,' the caller said. 'Take an educated guess at what it's worth now.'

Dunston gazed wildly up at the ceiling, as if he expected to find the answer written there.

'It's probably worth a thousand pounds,' he said finally. 'Maybe even a little more.'

The man on the other end of the line fell silent.

'Are you still there?' Dunston asked, as he felt the tears start to run down his cheeks.

'I'm still here. A thousand pounds, you say? Or maybe even a little more?'

'Yes.'

Another pause, then the man said, 'I suppose if that's all there is, it will have to do. Now listen carefully. There's an unpaved lane running along the back of your house—'

'I know.'

'I *know* you know. Don't interrupt again!'

'I'm sorry,' Dunston sobbed, and then, realizing that that could be interpreted as an interruption, said, 'I'm sorry,' a second time.

'Be on the lane in two minutes from now,' the caller said. 'If you're not there when I arrive, I won't wait for you.'

The line went dead.

Dunston picked up his suitcase, and headed towards the back door. Then, seeing his wife huddled in her armchair, he paused for a moment.

'I love you, Mary,' he said. 'I honestly do. And I'm *so* sorry.'

'Will you . . . will you be coming back?' his wife asked.

'I don't know,' he admitted. 'I hope so.'

He went through the kitchen, and into the back garden. It had gone completely dark now, but there was a moon, and he could see the path to the back gate quite clearly.

Once on the lane, he stood peering into the blackness. And then he saw the headlights – two shining, bright yellow eyes – moving slowly towards him.

As the vehicle got closer, he could see that it was a six-hundredweight van.

'A van?' he thought. 'That's not much of a getaway car.'

And suddenly, he was quite proud of feeling so calm – of being able to make a joke, even if it was only a weak one.

The van came to a halt beside him, and the driver reached across to open the passenger door.

'Get in,' he said.

Dunston manoeuvred his suitcase over the passenger seat into the back of the vehicle, and then climbed in.

The van pulled off again.

'Where are we going?' Dunston asked.

'You'll know when we get there,' the driver replied.

'Look, I'm paying for this, so I have a right to know now where we're going,' Dunston said, feeling more in control of himself now than he had since he'd seen the police press conference on the television.

'Where I'm taking you, all your worries will soon be over,' the driver said.

They had turned off the lane, and were on a paved road with street lights. For the first time, Dunston got a real look at his rescuer's face.

'I know you from somewhere,' he said.

'Do you?' the driver replied, his voice devoid of interest.

'Yes, I do.'

But *where* had he seen the man before?

Had they met on a professional basis, perhaps?

Was he one of the company's less important clients, whose account had been handled by one of the junior members of the firm?

Did he work for some other company, that Dunston's had audited?

Had they met in a pub, or at some sort of social gathering?

Or was the link even more tenuous than that?

And suddenly he had it.

'I know who you are,' he said triumphantly. 'You're . . .'

'That's right,' the driver agreed. 'I am.'

It was as the Vauxhall Victor turned a bend in the narrow lane that Jack Crane saw the patrol car a hundred yards ahead of him. It was parked at an angle – its bonnet pointing towards the drainage ditch on one side of the lane, its boot pointing in the direction of the ditch on the other side – and the flashing light on its roof was sending out demented orange rays in all directions.

It was a roadblock! Crane thought.

It couldn't be anything else.

But why would anybody set up a roadblock on this deserted country lane, at this time of night?

As he slowed his vehicle down, his mind ran through a series of rapid calculations. He was two or three minutes behind Forsyth's vehicle, he estimated – which was just about acceptable in terms of not losing him on a road where there very few turnings. But by the time the patrol car had performed the manoeuvre which would be necessary for him to get past it, he would have lost *another* two or three minutes. And that would make his task much more difficult.

A new – and very disturbing – thought came to his mind.

The patrol car must already have been there when Forsyth passed this way, but it had done nothing to stop him. So why was it blocking the lane now?

He brought the Victor to a halt a few feet from the police car, and wound down the window with one hand, while reaching for his warrant card with the other.

One of the uniforms, holding a torch, ambled over to him as if he had all the time in the world.

When he drew level with the car, he shone the torch directly into Crane's eyes and said, 'Good evening, sir.'

Squinting, Crane held out his warrant card.

'I'm following the car that just went through here – the Rover 2000 – and what I need you to do is to get your unit out of the way as quickly as possible,' he said urgently.

'Have you been drinking, sir?' the uniformed officer asked.

'Didn't you hear what I just said?' Crane demanded. 'I'm on a job. I need you to get out of the way.'

The second patrol car officer had joined them. 'There's no need to be abusive, sir,' he said.

'I'm not being abusive,' Crane protested. 'For God's sake, will you *listen* to me? I'm on a job!'

'And there's no need to shout at us, either, sir,' the first officer said.

Crane took a deep breath.

'Look, if you don't let me through soon, I'll lose the man I'm tailing,' he said, as calmly as he could.

'Would you mind stepping out of the car, please, sir?' the first officer asked.

'I've already explained . . .'

'If you refuse to obey my instructions, you'll leave me no alternative but to remove you forcibly.'

'This can't be happening,' Crane thought, as he got out of the car. 'It simply can't be happening.'

The first officer shone his torch on to the lane. 'What I'd like you to do now, sir, is to walk in a straight line,' he said. 'Do it slowly, placing the toe of one shoe against the heel of the one in front, and then . . .'

'I know how it works!' Crane told him. 'I was on motor patrol myself for six months.'

'Then you shouldn't have any difficulty following our instructions, should you, sir?'

Forsyth would be at least *five* minutes ahead by now, Crane thought.

'When *my* boss tells *your* boss about this, you'll get a real rocket for it, you know,' he said.

'That's as maybe,' the first constable said. 'But we can't be concerned about that for the moment. We're just doing our job, and what's required of you is to cooperate with us.'

There was no point in arguing – not with the patrol car parked across the lane. Crane walked the line, as he'd been instructed.

'What do you think?' asked the first constable.

'He's definitely under the influence,' replied the second.

'You've got to be joking,' Crane said. 'I promise you, I haven't touched a drop for over eight hours.'

'That's what they all say, sir,' the first constable told him.

It was only now that Crane noticed the badge which was painted on the side of the patrol car.

'You're not Lancashire police at all!' he said. 'You're from the West Yorkshire Constabulary!'

'That's right, we are,' the first constable agreed.

'So you're way outside your own patch!'

'That would be quite true, under normal circumstances,' the first constable said. 'But these circumstances aren't normal at all. We've been drafted in for the night. And we've got the paperwork to prove it.'

'Then I'd like to see that paperwork for myself,' Crane said.

'DC Crane would like to see the paperwork,' the second constable said to first.

'How did you know my name?' Crane asked.

'It's on your warrant card,' the second constable said.

'I know it is,' Crane agreed. 'But *you* weren't here when I showed it to your mate!'

'Do you want to see the paperwork, or not?' the first constable asked.

'Yes, I want to see the paperwork,' Crane said heavily.

The first constable went back to the patrol car, and returned with a document on a clipboard.

'Could you shine your torch on this, Tommy, so that DC Crane can get a proper look at it?' he asked the second constable.

'I'd be more than glad to,' the second constable replied.

Crane quickly scanned the document. It was written in the usual bureaucratic gobbledegook, but it seemed genuine enough, and the signature at the bottom – George Baxter, Chief Constable – was the clincher.

'Satisfied?' the first constable asked.

No, he wasn't, Crane thought. But he *was* resigned.

'My colleague will drive your vehicle to our station, and you will accompany me in the patrol car,' the first constable said. 'Now if you wouldn't mind putting your hands behind your back . . .'

'You're never going to handcuff me, are you?' Crane asked incredulously.

'Drunks can suddenly turn violent, and when there's only one officer in the vehicle with them, it's deemed safest to have them handcuffed,' the first constable said. 'It's normal procedure in a case like this.'

'I'm not drunk, and you both bloody know it,' Crane said angrily.

'What's the point in making this any harder than it has to be?' the first constable asked.

No point at all, Crane thought, putting his hands behind his back and feeling the metal bracelets click into place.

NINETEEN

It was the early-morning light, filtering in through the small, barred window of his cell, which probably woke Jack Crane up.

His first thought, as he turned over on an unfamiliar mattress, was that he hadn't been asleep at all. And yet, if he hadn't been, where had the hours gone?

He played back the events of the previous evening in his mind.

His arrest – and being handcuffed like a common criminal.

Failing a blood-alcohol test which he knew there was absolutely no way he *could have* failed.

Being photographed – full-faced and profile – while holding up a card which would later identify him as the subject of a mug-shot.

Having his fingerprints taken by a bored duty sergeant who had no idea how humiliating he found the whole process – and probably wouldn't have cared if he had.

He became aware that someone had entered the cell, and looked up to see a uniformed constable was standing next to the bed, with a tray in his hand.

'I've brought you your breakfast,' the constable said cheerily. 'A mug of tea, and a fried egg and sausage sandwich. I bet they don't feed you that well over in Lancashire.' He placed the tray on the small table next to the sink. 'Oh, and there's this,' he added, dropping a buff-coloured envelope on the bed.

'What is it?' Crane asked, still half-asleep.

'It's the record of your arrest, your mug shots, your finger-prints and the police doctor's report,' the constable replied. 'The duty sergeant thought that you'd like to know that there are no other copies.' He paused for a second. 'Is there anything else I can get you?'

Crane swung his legs off the bed, and stood up. 'I'm en-titled, by law, to make one phone call,' he said.

'So you are,' the constable agreed. 'But didn't you make it last night, when you were brought in?'

'No, I bloody didn't!' Crane said through gritted teeth. 'I asked if I could make it, but I was refused.'

'Oh, that's right!' the constable said. 'I remember now. The phones were on the blink. Nobody could ring in or out.'

That was bollocks, Crane thought – total and utter bollocks.

'Are the phones working *now*?' he asked.

'They most certainly are.'

'Then I'd like to make that phone call. And after that, I'd like to get the hell out of here.'

The constable gestured to the cell door. 'That's not locked, and you'll find a phone upstairs,' he said.

Crane quickly crossed the narrow cell, opened the door, and stepped into the corridor.

'You should eat your sandwich before you make that call,' the constable called after him. 'The fried egg won't taste half as good once it's gone cold.'

'Bugger the fried egg,' Crane said, over his shoulder.

The house was in a suburb much favoured by Whitebridge's moderately prosperous middle class. It had a double frontage and wide bay windows. The front garden was neat and orderly, and the central feature of it was a gnome, patiently fishing in a small wishing well.

The gnome would have been the chief constable's wife's choice, Paniatowski thought, as she walked up the path to the front door. George Baxter himself would never have indulged in such fey frivolity.

She rang the front-door bell, and it was the chief constable himself who answered it.

'For God's sake, Monika, what are you doing here at seven o'clock in the morning?' he asked exasperatedly. 'Can't whatever it is that's got you worked up into a state wait until I get to the office?'

'No,' Paniatowski told him firmly. 'It can't wait.'

'Who is it, George?' asked a voice from the hallway.

The woman who had spoken was about the same age she was, Paniatowski noted. She, too, was a blonde, and rather pretty – in an unassuming way.

Baxter sighed, and stepped to one side. 'Chief Inspector Paniatowski, this is my wife Josephine,' he said. 'Jo, this is Monika.'

The two women tentatively shook hands.

'She knows all about me!' Paniatowski thought, studying the other woman's face.

But that was hardly surprising. George Baxter was not the sort of man to keep his past hidden from his wife. George Baxter was straightforward and honest. Or rather, she amended, she'd *thought* he was straightforward and honest until she'd got the phone call from Yorkshire.

'Well, since you seem to feel an overwhelming urge to deal with police matters right now, I suppose you'd better come inside the house,' Baxter said to Paniatowski.

Mrs Baxter backed down the hallway, towards the kitchen, and Baxter led his chief inspector into a front room dominated by a large display cabinet full of delicate porcelain figures in pastoral poses.

'Nymphs and shepherds,' Paniatowski thought, running her eyes briefly over the cabinet. 'That'll be Jo's choice again.'

Once Baxter and Paniatowski had settled down on the two easy chairs of the cord three-piece suite, Jo appeared in the doorway.

'Would you like a drink, Chief Inspect— Monika?' she asked. 'Tea? Or would you prefer coffee?'

Paniatowski wondered how it must feel to have been courted on the rebound, and whether Jo sometimes felt that Baxter regarded her as no more than a consolation prize. She hoped – for all their sakes – that the thought had never even crossed the other woman's mind.

'I'd like a cup of tea, please,' she said. 'No milk, but a slice of lemon if you've got one.'

Jo didn't ask Baxter what he wanted. And why should she? She was his wife – his lifetime companion. She knew things about him that an ex-lover couldn't even begin to guess at.

Baxter waited until Jo had returned to the kitchen, then said, 'So what's this all about, Monika?'

'DC Crane was arrested last night,' Paniatowski told him. 'He was kept in the cells at Skipton Police Headquarters overnight, then this morning he was released. No explanations or apologies were offered – they just said he could go.'

'Did you really think that a green young detective constable like Crane could keep an eye on a man like Forsyth without being spotted?' Baxter asked, sounding slightly disappointed in her.

'What I thought – or didn't think – isn't the point,' Paniatowski replied as she felt the anger, which she'd promised herself she would contain, came bubbling to the surface. 'I want to know *why* Jack Crane was arrested.'

'He was arrested because Forsyth *wanted* him arrested.'

'And you went along with that quite happily, did you?'

'No, I didn't.' Baxter looked pained. 'And I'd have thought you'd know me well enough not to even feel the need to ask that question.'

'Hurt your feelings, have I?' Paniatowski taunted. 'Or is it just that I've shown you up for the man you really are?'

'I think you should remember who you're talking to, *Chief Inspector*,' Baxter said, his own anger starting to show.

'And I think you should stick up for the men under your command, *Chief Constable*,' Paniatowski countered.

The sound of footsteps in the hallway subdued them both, and they sat in glaring silence while Jo – pretending not to have noticed the atmosphere in the room – brought them their drinks.

Once his wife had left again, Baxter resumed, as if there had been no pause at all.

'I *did* stick up for the men under my command,' he said. 'Forsyth wanted to use Lancashire officers for the operation, and I refused.'

'So you washed your hands of it? You let somebody else do the dirty work instead. Well, why not? After all, it worked for Pontius Pilate.'

'Monika!' Baxter said warningly.

'But you didn't entirely keep your own men out of it, did you? Because *Jack Crane* is one of your men.'

'It was Crane I was thinking of when I asked the Yorkshire Police for their help,' Baxter said.

'Oh, it was, was it?' Paniatowski asked, sceptically. 'And would you mind explaining how having him banged up in Yorkshire for the night could possibly be called *thinking of him*?'

'All right, I will,' Baxter agreed. 'Forsyth didn't want to be followed last night, and what do you think would have happened if I'd refused to have any part in making sure he wasn't?'

'I don't know,' Paniatowski admitted.

'No, you don't, do you?' Baxter said, hectoring. 'You're so fired up with your own righteous indignation that you can't be bothered to stop for a moment and do some actual *thinking*. Now, do you want to hear about how I saw the situation or don't you?'

'I'm listening,' Paniatowski said.

'Well, that does make a pleasant change,' Baxter told her. 'It seemed to me that if I refused to help him, Forsyth would have brought in his own people from London to handle the job. And do you think they'd have treated Crane as gently as the Yorkshire Police did? Because I bloody don't!'

'I'm . . . I'm sorry, sir,' Paniatowski said contritely.

'And so you should be,' Baxter told her.

'Do you know what Forsyth was doing out well beyond Clitheroe, last night?'

'No, I don't. I haven't got a clue. It's no concern of mine. And it shouldn't be any concern of yours, either.'

Paniatowski felt a fresh wave of anger wash over her, but did her best to keep it damped down.

'Forsyth is interfering in my investigation, sir,' she said levelly. 'And I want to know *why* he's interfering.'

'All he's asking for is to be kept appraised of developments,' Baxter said. 'I fail to see how that could be called interfering.'

'That's because you don't know what he's doing behind the scenes,' Paniatowski argued.

'And do you?'

'Well, no.'

'Then isn't it just possible that he isn't doing anything *at all* behind the scenes?'

'You don't understand him like I do. He doesn't ever play a simple, straightforward game. He's always operating on at least three or four different levels.'

'Maybe he is. But how do you know that all – or *even one* – of those levels have anything to do with your case?'

'Tell me, honestly, sir, don't you resent him being here?' Paniatowski asked, sidestepping the question.

'Well, of course I resent him being here. But there's nothing I can do about it, so I'm just getting on with my job as best I can. And I'm ordering you – get that, *ordering you* – to do the same.'

*   *   *

When DS Cousins saw DS Gutterridge walking across the police canteen in his direction, he looked the other way.

But it was to no avail. Gutterridge came to a halt in front of his table, and said, 'Mind if I join you, Paul?'

'I do, as a matter of fact,' Cousins said, coldly. 'I'm rather particular who I share a table with these days.'

Gutterridge sat down anyway. 'What's happened to us, Paul?' he asked. 'We used to be real mates.'

'And the operative words there are *used to be*,' Cousins said.

'I was a good friend to you when Mary was . . . was . . .'

'When she was dying, Len,' Cousins said bluntly. 'When she was *bloody* dying.'

'That's right,' Gutterridge agreed awkwardly. 'When she was dying. Don't you remember what we did back then? My missus used to stay with your Mary, and I'd take you out for a drink.'

'And I appreciated it at the time,' Cousins said. 'But looking back on it, I've decided you were probably doing it more for yourself than for me.'

'More for myself? How do you mean?'

'You wanted an excuse to go out boozing, and I was it. Your Lily would never have let you out on your own, but if you were only going out to console poor old Paul, then it was all right.'

'You're not being fair,' Gutterridge protested weakly. 'And there's other things I've done for you.'

'Like what?'

'Well, for example, when you were . . . when you were starting to get ill yourself, I agreed to look after your dog for you, didn't I? I took him into my own home, and fed him out of my own pocket.'

'Yes, you did,' Cousins agreed. 'And then *he* went and bloody well died, an' all.'

'You can't blame me,' Gutterridge said. 'It was canine distemper that did for him.'

Cousins sighed. 'All right, let's say, purely for the sake of argument, that while my Mary was wasting away, you really did go out boozing solely for my sake,' he said. 'And let's say, for argument's sake again, that you gave my dog the best home a mutt could ever hope for.'

'Yes?'

'Does that excuse – in any way, shape or form – how you've treated me since they let me out of the nut house?'

'Ah, but you see, that was a difficult situation for me to know how to handle. I didn't want you to feel I was crowding you.'

'So to make absolutely sure you *weren't* crowding me, you completely bloody ignored me?'

'Like I said, it wasn't easy to know what the right thing to do was, and if I *seemed* to be ignoring you—'

'I had two or three other mates like you,' Cousins interrupted him, 'and it must have been difficult for them as well, because they also gave me the cold shoulder. And do you know *why* I think that was?'

'No, I . . .'

'I think it was because they didn't want to be seen knocking around with a nutter – because they were frightened that if they were, they'd be tarred with the same brush themselves.' Cousins paused for a second. 'I've got a new life now. It's not exactly a happy one, but it's got its compensations. I'm working on a new team, too, and while I don't exactly know my new team mates well, I know them well *enough* to be sure they'd never treat me like you did.'

'I've made mistakes,' Gutterridge admitted, 'and I'm very sorry I've made them. But can't we put the past behind us now? Can't we start again, and be mates like we were before?'

'All right, "mate", let's have a cosy chat, just like we used to do,' Cousins agreed. 'So what would you like to talk about?'

For a moment, Gutterridge looked like a man who had something he really needed to get off his chest, then he shrugged and said, 'I don't know. It's a bit difficult, isn't it?'

'Is it?' Cousins asked.

'I suppose we could talk about what bobbies like us always talk about to each other.'

'And what might that be?'

'The Job, of course.'

'Oh, I see!' Cousins said. 'You'd like to talk about your current investigation, would you? Maybe ask me for a bit of advice?'

Gutterridge smiled weakly. 'From what I've been hearing

on the grapevine, *your* current investigation is much more interesting than mine.'

'Maybe it is,' Cousins agreed.

There was perhaps half a minute's silence before Gutterridge said, 'Well, come on then, Paul, dish the dirt. How close are you to solving the case?'

'Isn't that the wrong question?' Cousins wondered.

'Then what's the right one?'

'If I was on the outside looking in, I think the thing I'd be most wondering about is *why* these men are being murdered,' Cousins said. 'And if I got the chance to talk to somebody who was actually working the case, I think the first thing I'd ask him is why *he* thinks they're being murdered.'

'Why do you think these men are being murdered?' Len Gutterridge asked dully.

'I've no idea,' Cousins replied. He counted out two beats, and then continued, 'And I've no idea where you go on Thursday nights, either.'

Gutterridge jumped, as if he'd just be electrocuted.

'Thursday nights?' he repeated.

'One of the victims, Simon Stockwell, always went missing on Thursday nights,' Cousins explained. 'It's more than possible that Andy Adair did, too. And when, a couple of minutes ago, you starting showing so much unnatural interest in the case, I began to wonder if *you* went missing on Thursday nights, too. Now I know you did. That's why you suddenly want to become mates again. Because *you* want to know what *I* know. Because you're in this – whatever *this* is – up to your neck. I'm right, aren't I?'

'I . . . I . . .' Gutterridge spluttered.

'If you tell me everything you can, I'll do my best to help you,' Cousins said. 'I can't promise you that you won't serve any jail time, because I've no idea what it is you've done, but I can promise you that I'll be in your corner for you every step of the way.'

'All you have to do is catch the killer,' Gutterridge said, his voice verging on the hysterical. 'Catch him, and the problems will go away.'

'Ah, but that's the difficulty, you see,' Cousins explained. 'We've absolutely no idea who the killer is. He could well strike again before we catch him – and next time his victim could be you.'

Gutterridge looked as if he were about to be sick. 'I can handle myself,' he said, unconvincingly.

'Andy Adair was ten years younger, two inches taller and about a hundred and fifty per cent fitter than you are,' Cousins pointed out. 'And look what happened to him.'

'You've no mercy, have you?' Gutterridge asked bitterly. 'No sense of compassion.'

'I've offered to help you out if you come clean with me,' Cousins said unyieldingly. 'That's the best I can do, and if I was in your shoes, I think I'd grab the opportunity with both hands. Besides . . .'

'Yes?'

'If you *don't* come clean now, I'm going to have to report this conversation to my boss.'

'You couldn't . . . you wouldn't . . .'

'I've no choice in the matter, Len. It's what they call *germane to the investigation.*'

'You're a bastard!' Gutterridge said. 'You're nothing but a bloody rotten bastard!'

'Maybe I am,' Cousins agreed. 'But I'm also too good a bobby to be able to pretend this conversation never happened.'

Gutterridge stood up so violently that his chair went flying away behind him, and he somehow managed to strike the underside of the table with his knee.

'That must have hurt,' Cousins thought, as he looked down at the rocking table.

But if Gutterridge was in any pain – any *physical* pain, at least – he showed no sign of noticing it, and as he fled from the canteen, he wasn't even limping.

Well, he'd done all he could for the man, Cousins told himself, reaching for the newspaper which someone had left behind on the table next to his.

And then he saw the headline which was screaming out at him from the front page, and any thoughts of Detective Sergeant Leonard Gutterridge immediately went out of his mind.

TWENTY

The first thing Monika Paniatowski noticed as she drove onto the Whitebridge Police Headquarters' car park was that DS Paul Cousins was standing in front of her parking place.

He wasn't there as the bringer of glad tidings, she guessed. Glad tidings – even *great* tidings – could have waited until she reached her office. He was there because the tidings were bad, and he wanted to deliver them as soon as possible.

Then she noticed the newspaper he was holding tightly in his right hand, and guessed that the tidings would be very bad indeed.

'It's the *Globe*, ma'am,' Cousins said, thrusting the paper at her even as she was getting out of her MGA. 'I think you need to read it.'

The story filled the front page.

Killer with a sense of justice?
By Mike Traynor
The Central Lancs Police have been searching for a link between the murders of Andrew Adair, who until recently was a member of Her Majesty's Armed Forces, and Simon Stockwell, who ran his own painting and decorating business. Perhaps they would have been wise to begin by examining both men's criminal records.

Had they done so, they would have discovered that both Adair and Stockwell have been charged, in the past, with assaults on young girls well under the age of consent, and have served terms in prison as a result.

But if the police were in ignorance of these facts, as they seem to have been, perhaps the killer wasn't. Perhaps that was what motivated him to carry out the killings in

the first place. Perhaps that was why he stripped their
bodies naked once his grisly work had been completed.

Neither this newspaper nor this reporter would endorse
what the Americans call "vigilante killings", yet it is
hard not to feel, in some small way, that these men got
what they deserved.

'I'll have his balls for this,' Paniatowski said angrily. 'Do you
realize how much it could impede the investigation?'

'I do, ma'am.'

'And it's a complete fabrication! He can't back any of it
up, because there's not an ounce of truth in it.'

'You're right that there's not an ounce of truth in it, but
you're wrong that he can't back it up,' Cousins said grimly.

'What are you talking about?' Paniatowski demanded. 'I've
seen Stockwell's criminal record, and there's no mention of
child abuse in it.'

'There wasn't yesterday, but today there is,' Cousins said.
'And I'd be willing to bet that there's some mention of it in
Adair's army record, as well.'

'Bloody Forsyth!' Paniatowski said.

'Yes, ma'am, it just has to be his handiwork, doesn't it?'

'We can easily prove the documents are complete forgeries
– because however skilfully they've been done, they're simply
not supported by the facts,' Paniatowski said stubbornly.

'We *can* prove they're forgeries, but not *easily*,' Cousins
told her. 'The officers who are down in the new record as
having arrested Stockwell for child abuse were Inspector Fred
Meade and DS Pat Donovan. And what do you know about
those two, ma'am?'

'Meade died about three years ago,' Paniatowski said. 'Heart
attack, wasn't it?'

'That's right, ma'am. And Donovan died in a car crash, two
years ago. So they're not going to dispute the facts, are they?'

'No, but there'll be others who can. It's not just the arresting
officers who would have been involved in a case like that.
There's a whole legal process to be gone through.'

'Yes, there is,' Cousins agreed. 'And they'll have doctored
that, too. I haven't had time yet to check on who was the
judge in this supposed prosecution, but when I do I'm sure

I'll find that he's either dead himself or has retired and gone to live with one of his children – in somewhere like Australia.'

'Wherever he's living, we'll send officers to interview him, and expose all this for the lie that it is,' Paniatowski said, with mounting fury.

'With respect, ma'am, I don't think you've quite grasped the big picture yet,' Cousins said.

'Haven't I? Then you'd better explain it to me.'

'I've no idea what it is that Forsyth hopes to achieve by all this, but I do know that he doesn't care *what* you can prove in a month's time, because he'll be long gone by then. You see, this isn't a long-term strategy he's employing – it's just a short-term tactic.'

'And one that's going to backfire on him straight away,' Paniatowski said, with grim satisfaction. 'Because we don't need judges or prison officers to prove this is a tissue of lies – all we need is Mrs Stockwell. She knows Simon never went to prison for child abuse – and even if she hates him, she's not going to allow his reputation to be smeared in this particularly nasty kind of way.'

'That occurred to me, too,' Cousins said. 'That's why the first thing I did after I'd read the article was to drive to Mrs Stockwell's house. And do know you what I discovered when I got there? That she'd gone!'

'Gone?'

'The neighbours said she'd taken her kids away on a holiday.'

'A holiday?' Paniatowski repeated. 'She wouldn't think of going on a holiday with her husband still to be buried. Besides, she can't *afford* to go on a holiday. She's up to her neck in debt.'

'I suspect that she *isn't* in debt any longer,' Cousins said. 'I think you'll find that her debts have all been paid off. And she's definitely gone away – the neighbours saw her leave early this morning in a big black chauffeur-driven car.'

Paniatowski flung open the door of Forsyth's temporary office, and saw the man from London was already at his desk, and had an amused smile playing on his face.

'I've been expecting you, Monika,' he said. 'In fact, I'm surprised it's taken you quite so long to get here.'

'You planted this story in the newspaper, didn't you?' Paniatowski demanded, slamming the copy of the *Daily Globe* down on the desk.

'Yes, I did,' Forsyth confirmed. 'But it was your fault that it *had to be* planted.'

'How could it be my fault?'

'You were given the opportunity, at your press conference yesterday, to deny any possible IRA involvement in the killing of Andy Adair. And you didn't take that opportunity, did you?'

'You're right, I didn't. Because although it's a long shot that the IRA did it, I still can't rule it out entirely.'

'Do you *really* think that if the IRA were involved, I wouldn't know about it?' Forsyth asked.

'It's possible,' Paniatowski said. 'You love to play up the image of the all-seeing, all-knowing super-spy. You probably even believe it yourself, by now. But has it never occurred to you that it might be no more than that – an image?'

'I would know if they were involved,' Forsyth said firmly. 'And if they *were* responsible for Adair's murder, do you seriously believe I would ever have allowed the case to be assigned to a country bumpkin chief inspector like yourself?'

Paniatowski felt her anger flaring up again, then realized that was just what Forsyth wanted to happen, and forced a smile to her face.

'You really know how to hurt a girl,' she said. 'But if you're right, and the IRA *aren't* involved in the case, what was the point of planting the false newspaper story?'

'I did it because, for operational reasons, I don't want there to be a hint – not even the merest wisp of a suggestion – that this murder had anything to do with Andrew Adair's experiences in Ireland. And in order to ensure that *is* the case, I had to do something which would shift the focus of attention away from any such speculation.'

A new possibility – so horrific she didn't really want to contemplate it – came to Paniatowski's mind.

'Did you have Simon Stockwell killed?' she asked.

'Why should I have done that?'

'Precisely because Stockwell *didn't* have an Irish connection, so there could be no suggestion *he'd* been killed by the IRA. And if *he* hadn't been killed by them, then Adair – who was murdered in exactly the same manner – couldn't have been killed by them either.'

Forsyth smiled again. 'My congratulations,' he said. 'You're finally starting to think like someone who could be of some use in the security services.'

'Answer the question,' Paniatowski demanded.

'No, I didn't have Simon Stockwell killed.'

'But if you had, you'd have denied it just as convincingly as you're denying it now?'

'Quite so,' Forsyth agreed. 'By the way, I've recently received some information from Poland that might be of great interest to you, Monika.'

'So now we're playing *Change the Subject*, are we?' Paniatowski asked. 'Well, you should have chosen a better subject to change to, because I'm not *interested* in Poland.'

She was not lying. She had not thought seriously – or at any length – about Poland for years. And yet there was something in Forsyth's tone which suggested that this particular piece of information *would* be of interest to her, and already her stomach was starting to knot up.

'Very well, if you don't want to talk about Poland, let's talk about something else,' Forsyth said mildly.

Damn the man, Paniatowski thought – and wished she still believed in hell, so that she could picture him being burnt in it for all eternity.

'Monika?' Forsyth said.

'You might as well tell me,' Paniatowski said indifferently, knowing she was fooling neither herself nor Forsyth.

'The Polish authorities have recently been doing some excavations on the site of one of the early battles of the Second World War,' Forsyth said. 'And one of the many things that they've uncovered is a mass grave of Polish soldiers – specifically, of Polish cavalrymen.'

Paniatowski found her mind was suddenly travelling back in time. She was no longer a woman in her late thirties – a senior detective, involved in a battle of wits with a spook from London. Instead, she was a small girl, sitting on the firm, well-muscled knee of a man dressed in an immaculate cavalry officer's uniform. She could feel his fingers running gently through her hair. She could smell his cigar and his highly polished leather boots.

'No, please!' she thought. 'It couldn't be anything to do with him. It just *couldn't* be.'

'Often, in such cases, the corpses would be stripped of anything of value before they were interred, but this particular burial seems to have been a very hurried affair, which means that it is much easier to identify the bodies than it would normally be,' Forsyth continued. 'One of the dead has been identified as a Colonel Andrej Paniatowski. That would be your father, would it?'

'Yes,' Paniatowski gasped, feeling as if she were choking.

'Initially, the Polish authorities were very keen to publicize their discovery. It would make the West Germans feel guilty, you see – and they just *love* making the West Germans feel guilty. Their Russian masters, however, were altogether less eager, since it would probably also revive, in the public mind at least, memories of the Katyń Forest Massacre, in which they themselves murdered a goodly number of Polish officers. So, for the moment, it is as if the discovery never occurred. But it *did* occur.'

'Why . . . why are you telling me this?' Paniatowski asked.

'Because I thought you'd like to be able to bury your father's body in England,' Forsyth said.

'And you're saying that you could get it for me?'

'Yes, I am. It won't be easy – but it can be done.'

'And what do you want from me in exchange?'

'I want you to start behaving yourself. And I mean *really* behaving yourself. No more attempts to find out what I'm doing here. No more amateur spying excursions for your subordinate, Secret Agent Crane.'

'If you're offering me this, I must really have you worried,' Paniatowski said.

'Don't overrate your own importance, Monika,' Forsyth told her. 'When a mechanism is delicately balanced as this one is . . .'

'As *which* one is?'

Forsyth smiled. 'There you go again – trying to be too clever by half. It'll be your downfall some day, Monika. It may even be your downfall *soon*. Now what was I saying?'

'You were talking some shite about delicate mechanisms,' Paniatowski told him.

'So I was. When a mechanism is as delicately balanced as

this one is, even something as insignificant as a fly can tip it over. And all I am doing here – through this offer of mine – is attempting to ensure that one of the more persistent of the flies keeps away.'

'You'd really have my father's body brought to England?' Paniatowski asked.

'I would. And I can see, from the expression on your face, just how much that would mean to you.'

Paniatowski stood up. 'My father was an honourable man,' she said. 'He lived *by* his honour, and he died *for* his honour.'

'I'm sure that's a goal we all seek to attain.'

'And if I made a deal with you, I wouldn't be *fit* to be the custodian of his remains.'

'So you're turning me down?' Forsyth asked, disappointedly.

'I'm telling you that you take your offer and stick it up your tight upper-class arse,' Paniatowski replied.

TWENTY-ONE

In big places, like London and Manchester, people disappeared all the time, but even in a relatively quiet backwater like Whitebridge such things were not entirely unknown.

Some of these people – a few – would never be seen or heard of again, but in most cases the disappearance would be so temporary that it could hardly be counted as a disappearance at all.

A husband would go out for a drink with his mates, get legless and then be either too incapable – or too frightened – to go home. So he'd crash out on one of his friend's sofas and – when he appeared, shamefaced and overhung, at his own door sometime around noon the next day – would be amazed to discover that he'd been reported missing.

A young girl would tell her parents that she was staying with a friend overnight, when the truth was that she was going to a disco in a nearby town. She'd miss the last bus home, and – not having the money for a taxi – would have no way of returning to Whitebridge before morning.

An old man, going a bit soft in the head (as they said locally), would forget his own address and spend the night sleeping on one of the benches in the Corporation Park.

All very mundane! All very *domestic*!

Which explained why, once the duty sergeant at Whitebridge HQ had taken down the details of the first disappearance that day, he pushed the whole matter to the back of his mind.

Then a second disappearance was reported . . . and a third . . . and a fourth . . . and what had started out as a gentle trickle of mild concern was, the sergeant thought colourfully, rapidly turning into a fast-flowing river of worrying shit.

And it was at that point that he began to wonder if all these disappearances had anything to do with DCI Paniatowski's murder investigation.

*   *   *

Colin Beresford stared gloomily down at the thick pile of missing-person reports.

Maybe, looking back at it later, it wouldn't seem as bad as it did now, he thought.

Maybe, seen in retrospect, it would be viewed as the moment when the team got the first big break in a case which, up until that point, hadn't really been going anywhere.

Maybe!

Or maybe they'd come to acknowledge it as the point at which the investigation began its almost inevitable disintegration.

He drummed his fingers impatiently on the desk. He needed to talk to Monika about it – *really* needed to talk to her – and she was still in her meeting with Mr Forsyth.

He heard the sound of her footsteps along the corridor – that click-click-click of her high heels – and breathed a sigh of relief.

The boss was back. The boss would know what to do.

The door opened, and Paniatowski walked into the office.

'Things are going pear-shaped, boss,' Beresford began. 'Since eight o'clock this morning, we have seven reports of . . .'

And then he stopped.

Stopped because, even as distracted as he was, he had noticed the change in her.

Stopped because he was *shocked* by it.

It was nothing external, this change. Apart from a slightly worried, slightly abstract expression of her face, she looked much as she always did.

But as a man who had known and worked with her for a long time – and who sometimes wondered if he might actually be in love with her – he sensed something cataclysmic had happened to her in the previous half-hour.

Paniatowski sat down opposite him, and lit up a cigarette with trembling hands.

'What the hell has that bastard Forsyth just put you through?' Beresford asked, aware that by even asking the question he might be treading in an emotional mine field.

Paniatowski shrugged. 'Put me through?' she said with a casualness which didn't fool him for a minute. 'Nothing!'

'Nothing?'

'The meeting was very straightforward. I asked him about

the story in the *Globe*, and he admitted he'd planted it in an attempt to scotch any speculation about an IRA link to Adair's murder.'

She delivered the words in a flat, unemotional – almost *dead* – tone of voice. And that wasn't the Monika who Beresford knew. The Monika *he* knew would have been furious!

'Are you sure there wasn't anything else said?' he risked asking.

'If there'd been anything else, I'd have told you,' Paniatowski replied, with a growing irritation in her voice which he suspected she was using to mask something else.

They sat in silence for perhaps half a minute, then Beresford said, 'I'd started to tell you about what's been happening while you were in your meeting, boss. Shall I go on?'

'All right,' Paniatowski agreed.

'At five to eight this morning, the duty sergeant got a call from a Mrs—' Beresford began.

'Actually, *don't* go on,' Paniatowski interrupted him.

'Sorry, boss?'

'Aren't we due to have a meeting with DS Cousins and DC Crane sometime soon?'

'Well, yes, we are – but we've got five minutes to spare, and that's just long enough to get you up to speed on . . .'

'If it's only five minutes, we might as well wait until they get here,' Paniatowski said.

What the bloody hell was going on, Beresford wondered. Who *was* this stranger sitting opposite him?

The stranger turned away from him, and gazed fixedly at the wall. Her face still gave away nothing, but he was now more convinced than ever that she was fighting a tremendous battle within herself.

Suddenly, she swung round again, looked him straight in the eyes, and said, 'Is it important to you where your mother's going to be buried, Colin?'

The question caught him completely off-guard, and all he could think to say was, 'I beg your pardon, boss?'

'Your mother *is* going to die eventually, isn't she?'

'Well, yes. We all are.'

'And when she does die, will it matter to you whether or not she's buried close to home?'

'I don't know,' Beresford admitted. 'I can't say I've ever really given it much thought.'

'You see, it *shouldn't* matter whether you can visit the grave or not,' Paniatowski continued, and he began to understand it was not his mother she was talking about at all. 'Because, when all's said and done, it's only a few old bones we're talking about, isn't?'

'Yes, ma'am, but I don't see quite where you're going with . . .'

'Yet somehow it *does* matter! You realize that, when you're actually given the choice. But what if that choice comes with strings attached? What if, by choosing, you have to betray everything you ever believed in? And what kind of monster does that make the man who *offered* you the choice?'

There was a knock on the door.

Beresford waited for Paniatowski to tell Cousins and Crane to enter the room, and when it became plain that she wasn't about to do so, he said, 'Come in,' himself.

The two new arrivals took their usual seats, and Paniatowski gazed down at the desk-top.

So what happened next, Beresford wondered.

'Ma'am?' he said aloud.

Paniatowski jumped. 'What?'

Beresford slid the file across the desk. 'The information's all in there. If you'd like to take a couple of minutes to read it, and then you can tell us what you think we should . . .'

Paniatowski pushed the file back to him.

'Wouldn't it be simpler if, instead of me doing that, you just briefed all three of us?' she suggested.

Except it wasn't a suggestion at all.

Beresford cleared his throat.

'At five to eight this morning, a Mrs Duggan rang,' he began. 'She said that her husband, a teacher at the grammar school, had told her that he had to attend a parent-teacher meeting last night. She was expecting him home by ten. When he still hadn't arrived at eleven, she went to bed – no doubt believing he'd gone out for a drink with the other members of staff, and promising herself she'd give him hell in the morning. She woke up expecting to find him in bed beside her. But he wasn't. That was when she noticed the wardrobe door was open, and some of his clothes were missing. So what do you think she did next?'

'I expect that, like most women, she keeps a bit of money hidden somewhere in the house, and she went to see if it was still there,' Cousins suggested.

'Spot on,' Beresford agreed. 'And it wasn't. At nine o'clock, we had a call from a Mrs Booth. Her husband is a clerk in the town hall. She said he's been acting very strangely since yesterday afternoon. Then, last night, he told her he had to go away for a while, but he wouldn't tell her where he was going. She's worried he might try to hurt himself.'

Beresford broke off, and glanced across at Paniatowski. She *looked* as if she might be listening, but he couldn't tell for sure.

'We've had five more calls since then,' he continued. 'The circumstances are a little different in each case, but the basic story's the same. So I sent officers round to each of the houses. Their instructions were to collect as much information on the missing man as they could – everything from his date of birth to where he banks his money – so we can find out what it is that connects them. I haven't had time to do a detailed analysis myself yet, but I've already found one link – none of them was usually with their wives on Thursday nights.'

Cousins coughed awkwardly. 'I think there's one more name you can add to that list of yours, sir – Len Gutterridge.'

'*DS* Gutterridge?' Beresford asked, surprised.

'Yes.'

'But I worked with him when I was in uniform. He's a good solid bobby – the salt of the earth.'

'If you'd asked me about him yesterday, I might have agreed with you,' Cousins said. 'But you should have seen him this morning, when he came asking me about how the investigation was going. He was as nervous as a rabbit that's just spotted a stoat, and when I mentioned Thursday nights, it was just like I'd stuck a hot needle in him.'

'So what did you do?'

'What I *wanted* to do was pull him in for questioning then and there, but he's a sergeant, with the same authority as me, and I had no *proof* of anything. So I did the best I could in the circumstances. I tried to scare him into helping the investigation, and I thought, at the time, that it had almost worked. But now I think I made a big mistake. Now, I think I should have said nothing at all to him, and just passed the information

on to you and the chief inspector – because you've got the
clout to do what I couldn't do.'

'No harm done,' Beresford said. 'Based on what we've
learned this morning, we can pull him in now.'

'That's the problem,' Cousins said. 'You can't. I went
looking for him half an hour ago. I wanted to see if, now he's
had time to think about it, he was ready to come clean. But
he wasn't in his office, and the desk sergeant told me he'd
taken a sick day. Then I rang his home, and his missus, Lily,
was almost in hysterics. Said he'd packed a suitcase and left.
Said she'd no idea where he'd gone.' Cousins paused for a
moment. 'I've been telling myself that I'm as good a bobby
as I ever was before my breakdown, sir. But I'm not. I'd never
have made a mistake like that a few years ago, and I'm very
sorry for having let the team down.'

'That's utter bollocks!' Beresford told him. 'You *haven't*
let the team down at all, Paul. You made a judgement call,
like we all do, and it just didn't work out this time. There's
not a bobby on the Force who hasn't had that happen to him.'

'Thank you, sir,' DS Cousins replied humbly. 'I really appreciate you saying that.'

And it had to be said, Beresford thought. But it shouldn't
have needed to be said by *him*. It was the *boss*'s job to keep
up morale – and she simply wasn't doing it!

Was he being *too* critical, he wondered. He wasn't beyond
reproach himself, especially after having abandoned his central
role in the incident room the day before, in favour of going
off and playing detective sergeant.

But he wasn't the *leader* of the team – he wasn't the
lynchpin. If he stepped out of line, the boss could pull him
back on to the straight and narrow. And she had done!

But who was there with the necessary weight to pull *her*
back?

Not him!

Not anybody!

He reached into the folder in front of him, and handed each
of the team several sheets of typed notes.

'This is all the information we have on the missing men,'
he said. 'I'd like you to go through it, and see if you can find
any link that I haven't found myself yet.' He looked across at
Paniatowski again, hoping to see that some of her old spark

had returned. 'At least, that's what I'd like them to do if it's all right with you, boss,' he added hopefully.

'It's fine with me,' Paniatowski replied, with no discernable sign of interest that Beresford could detect.

The first thing that DS Len Gutterridge was aware of when he regained consciousness was a pounding headache which seemed to stretch all the way from his forehead to the base of his skull.

Then – slowly and hazily – he began to notice other things about his current condition.

He was lying on his side – but not in a bed, because if there'd been a mattress under him, his right hip wouldn't be complaining so much.

His hands were behind his back, and when he tried to move them, he found he couldn't. And he knew just why that was, because he could feel the cord biting into his skin.

His ankles seemed to be bound together, too. Not just bound together, but bent up unnaturally into the small of his back. And when he tried to move *them*, he felt a pain in his wrists.

There had to be a third cord, he realized – and that cord connected the bonds on his wrists with the bonds on his ankles.

Hog-tied, he thought, remembering the cowboy films of his youth.

He was still trapped in a fuzzy, undefined zone that existed between the conscious and the unconscious, but even so, he understood enough to know that this was not normal.

'Need to think,' he told himself. 'Need to work out how I got here.'

He had arranged to meet somebody.

He remembered that.

Only he couldn't *quite* remember who that somebody was.

'That'll be because I'm suffering from concussion,' he thought – and felt quite pleased with himself.

So if he couldn't remember *who* he had met, could he at least work out *where* that meeting had taken place?

He was almost sure it had been on the edge of the moors.

Step one!

And what had happened next?

This *person* had asked him to get something from his car, and it was when he was opening the door that everything had gone black.

That would be when he was hit over the head!

So far, so good. That was what had happened. But *why* had it happened? Who on earth would have wanted to hit him over . . .

The killer! He was in the hands of the *killer*!

'I should have listened to Paul Cousins,' he sobbed softly to himself. 'I should have accepted his help when he offered it.'

What would it have mattered if, by confessing to Cousins, he had lost his job and had to spend a few months – or even a couple of years – in jail?

That was nothing – *nothing!* – compared to what he feared was in store for him now.

He had kept his eyes closed the whole time he had been thinking things through, but now he forced himself to open them.

He was lying on a floor of compacted earth, and where it came to an end there was a solid rough-stone wall which looked at least a hundred years old.

He was probably in an old barn, somewhere on the moors, he thought. But if it was a barn, he didn't recognize it – was sure he had never been there before.

He listened carefully for any noises from the outside which would tell him where he was.

But there was nothing to hear except the silence.

Which meant that the killer was not there, he told himself, with a sudden surge of hope.

Because if the killer *had been* there, he'd have heard his breathing!

So all was not yet lost. There was still a chance he could escape – if only he could bring himself to put his mind to it.

The first thing to do was to test the strength of his bonds, and the best way to do that was by moving.

He thought of rolling over onto his back, but given the way he was trussed up, that would probably be too painful. It might be easier – not quite so agonizing – if he rolled over onto his stomach, he decided.

He tensed himself, and rolled. His bonds showed no signs of giving, but at least now he could see the big, dilapidated door through which most of the light was streaming.

Escaping from the barn would be easy enough, he thought
– untying himself was the hard part.

He rolled again, onto his left side this time – and that was
when he saw the eyes.

They were large and wide and terrified – and they were
quite dead.

He screamed, and closed his own eyes. Then, slowly and
cautiously, he opened them again – because he knew he had
to.

The dead eyes were still there – but now he could see
beyond them.

To the head which housed them, with its mouth twisted in
frozen, agonized fear.

To the throat, which had been ferociously ripped open.

To the dead man's naked body, draped over a packing case
in such a way that the hands and knees touched the ground.

And what made it truly horrific was not the fear in the eyes,
not the gash across the throat, not the way in which the corpse
had been posed – it was that Gutterridge *knew* this man, recognized him as Edward Dunston, another member of the Langley
Club.

'Save me!' the sergeant screamed. 'Please save me!'

He had no idea who he was addressing the scream to. It
could have been God. It could have been DS Cousins. It could
even have been the man who delivered his morning milk.

It didn't matter who it was, as long as *somebody* would
save him!

TWENTY-TWO

The only sounds in Paniatowski's office for the last half-hour had been those of pages being turned over and cigarettes being lit.

Now, finally, DS Cousins broke the silence

'There *is* no bloody link between the missing men, sir!' he said exasperatedly. 'We've got everybody from a builder's labourer to a chartered accountant on this list. These men all move in entirely different circles. They could live their whole lives in Whitebridge without ever coming into contact once.'

'There is *one* thing that connects them,' Crane said tentatively. 'As far as I can see, none of them are Catholics.'

'Is that *so* surprising?' Beresford asked. 'Most people in this town are Protestant – if they're anything at all. As far as I can recall, there are only three Catholic churches in the whole of the Whitebridge area.'

'The thing is, sir, even though the Catholics here are in a minority, they're not a *segregated* minority,' Crane persisted.

Beresford waited for Paniatowski to speak, and when it was clear that she wasn't going to, he said, 'Go on, Jack.'

'You know what it's like in Northern Ireland, if only from seeing it on the telly,' Crane said. 'There are Catholic housing areas and Ulster Protestant housing areas, and not only do the groups not live side by side, sometimes they don't even dare walk down each other's *streets*. And it goes beyond that. Catholic firms don't employ Ulstermen, and Protestant firms don't employ Catholics. Over there, you wouldn't even think of letting a barber cut your hair before you knew which religion he followed.'

'So?'

'So it isn't like that in Whitebridge at all. I play squash, and some of the members of my squash club are Catholic. I also belong to a writers' group, and there are Catholics in that, too.'

'And the pubs aren't segregated, either,' Cousins said, giving his support to the argument. 'In the Drum, a man's worth is measured by how many pints he can sink without falling over, not which church he worships at.'

'So what I'm saying is that if you take any sort of group or social gathering, you'd expect to find at least one Catholic in it,' Crane concluded. 'But that's simply not true of this lot!'

'It all leads back to Forsyth,' Paniatowski said, suddenly and unexpectedly coming to life.

It was the *way* she said the name which troubled Beresford. There was vehemence to her tone which verged on hatred. It was almost as if she'd selected the Londoner as her own personal demon – and nothing else seemed to matter to her any more.

'I'm not entirely sure that it *does* all lead back to Forsyth, ma'am,' he said dubiously.

'Well, if it doesn't, where the hell else *does* it lead?' Paniatowski demanded aggressively. 'What's the government's policy on Northern Ireland, Colin?'

'I suppose it's to hold on to the province at all costs,' Beresford said. 'To do anything that's necessary to prevent it from breaking away and forming a union with the Republic of Ireland.'

'Exactly. And while we'll probably never be told the full extent of the security services' involvement in holding the province together, it's a pretty safe bet that the involvement's huge.'

'Yes, we can agree on that, at least,' Beresford said.

'And when an ex-soldier is murdered, that bastard Forsyth immediately appears on the scene. Not only that, but he'll go to any extreme – and I mean, *any* extreme – to avoid Adair's death being linked with the IRA.'

'Have you got anything in particular in mind when you say *any* extreme?' Beresford wondered.

'That doesn't matter,' Paniatowski said dismissively. 'The question you should be asking is *why* he seems willing to do it.'

'I don't *know* why,' Beresford admitted.

'And neither do I. But I *do* now know there's some sort of secret society – made up entirely of Protestants – which met every Thursday night, and that now Adair and Stockwell are dead, the rest of the members are running for their lives.'

'So you're suggesting that the government was using this society to somehow further its ends in Northern Ireland?' Beresford asked.

'Yes.'

'It's a bit of a tenuous link, isn't it, boss?'

'Then come up with something better for me to get my teeth into,' Paniatowski challenged.

'I can't,' Beresford conceded. 'But I still don't see how a very mixed bunch of people like the ones we've got these reports on could have been used by the government.'

'Neither do I. But I'm going to bloody well find out.'

'How?'

'By discovering exactly what Forsyth was doing last night. Because whatever it was, it was important enough for him to go to great efforts to make sure that *we* knew nothing about it.'

'But we don't have even a glimmering of an idea about what it might have been,' Beresford protested.

'No, we don't,' Paniatowski agreed. 'But while we might not know what it was, we know where it *happened*, don't we?'

'Do we?'

'Yes, we do. Or, at least, *I* do.' Paniatowski took a map out of her drawer and laid it on the desk. 'This is the road that Forsyth took last night,' she continued, tracing it out with her finger. 'This is where the West Yorkshire Police pulled DC Crane up. Now where is the road leading to?'

'You could get to Skipton by it,' Beresford suggested.

'You *could*, but Forsyth was already on a faster road to Skipton when he turned off onto this one. So where else could he have been going?'

'There are two or three small villages just off the road,' said Beresford, studying the map.

'And the key word here is *small*,' Paniatowski said. 'They probably all have a post office-general store. They may even have a pub. But that's it! So what possible interest could Forsyth have in visiting any of them – especially late at night?'

'I don't know.'

'Use your bloody brain!' Paniatowski urged. 'What else is there on that road, Inspector?'

'Well, there's the moors.'

'Yes, there are,' Paniatowski agreed. 'What we've got here is one of the remotest parts of Lancashire, which shouldn't have been of any interest at all to a man like Forsyth. But it was! Something was happening on the moor last night that he felt he needed to take a special interest in. And I want to find out what that something was.'

'But since it *did* happen last night, and is therefore over and done with now, you've no chance of finding out, have you?'

'Unless it happens again, *tonight*.'

'But you've no reason to think it will.'

'And you've no reason to think it *won't*.'

'You're clutching at straws, boss,' Beresford said.

'It is a long shot,' Paniatowski admitted reluctantly. 'But let's be honest, until we can track down one of the men who went missing this morning, the investigation's pretty much stalled anyway – so why shouldn't I go after a long shot?'

'Because by doing that, you'll be as good as proclaiming from the rooftops that you're not actually very interested in solving the murders any more,' Beresford thought. 'By doing that, you'll be showing that all you care about now is getting something on Forsyth.'

'I asked you why I shouldn't go after it?' Paniatowski repeated.

'And just how do you *propose* to "go after it", ma'am?' Beresford wondered. 'Let's just suppose that Forsyth does make the same journey tonight – and that's a *big* supposition. If you follow him, you'll be stopped just as DC Crane was yesterday, which means that all you'll get out of the experience is a night in the cells at Skipton Police Station.'

'And that's precisely why I have no intention of *following* him,' Paniatowski said.

'Then how do you expect to . . .?'

'I'm going to get there *ahead* of him.'

'It'll be a waste of time,' Beresford said.

'Perhaps it will. But it will be *my* time I'm wasting.'

'You shouldn't be putting me in this position, Monika,' Beresford thought. 'You shouldn't be making me say something I never thought I'd *have* to say.'

He took a deep breath.

'With respect, ma'am, it won't be *your* time you're wasting at all,' he told her. 'It will be the *investigation*'s time.'

*   *   *

She'd known Colin Beresford since he was a young bobby
still wet behind the ears, Monika Paniatowski thought, as she
moodily sipped at her vodka in the public bar of the Drum
and Monkey. She'd helped him, she'd encouraged him – she'd
played a big part in making him into the kind of bobby he
was. And now he'd openly rebuked her – in front of a sergeant
and detective constable, no less.

And she deserved it, she conceded. She deserved that – and
more. She'd let him down in a way she wouldn't have believed
possible even a day earlier. And the worst thing of all was
that she was going to *continue* letting him down.

'Are your lads not comin' in today, Chief Inspector?' the
landlord called from across the counter.

'Shouldn't think so,' Paniatowski replied.

Her lads! Even now, before she'd even started on the course
she had plotted, those words were starting to acquire a hollow
sound.

She was taking on the British Secret Service single-handed,
and if things went wrong, she wouldn't *have* her lads any
more. And even if her career survived the night – even if the
team remained intact – would things ever be the same again?

She became aware that someone had walked over to the
table and sat down opposite her, and looking up saw DS
Cousins with a pint of best bitter in his hand.

'Me and DC Crane have been talking it over, and we don't
think you should go out on to the moors alone,' Cousins said.

'Well, you and DC Crane can mind your own bloody business!' she snapped back at him. Then the last word of his
comment finally registered in her mind. 'Did you say *alone*?'
she asked.

'That's right, ma'am,' Cousins agreed. 'We think you might
need backup, and we decided we're just the men to provide it.'

'Why?' Paniatowski asked.

'Why, ma'am? Because if it comes to a punch-up, you'll
need a chunky feller like me by your side, and even young
Crane – who doesn't look as if he could fight his way out of
a paper bag – will come in useful, because we'll need somebody to hold our coats for us, won't we?'

Despite herself, Paniatowski smiled. 'Why do you want to
come with me?' she said. 'Is it because, unlike DI Beresford,
you think I might actually be on to something?'

'Jack Crane thinks you might be on to something,' Cousins said evasively.

'And you?'

'I'm older, and inclined to be a bit more cautious,' Cousins admitted. 'But that doesn't mean I've quite given up hope that you'll still manage to pull a rabbit out of the hat,' he added hastily.

Which was about as much of a vote of confidence as she was likely to get from him on this particular matter, Paniatowski thought.

'If you don't really believe we'll find anything, why do you want to come along?' she asked.

'For the ride,' Cousins said lightly. 'And because you're my boss,' he added, more seriously.

'Tangling with the security forces could ruin your careers, you know,' Paniatowski cautioned.

'We *do* know,' Cousins replied. 'And we're prepared to chance it.'

It was tempting to accept the offer, Paniatowski thought – because nobody likes to meet the Devil on their own.

She shook her head. 'I'm sorry, Paul, I can't allow it.'

'With respect, ma'am, this is a free country and there's nothing you can do to stop us,' Cousins said. 'We're going up to the moors *whatever* you say, so the only question you have to ask yourself is whether you're going to have us floundering around there on our own, or whether you're willing to provide us with some leadership.'

'If it looks like things are turning nasty up there, and I order you to go, you *will* obey that order, won't you?' Paniatowski asked.

'Of course, ma'am,' Cousins replied, unconvincingly.

Cousins was right, Beresford thought, forcing himself to gaze down, once more, at the file on the desk – the missing men could have lived their whole lives without their paths ever crossing. And Crane was right, too, there wasn't a Catholic among them – though, by all the laws of probability, there certainly should have been.

So what was the message of these files?

And why couldn't he see it?

He became aware of someone watching him from the

doorway, and looking up, saw Monika Paniatowski standing there.

She looked so very sad, he thought.

'I'm sorry, Colin,' she said.

'Sorry, ma'am? What for?'

'You *know* what for. For not giving the team the leadership it needed, and leaving it up to you instead. For wasting time by going off on what will probably be a wild-goose chase.'

'For wanting to find some way – *any* way – to hurt Forsyth as he's so obviously hurt you?' Beresford suggested.

'Yes, I suppose that's what it does boil down to in the end,' Paniatowski admitted. 'I have to do it, Colin. I don't want to, but I *have to*. But I promise you that after tonight, that's it. Whatever happens, you'll have the old Monika back with you in the morning.'

'I'll hold you to that,' Beresford said.

'I know you will.' Paniatowski replied. She paused for a second, before adding, 'When I drive out to the moors, DC Crane and DS Cousins want to come with me. They were quite insistent on it.'

'Were they?' Beresford asked, noncommittally.

'But they couldn't do that if you assigned them a duty that kept them in Whitebridge, could they? So why don't you come up with something?'

Beresford thought about it. 'If you must go off chasing phantoms, I'd be happier if you had them with you,' he said finally.

'And I'd like to be there myself,' he thought, 'but *somebody* has to hold the fort.'

'I could order you to assign them duties,' Paniatowski pointed out.

'You could,' Beresford agreed. 'But it's not an order I'd obey.'

Paniatowski shook her head slowly from side to side. 'Well, I suppose that when you stop *acting* like the boss, you lose the right to be *treated* like the boss,' she said.

'So it would seem,' Beresford concurred.

'I'll see you in the morning, then,' Paniatowski said.

'Yes,' Beresford replied, pointedly turning his attention back to his notes. 'I'll see you in the morning.'

From the corner of his eye he saw her turn, then heard the clacking of her heels as she walked away.

He stood up, though he'd never intended to, and rushed over to the door. By the time he reached it, she was almost at the end of the corridor.

'Good luck, boss!' he called after her.

She turned, and smiled gratefully at him.

'Thank you, Colin,' she said.

TWENTY-THREE

They had used Crane's Vauxhall Victor for their journey out to the moors, and Paniatowski had decided to leave it parked at the far side of a small hillock, some distance from the road and invisible to traffic travelling in either direction. Once that job was completed, she'd selected the crest of that same hillock as her observation post, and that was where she sat now, with the seemingly endless rugged moorland stretched out in front of her.

'Me and the missus used to come out here with the dog, ma'am,' she heard DS Cousins say wistfully, as he looked down at the parched grass and sea of purple heather. 'We'd walk for bloody miles, trying to tire the young bugger out, but he'd still be as playful at the end of it as he was at the beginning. Sometimes, I'd get quite cross with him over it. But my Mary didn't. She hardly ever got cross with anybody or anything.'

'I can't imagine how much you must miss her,' Paniatowski said.

'And I miss Bob,' she thought. 'I miss him desperately! But at least *I've* got Louisa to console me.'

Cousins sighed. 'Do you know, even after two years, there's still always a moment – just after I wake up – when I expect to find her lying there next to me.' He took a deep breath and squared his shoulders. 'Look at Jack Crane over there,' he continued, pointedly changing the subject. 'He's another bugger who refuses to be tired out.'

There was no disputing that. Ever since they'd arrived at the hillock, an hour earlier, Crane had been scouring the area around it like an eager Boy Scout out on a treasure hunt.

Ah, to be young again, Paniatowski thought, as she watched the detective constable climb the slope towards them with an effortlessness which, though athletic herself, she found enviable.

'I've checked our position from all vantage points, ma'am,' the detective constable said, when he'd reached the crest.

'Have you?' Paniatowski asked.

And she was thinking, 'You could at least pretend to be *a little* out of breath, Jack.'

'The thing is, ma'am, anybody with a pair of binoculars could pick us out from miles away,' Crane continued.

'That doesn't matter,' Paniatowski told him. 'Forsyth won't come until night has fallen, and the darkness will give us all the cover we need.'

'Are you sure he *will be* coming?' Crane asked.

'So even *you* are losing confidence in me now, are you, Jack?' Paniatowski thought.

'I'm not sure of *anything*,' she confessed. 'It's just a gut feeling.'

'Oh, I see,' said Crane, weakly.

'Besides, if he came last night, why *shouldn't* he come again tonight?' Paniatowski asked.

'True, but then again, why *should* he?' Crane countered, echoing her earlier argument with Colin Beresford. He paused for a moment, they continued, 'But supposing he *does* come, ma'am?'

'Yes?'

'What do you think will happen when he arrives?'

'I don't know,' Paniatowski admitted to herself. 'I've absolutely no idea!'

Gut feelings like the one she had now simply didn't work like that. They might be hard task masters, but they were rarely very specific.

Still, she had to tell Crane *something*.

'My best guess is that he'll be coming here to meet some of his mates from the security services' dirty tricks department,' she said.

'But why here?' Crane persisted. 'Why not hold the meeting back in Whitebridge?'

'I imagine that's what he would do, if all their nasty little games were *centred* on Whitebridge. But as far as we know, Forsyth is the only spook in town. The rest of his team are probably spread throughout the north, which makes this area very convenient for a rendezvous, doesn't it?'

'I suppose so,' Crane said dubiously.

'And from the security viewpoint, it's perfect, isn't it?' Paniatowski continued, aware, even as she spoke the words, that she was arguing the case as much to convince herself as to convince the detective constable. 'If they met in a pub somewhere, for instance, they'd be running the risk that somebody would remember them, but they had this place to themselves until we arrived.'

'Do you think it will be a big meeting, ma'am?' Crane asked.

Damn the child! Why did he have to keep persecuting her like this?

'I don't know how big a meeting it will be,' Paniatowski said. 'We'll have to wait and see, won't we?'

As the sun sank lower on the horizon, the brilliant purple of the heather became more muted, and then was finally lost in the darkness.

With the onset of night, different forms of life began to emerge. An owl hooted somewhere in the distance, insects began to chirp busily from the undergrowth, and small furry creatures darted hither and thither.

The moon rose, casting a pale, silvery glow over the moors, and Paniatowski, sitting there and watching it, found her mind drifting back to the past.

It was not only DS Cousins who had memories of this moor, she thought. She and Bob had often visited it – lying down in the heather and making passionate love, all the while aware that when it was over her lover's sense of duty would drive him back to his blind wife.

She could almost smell the crushed heather of that lovemaking now – could almost feel it sticking to her legs and breasts. She wondered if she would ever get over Bob, and decided she probably wouldn't – decided that, even if she did find love again, she would never be able to banish him entirely from her heart.

A dark shape, which had been sitting at the other end of the hillock, stood up and walked over to her.

'Do you mind if I sit down, ma'am?' it asked.

Paniatowski smiled into the darkness – partly through amusement, partly through relief.

'For God's sake, Jack, you don't need to ask my permission,' she said. 'This is the bloody moors, not my office,'

'Oh right, ma'am,' Crane said. He sat down next to her

– though not *too* close. 'There's something I've been wanting to get off my chest, ma'am,' he continued. 'Or rather, there's something that DS Cousins has advised me I *should* get off my chest.'

'I'm listening,' Paniatowski told him.

'I've . . . er . . . been lying about my education, ma'am. Well, not so much lying, as concealing the truth, which I suppose *is* lying in a way, and I thought it would be best if I . . .'

'Vehicles approaching!' DS Cousins called out, ending Crane's confession before it had even really got started.

They came from the north, cutting through the darkness with their headlights. There were five of them – and even from a distance, it was clear from the height of those headlights that whatever the vehicles were, they were much bigger than cars.

'Bloody large meeting, ma'am,' DS Cousins said. 'More like a party, if you ask me.'

'Maybe they're just passing through,' Paniatowski replied.

But she didn't believe they were, because this road was no short-cut to anywhere, and besides, her gut was starting to send out messages of self-congratulation.

The lorries – and they could definitely see that they *were* lorries now – pulled off the road about a mile away from the hillock, and, despite all the space available to them, parked in a straight line.

'Bloody hell, it's the army!' Cousins exclaimed. 'With that sense of neatness, it has to be.'

It certainly looked like it, Paniatowski thought.

But what business could Forsyth possibly have with the army?

'And here comes our mate the super-spy,' Cousins said, pointing to a set of much lower-slung headlights approaching from the Clitheroe end of the road. 'He's turned up, just like you promised he would. I'm proud of you, ma'am.' He paused. 'Sorry, ma'am. Not my place to say something like that.'

'That's all right,' Paniatowski assured him. 'I'm just a little proud of *myself*, too.'

The car reached the area where the lorries were parked, and pulled in beside them.

'We need to take a closer look,' Paniatowski said, with a sense of urgency in her voice. 'Paul, you approach them from the left-hand side. Jack, you go in from the right. Get as near as you safely can, but for God's sake don't push it too far, and end up getting yourself spotted.'

'I've got a question, ma'am,' DC Crane said.

Of course he had, Paniatowski thought.

And it would be an awkward one – because Jack Crane's main purpose on earth seemed to be to ask her awkward questions.

'Go ahead,' she said resignedly.

'Just what am I supposed to be *looking for*, ma'am?' Crane asked.

'I don't rightly know,' Paniatowski replied. 'But I'm sure you'll recognize it when you see it.'

Running in a crouched position was taking its toll on her calf muscles, and the unevenness of the ground meant that twice she'd slipped, and had to break her fall by holding her arms out in front of her. Even so, it was less than fifteen minutes before she was close enough to the lorries to be able to establish that if they weren't actually *army* vehicles, they were certainly very similar to them.

She hunkered down, and considered her next move.

There was no camp fire lighting up the darkness. She could detect no signs of human movement, and could hear no voices. So perhaps the soldiers – or *whatever* they were – had bedded down for the night.

But that made no sense at all, because Forsyth would not have made the trip out from Whitebridge just to watch other men sleep.

There was the sudden sound of gunfire in the distance, and turning her head she saw the bright red light of tracer bullets flying through the air.

'Oh my God, what the hell have I got my lads into?' she asked herself worriedly.

She heard the tread of the footfalls behind her just a split second before a heavy boot struck her in the middle of her back, sending her pitching forward. It was her shoulder, rather than her face, which hit the ground first – but it still hurt like buggery.

'Move an inch, and I'll fill you full of holes, you bastard,' said a harsh voice with a strong Ulster accent.

A beam of light lit up the ground just by her head.

'Get up – but do it slowly,' the voice said. 'And the instant you're standing up, I want to see your hands behind your head.'

There were two of them, she noted when she was back on her feet. One had his hands dangling by his sides, as if he was not quite sure what to do with them, but the second was holding a torch in one hand and a pistol in the other – and both those objects were firmly pointing at her.

'Jesus, Johnny, but it's only a woman,' said the one with his hands by his sides.

'What are you doing here?' demanded the one with the pistol.

'I'm a police officer, *Johnny*,' Paniatowski said. 'And that means *I'm* the one who's going to be asking the questions.'

'It doesn't work like that out here in the middle of nowhere,' the Ulsterman said harshly. 'You might have a warrant card, but I've got a gun – and that puts *me* in charge.'

'You know you wouldn't dare shoot a bobby, so why pretend?' Paniatowski countered.

'Wouldn't dare?' the Ulsterman repeated. 'I wouldn't be so sure of that, if I was you. When a man knows he can get away with it, there's no telling what he's capable of – and when he has powerful friends, like I have, he can get away with almost anything.'

'I believe him,' Paniatowski thought, as she felt a shudder run through her body. 'Or, at least, I believe that he *believes* it – and that's just as dangerous.'

'Search her, Michael,' Johnny told his companion. 'And don't go easy on the search just because she's a woman. She looks old enough to be well used to having her tits felt up.'

Michael stepped forward, and ran his hands quickly up and down Paniatowski's body.

She did not resist.

'She's clean,' Michael said, when he'd finished.

'Right,' Johnny said. 'Now we've got that bit of business out of the way, we'll all go over to the trucks, and find out just what Mr Smith wants us to do with you.'

TWENTY-FOUR

Paniatowski was standing with her back pressed against the wheel arch of one of the lorries. Johnny was positioned less than six feet away from her, his feet wide apart and his pistol unwaveringly aimed at her chest. Neither of them had spoken since Michael had left. And why should they have done? They both recognized that they were merely minor players in the unfolding drama, and that what happened next was entirely in the hands of 'Mr Smith'.

Michael returned. 'Are you Chief Inspector Pania . . . Pania . . .?' he asked falteringly.

'Paniatowski,' Monika supplied. 'Yes, I am.'

'A Polack!' Johnny said, with evident disgust. 'A bloody Catholic!' He spat on the ground. 'I knew it! I just bloody *knew* it! I can smell you Papist bastards from a mile away.'

'Mr Smith wants to see her, Johnny,' Michael said. 'He's waiting for her in his car.'

'Then we'd better take the heathen bitch to him, hadn't we?' Johnny replied.

The two men led Paniatowski past the lorries, to where the Rover 2000 was parked.

Johnny opened the passenger door, and said, 'Get in there, you filthy foreign whore!'

Forsyth was sitting in the driver's seat, with his leather briefcase neatly on his lap.

'Good evening, *Mr Smith*,' Paniatowski said.

'Oh, that's not my real name, as you well know,' the man replied. 'But then, of course, neither is Forsyth.'

He opened the briefcase, took out his hip flask and two small glasses, and placed them on the dashboard.

'On this occasion, all I can offer you is malt whisky,' he said apologetically. 'I didn't bring the vodka with me, because I never imagined you'd be stupid enough to pull a stunt like this.'

'Who are these men?' Paniatowski asked, ignoring the comment.

Forsyth poured out two glasses of malt, and handed one to
Paniatowski. When he saw her knock it back in a single gulp,
he couldn't resist a faint smile.

'Who are these men?' he repeated. 'Well, they're Ulstermen,
obviously. In fact, they're part of the Ulster Freedom Force.'

Paniatowski nodded, unsurprised.

'The Ulster Freedom Force,' she said, rolling the words
carefully around in her mouth, as if they were an unexploded
bomb. 'In other words, they're part of a terrorist paramilitary
organization which your *own* government has declared illegal.'

'It's *your* government, too,' Forsyth reminded her.

'And you're in charge of training them, are you?'

'Of course not!' Forsyth said disdainfully. 'I wouldn't even
know how to begin. My military experience was all in the
Guards, and we fought a much cleaner, more gentlemanly
kind of war than the one these chaps will be fighting. All *I'm*
doing here, Monika, is *facilitating* their training.'

'So who *is* training them?'

'A number of ex-soldiers who've had experience of serving
at the sharp end in Northern Ireland.'

'Men like Andy Adair.'

'Yes, he was one of the instructors.'

'And that's why he was killed?'

Forsyth sighed. 'As I've told you at least a dozen times
already, Monika, Adair's death had nothing to do with the
IRA.'

'Then who *did* kill him?'

'I really don't know. But there must be plenty of people –
people with no interest in politics at all – who would have
wanted him dead.'

'Why?'

'Because he was the kind of man who made enemies easily.
Adair was both greedy and unscrupulous, and in a place like
Ulster – where there are few rules, and even less restraints –
he must have felt right at home.'

'You're telling me that he was involved in some kind of
criminal activity over there, are you?'

'I'm telling you that he was involved in a *myriad* of criminal activities. He sold goods on the black market. He provided
the protection for a prostitution ring. He may even have been
involved in drug dealing. I don't know about that. But I do

know that if he hadn't left the army when he did, he'd probably have ended up being court-martialled.'

'Yet, despite all that, you recruited him for this job.'

Forsyth laughed. 'You've got entirely the wrong end of the stick. It's *because* of all that I recruited him. He knows the way Ulster works. He knows what buttons to push to get the desired outcomes.'

'The desired outcomes!' Paniatowski repeated scornfully. 'What a nice, neutral, antiseptic phrase that is.'

'Yes, isn't it?' Forsyth agreed.

'When what you really mean is that he's been training a bunch of mad dogs who, once you think they're ready, you'll set loose on Ulster, to intimidate, torture and murder at will.'

'Scarcely *at will*,' Forsyth corrected her. 'There have to be some limits set on their behaviour, even in a place like that.'

'But the simple truth is that they'll be doing the dirty work for you – work you daren't have the army implicated in.'

'Essentially, yes.'

'And innocent people will die.'

'It's a war we're fighting over there, Monika. And in a war, innocent people on *both sides* die all the time.'

'I can see now why you were so keen to dispel any rumours that Adair was killed by the IRA,' Paniatowski said.

'Can you?'

'Yes. It would have been very bad for the morale of these men to think that the Republicans could get at one of their instructors so easily.'

'Quite so.'

'But what I *don't* see is why, once Adair had been killed, you didn't pull them out immediately.'

'It's very simple,' Forsyth told her. 'When their training period is over, we'll be putting these men back into a war zone, where not only they, but also their families, will be at risk. They have to be confident – in a situation like that – that they have our full and unqualified support.'

'And do they?'

'Of course not! If they do something particularly horrific – and they will – or end up in serious danger – and that will happen too – we'll say we never heard of them. Their value to us, you see, is based almost entirely on their deniability. But *they* mustn't know that.'

'I still don't see . . .'

'We have promised them that they will have the full force of the British government behind them. And how strong would that government look if, just because the police were investigating the murder of one of their instructors, we made them cut and run?'

'So they're still here simply to prove they *can* still be here?'

'Exactly. I suppose that, in some ways, Andy Adair's murderer did us a favour.'

'A favour?'

'Indeed – because it presented us with the opportunity to show these men just how determined we are to give them our full backing.'

'Even though you're not.'

'Even though we're not.'

'So what happens next?' Paniatowski asked.

Forsyth opened his briefcase and took out three forms. 'Now, you and your colleagues . . .' He paused. 'I did mention that we'd also caught your colleagues, didn't I?'

'You know you didn't.'

'Well, we have. DS Cousins, isn't it? And, of course, DC Crane, my friend from *last* night's little adventure.'

'Sometimes you sound just like a big kid,' Paniatowski said, with utter contempt.

Forsyth smiled. 'You seem surprised at that. I'd have thought you would have realized, long before now, that the security service is the natural home of overgrown schoolboys. Who else would throw themselves with such relish into a game which, in the long run, we're bound to lose?' An expression of deep sadness crossed his face, and then was gone, leaving no trace. 'But to return to my point,' he continued, 'what happens next is that you and your colleagues sign the Official Secrets Act. And once you've done that, of course, you can leave.'

'Just like that?'

'Yes. At this delicate stage of the operation, the last thing I'd like to have on my hands is the unexplained disappearance of three police officers, and so I've decided to let you go.'

'As long as we sign the Act?'

'Exactly.'

'Why does it matter if we sign it or not? An official secret is an official secret, and if we reveal what we've seen, we'd go to jail whether or not we'd put our names to a piece of paper.'

'Indeed you would,' Forsyth agreed. 'You would not be the first to suffer, of course – other heads would roll before yours . . .'

'Yours, for example,' Paniatowski taunted.

'Yes, mine would probably be the first, rapidly followed by those of some quite influential men in the Ministry of Defence,' Forsyth admitted. 'But your turn would come. You'd be given a long sentence for breaching national security – but it's not really the *length* of your sentence you should worry about.'

'Isn't it?'

'Oh dear me, no. The security services have considerable influence in our prison system, and they'd make sure you had a very hard time while you were inside. You'd be raped, probably with some rather unpleasant kitchen implement. You'd be beaten on a daily basis. I honestly doubt you'd survive the experience.'

'Why would your mates in the security services want *that* to happen?' Paniatowski wondered. 'Is it because they're *all* sadistic bastards like you?'

'Of course not! Overgrown schoolboys we may be, but we rarely have the luxury of doing things simply for our own pleasure, Monika,' Forsyth said. 'You would be made to suffer as an example – and the *more* you suffered, the better the example would be. You would serve, if you like, as a deterrent to others who might be contemplating following in your footsteps.'

'You still haven't answered the question I asked earlier,' Paniatowski said.

'That was very remiss of me,' Forsyth said. 'Remind me what that question was.'

As if he needed reminding! Paniatowski thought.

'Since it's illegal to reveal official secrets under *any* circumstances, why do you *need* me to sign the Act?' she asked.

'I suppose there are two main reasons,' Forsyth said, speaking in slow, measured terms, almost as if he were delivering an academic lecture. 'The first is that this country unaccountably still believes in trial by jury – an archaic system in which those least able to reach a verdict are given the sole right to do so

– and these juries feel happier convicting if the prisoner in the dock has signed the Act. It is almost, in their poor muddled terms, as if he or she had signed a confession.'

'And the second?'

'The person who has signed the Act almost invariably feels as if it has put him or her under a moral obligation. It isn't logical, of course, but I have seen it happen too often to deny that it's the truth.'

'That's not it,' Paniatowski said firmly. 'That isn't why *you* want *me* to sign.'

'Then why *do* I want you to sign?'

'As an act of submission – as proof that I'm prepared to bend my will to yours. I wouldn't be just signing away my right to speak – I'd be signing away part of myself.'

'In one way, you're right,' Forsyth conceded. 'That *is* part of the process. But you're wrong to see it – as you so obviously do – in personal terms. I have no desire to bend your will to mine – I merely wish to bend the will of a British subject to that of the British government.'

'You're a bloody liar,' Paniatowski said. 'You're a bloody liar and I *won't* sign.'

'Then you'll never get your father's remains back,' Forsyth said. 'In fact,' he continued, his voice hardening, 'I'll see to it personally that they're flushed down the sewer.'

There was always excitement in the house when the colonel was coming home.

The mistress would go through her entire wardrobe, rejecting each and every dress as being unworthy to greet him in, and finally, out of desperation, select one which she hoped would more or less pass muster.

On the floor below her, the maids rushed around in a flurry, searching out even the most minute particle of dust and vanquishing it. In the kitchen, the cook laboured long and hard, striving to produce the best meal the master had ever tasted. In the stables, the grooms brushed the horses. In the grounds, the gardeners removed plants which were only just past their best, and replaced them with new ones in their full glory.

And little Monika?

She would post herself at an upstairs window, hours before he was due to arrive, in order to ensure that she was the very first person in the entire household to catch sight of him.

Finally, he would appear, riding his magnificent black stallion down the long avenue of plain trees. The horse would be moving at no more than a steady trot – for it would have been unseemly for the colonel to appear to be in a hurry. But the man himself would have his eyes fixed on that upstairs window from which he knew his daughter would be watching.

'Did you hear what I said about your father's remains?' Forsyth asked.

He'd been a wonderful man, Paniatowski thought. Though he'd died when she was no more than a child, he had largely made her the woman she was. It was he who'd given her a fighting spirit, and without his example, she'd have gone under long ago.

'Monika?' Forsyth said, with just an edge of irritation slowly creeping into his voice.

'Do it!' she told him.

'I beg your pardon?'

'Flush his bones down the sewer. Go even further than that, if it'll make you happy. Feed his bones to the dogs. Pay some poor sod to spend the next twenty years daubing them with shit every day. I don't care!'

'You *do* care, Monika,' Forsyth contradicted her.

'You're right, I do care,' Paniatowski admitted, fighting back the tears. 'It's important to me. But I'm not prepared to sell my soul for it.'

Forsyth sighed again. 'I just knew, when that Irish thug told me they'd captured you, that you were going to be difficult,' he said. 'And now, you see, by turning down my offer, you're forcing me to say something I'd hoped to avoid having to say at all.'

'Let's hear it,' Paniatowski challenged.

'If you sign the Official Secrets Act, I will instruct one of the Volunteers to go and collect your car from wherever it is you've hidden it. And once he has done that, we will drive back to Whitebridge together.'

'And if I don't sign?'

'Then I'll drive back to Whitebridge alone.'

'And what will happen to us?'

'I don't know.'

'But you can guess.'

'As can you.'

'In other words,' Paniatowski said, 'if we don't sign the act, you'll have us killed?'

'No,' Forsyth replied emphatically. 'If you don't sign, I'll do nothing to *prevent* you from being killed. The ultimate responsibility for your men rests with you and the decisions you chose to take, Monika. So ask yourself – do you really want to go to your own death knowing that you've caused their deaths, too?'

'You win,' Paniatowski said.

'Of course I do,' Forsyth agreed.

He reached into his briefcase again, and produced a thick folder. For several seconds he held it his hands, as if weighing not just the folder itself but also his own options.

'I had almost decided not to give you this, Monika,' he said finally, 'but it is sometimes necessary to allow even the vanquished to walk away with some small sense of victory, and this can be yours.'

'What is it?' Paniatowski asked.

'The information you asked me to collect on Sir William Langley,' Forsyth told her. 'I think you might find it very interesting reading.'

TWENTY-FIVE

Whitebridge Rovers FC had languished in the Football League's Third Division for over thirty years. Sometimes, when the season came to an end, they would be clinging to the middle of the division, like a thwarted mountaineer. Sometimes, they could be found hovering shakily just above the relegation zone at the bottom of the table. But never, in the memory of their younger fans, had they breathed the heady air at the top.

Last season had been different. Last season, the team had played like men inspired, become division champions, and gained automatic promotion to the Second Division.

The promotion would bring with it big changes. When the new season opened, the Rovers could look forward to higher attendance rates, and more appearances on television.

'In other words,' said Thad Rogers, the chairman, who was a prosperous local businessman and had been running the club as a loss-making hobby for over a decade, 'we'll finally see some money start to come in.'

But before the money could be earned, money needed to be spent, especially on the pitch. For though visiting Third Division teams had complained about it, they were well aware of their own place in the scheme of things, and had not – in all honesty – expected much better. The promotion had changed all that. Now the club had moved up the ladder – now they finally had their chance to play with the big boys – and it was clear to everyone that before Second Division players deigned to put their studded boots on it, the pitch would have to be radically improved.

It was in order to work towards this aim that Brian Dewhurst, the Rovers' head groundsman, arrived at the stadium at eight o'clock that Friday morning. He did not go straight onto the pitch, as he'd originally planned, because it occurred to him that since he'd recently been entrusted with the key to the directors' box, he might as well take advantage of the fact, and start his day with a small shot of the chairman's vintage brandy.

The small shot – as it happened – turned out to be not quite so small after all, because when you were drinking out of one of those big balloon glasses, Dewhurst explained to himself, you had to pour a fair bit into it before you could even *see* the brandy.

And since a drink like that couldn't be rushed – it would have been almost criminal to gulp it down – it was not until twenty-five past eight that Dewhurst forced himself to rise from the chairman's sofa and walk over to the picture window which looked out onto the pitch.

And that was when he saw it!

From their position halfway up the stand, Paniatowski and Beresford looked down at the two naked men – both on their hands and knees, and both undoubtedly dead – who were facing each other in the centre of the pitch.

'Did you know DS Gutterridge, boss?' Beresford asked.

'Only by sight,' Paniatowski replied. 'Who did you say the other one was?'

'Edward Dunston. He was an accountant.'

'And was he one of the men whose whereabouts were unaccounted for on Thursday nights?'

'He was.'

Paniatowski lit up a cigarette. 'What does it all mean?' she asked, exasperatedly. 'What message is he trying to send us?'

'Is he trying to send *us* a message at all?' Beresford replied. 'Or is it aimed at any members of the Thursday-night brigade who still haven't left town?'

'*Last* night was Thursday night,' Paniatowski pointed out. 'Do you think *that* means anything?'

'Might do,' Beresford said.

'And then again, it might not.' Paniatowski sighed. 'Not that that's the only question we need an answer to. I can think of another three just off the top of my head. Why are there two of them this time? Why did he choose to position them like that? And why did he leave them here, rather than anywhere else?'

'I think there are two of them because it's his swansong,' Colin Beresford said.

'Go on,' Paniatowski encouraged.

'He's been lucky so far. He *could have* been spotted when

he kidnapped one of his victims. He *could have* been seen when he was dumping them. He might even have been caught driving around in one of the vans that he stole. But his luck can't last forever – and he knows that as well as we do. So I think this is his grand finale – the firework display at the end of the show.'

'Are you saying he *won't* kill again?'

'No, I'm not. If the opportunity presents itself, he'll take it. But I don't think *he* thinks he'll get the opportunity. I think he can feel the net closing in on him.'

'If only it was,' Paniatowski thought. 'But we're no closer to catching him than we were three days ago.'

'I also think he *wants* to be caught,' Beresford added. 'I think he's had enough.'

'What makes you say that?' Paniatowski wondered.

'Nothing tangible,' Beresford admitted. 'It's just a gut feeling. I'm allowed to have one of my own, you know, now that I'm an inspector.'

He was grinning as he said the words, Paniatowski thought. But behind the grin, was he still angry with her for going out onto the moors the night before?

'You were right,' she said. 'Last night was a waste of time.'

'So nothing happened, and nobody turned up?'

It should have been easy to nod, but Colin Beresford was more than just her inspector, he was her friend.

'I didn't say *nothing* happened,' she told him.

'Well, then . . .?'

'But I can't talk about it. I can't even tell you *why* I can't talk about it, so don't bother to ask. And don't ask DC Crane or DS Cousins, because they can't talk about it, either.'

'So much for team spirit,' Beresford said, sourly.

'Nothing that happened had anything to do with the case, you have to trust me on that, Colin,' Paniatowski said. And then she realized she was not being entirely truthful. 'There was one thing I learned,' she amended. 'When Andy Adair was serving in Northern Ireland, he did a number of things that could have earned him a fairly lengthy prison sentence if he'd been found out.'

'Who told you that? Forsyth?'

'Yes.'

'So he *was* there.'

'As I said earlier, I'm wondering why the killer positioned his victims facing each other,' Paniatowski said, changing the subject. 'It's almost as if they were squaring up to have a fight, isn't it? And *is* there any significance to leaving them in the Rovers' ground?'

'There must be,' Beresford said, understanding what was going on and deciding not to fight it. 'There are a hundred places he could have dumped them that would have been easier to get into than this stadium.'

'We think he left his last victim in Ashton Court because he wanted Sir William Langley himself to find him, don't we? So who did he want to find this pair? Thad Rogers?'

'The chairman? I wouldn't expect him to be here at this hour of the morning, and I don't think the killer would, either.'

'Then there's only one other possible explanation, isn't there?' Paniatowski said. 'He must have left them for the groundsman to find.'

Brian Dewhurst was in his late fifties, Paniatowski guessed. He had large, work-hardened hands, and there was the smell of alcohol on his breath.

'It were the shock of my life, seeing them two dead men,' he told the chief inspector. 'I thought it were a joke at first, but the more I looked at them, the more I knew it wasn't.'

'Did you know either of the victims?'

'I can't say for sure. To be honest with you, I didn't look at them any closer than I had to.'

'Then let me ask you this – do the names Edward Dunston and Len Gutterridge mean anything to you?'

Dewhurst scratched his head. 'I used to know a *Sid* Gutterridge,' he said.

'But not *Len*?'

'I don't think so.'

He was either a bloody fine actor or he was telling the truth, Paniatowski decided.

'Can I ask you where you were last night, Mr Dewhurst?' she said.

'Last night?' Dewhurst asked, showing some signs of alarm. 'Here, you're surely not suggesting I had anything to do with them two dead fellers, are you, Chief Inspector?'

'No, I'm simply asking you where you were last night.'

'I was in the public bar of the Dog and Partridge,' Dewhurst said, with the reluctance of a man who believed you should never give the authorities more information than you absolutely had to.

'And can anyone confirm that's where you were?' Paniatowski asked.

'Yes,' Dewhurst replied, and now there was an edge of aggression creeping into his voice. 'My whole bloody darts team can confirm it. An' the visiting team, which came from the Tinker's Bucket, an' all.'

'And is that what you *usually* do on Thursdays?'

'It's what I *always* do on a Thursday. I've not missed a single match all season.'

'And once the match had finished? What did you do then?'

'I was home by a quarter to twelve, and in bed by a quarter *past*. And if you want confirmation of that, you've only to ask my missus. She'll remember, all right.' Dewhurst's mood changed again, and he chuckled. 'To tell the truth, last night I was bit like one of them sexual athletes you read about – I usually am when we win the match, especially if I finish my own game with a double top.'

So whatever the killer's reason for leaving the bodies in the stadium, it had nothing to do with Brian Dewhurst, Paniatowski decided.

But what other reason *could* there he have been? What point was he trying to *make*?

'The panic's spreading,' Beresford told Crane, as they sipped from their mugs of industrial-strength tea in the police canteen. 'Since yesterday afternoon, four more men have gone missing. And when the news is released that another two bodies have been discovered at the Rovers' ground, I wouldn't be surprised if there wasn't a positive bloody exodus.'

'Are all the newly missing men linked by Thursday-evening absences, sir?' Crane asked.

'*Are all the newly missing men linked by Thursday-evening absences,*' Beresford repeated to himself.

There were times, he thought, when Jack Crane didn't sound like an ordinary bobby at all.

'Three of them regularly went off on their own Thursday nights, and the fourth one did occasionally,' he said aloud.

'I wonder where they went,' Crane mused. 'When men slope off together in a group, it's usually a good guess that they're off to a strip club. But people don't get killed for going to a strip club.'

'Maybe you should ask your mate Mr Forsyth if he's got any ideas,' Beresford suggested.

'I . . . er . . . don't think Mr Forsyth is very interested in who the killer is, sir,' Crane said awkwardly.

'Then what *is* he interested in?'

'Other things,' Crane said, gazing into his mug.

'Well done, Colin,' Beresford thought to himself. 'You've actually sunk to the level of trying to wheedle information out of a junior officer – a lad who's only been on the job for five minutes. Call yourself an inspector? A leader of men? Because I bloody don't!'

Yet what else was he supposed to do? He had worked with Monika for nearly a decade. He had relied on her, and she had replied on him. Now she'd cut him out of the loop – and he felt like an orphan.

Crane was looking at him nervously – as if he was expecting the interrogation to continue.

'Let's talk about something else,' Beresford suggested. 'And, just for a change, let's make it something totally unconnected with work.'

The obvious relief on Crane's face could have been spotted from the other end of the canteen.

'All right,' he agreed.

But talk about *what*, Beresford wondered. How easy would it be to think of another topic of conversation, when all he was really interested in was what had happened on the moors the previous night.

Crane was still waiting for him – the inspector – to take the lead.

'So what do you do with your free time?' Beresford asked finally.

'I do a lot of reading,' Crane said.

'Oh, you're a big fan of the football magazines, are you?'

'No,' Crane thought. 'I'm a big fan of the metaphysical poets and Marcel Proust.'

'That's right,' he agreed. 'But I also like to go out dancing,' he added quickly, on the off-chance that Beresford would decide to pursue the idea of football magazines further, and thus expose his total ignorance on the subject.

'Who do you go dancing with? Do you have a regular partner? A steady girlfriend, perhaps?'

Crane grinned. 'I don't *take* girls to dances, sir. I go to dances to *pick up* girls.'

'And then you probably take them back your flat, and give them a bloody good rogering,' Beresford the still-virgin thought enviously.

This was not turning out to be a good day, he decided – it wasn't turning out to be a good day at all!

When Beresford returned to the office, he found Paniatowski absorbed in a bulky folder that he didn't recall ever having seen before.

The chief inspector looked up. 'Anything I need to know?' she asked.

'I've had the Rovers' ground sealed, and there's a forensic team combing through it right now,' Beresford said. 'I've got lads out on the street looking for witnesses, but I'm not holding out much hope of them finding any. There's no sign of a break-in, so another team is out checking on the Rovers' key-holders. There's no report from Dr Shastri yet, either, but even when we get it, I'd be surprised if it contains anything new, because our killer's too careful to go leaving any clues.' He paused for a second. 'What's in the folder, boss – or is that something else I'm not supposed to know about?'

Paniatowski sighed. 'It's all about Sir William Langley,' she said.

'Is it, now,' Beresford said, noncommittally.

'What it's mostly concerned with is his financial dealings,' Paniatowski told him. 'Langley might come over as a bit thick when you talk to him, but he's certainly not stupid when it comes to handling his money. He's not exactly what you might call straight as a die, either. He's set up dozens of dummy companies, all over the world. Most of them show a large loss on their annual balance sheets, and so they don't pay any tax at all. But the *reason* they show a loss is that Langley's already siphoned the money off.'

She was expecting him to ask her where she got this information from, Beresford thought. But why the hell *should* he?

'If Langley's as bad as that, I'm surprised the Inland Revenue hasn't caught up with him years ago,' he said, almost disinterestedly.

'*I'm* not surprised at all,' Paniatowski replied.

'Aren't you? The Revenue's been given powers that bobbies like us can only dream of having. *It* doesn't have to go sweet-talking a magistrate every time it wants to enter private property. If it feels like it, it can seize your account books or shut down your business while it audits you – and all without having to produce a single shred of evidence as justification.'

'You're right,' Paniatowski agreed. 'But even though it *does* have all those powers, it still has to work *within* the law. And that's not a restraint that Forsyth's mates seem to think applies to them.'

Beresford sniffed. 'I might have guessed the information came from Forsyth,' he said.

It was no good, Paniatowski decided, she couldn't keep it a secret any longer– not from Colin.

'Forsyth's training Protestant paramilitaries on the moors,' she said in a rush, before she had time to change her mind again. '*That's* what we found out last night – and I don't think it has anything at all to do with the murders.'

'So why wouldn't you tell me that earlier, when we were at the football ground?' Beresford asked, unyielding.

What did he want from her, Paniatowski thought angrily. What did he bloody *want*?

'I didn't tell you earlier because Forsyth made me sign the Official Secrets Act, and if he *found out* I'd told you, I could go to jail.'

'How *could* he have found out?' Beresford asked, reddening. 'Do you think *I* would have told him? Or that I'd have told anybody else, for that matter? Do you think I would *ever* have done *anything* that I knew would land you in trouble?'

Paniatowski felt her anger draining away. 'You're right,' she admitted guiltily. 'Charlie Woodend would have told *me* about it straight away, and I should have done the same with *you*. If we don't trust each other completely, then the team means nothing.'

She paused, to give Beresford the chance to say something conciliatory, but he kept determinedly silent.

'Give me a break, Colin,' she pleaded. 'I'm new to the job. I'm still feeling my way.'

The inspector's stony expression melted away, and a smile came to his face 'Of course you are, boss,' he said. 'We're *all* just feeling our way.'

It was going to be all right between them again, Paniatowski thought with relief. It would take some working on, but it was going to be *fine*.

'Anyway,' she continued, doing her best to cover her emotions with an official crispness, 'I asked Forsyth to compile this dossier on Langley, and last night, on the moors, he gave it to me.'

'Why?' Beresford asked.

'Why did I ask him to compile the dossier?'

'Why did he give it to you last night?'

Paniatowski shrugged. 'He *said* it was a sort of consolation prize for having made me jump through the hoops, but with a man like him, you can never be sure. He's probably got five or six other devious reasons for giving it to me – reasons that I couldn't even begin to guess at.'

'Do you think he'd have given it to you even if you *hadn't* caught him red-handed with the paramilitaries?' Beresford asked.

'No, probably not,' Paniatowski said.

'Then your instincts were right after all, weren't they?'

'I'm sorry?'

'If you hadn't gone out onto the moors, you'd never have got your hands on what could turn out to be a valuable lead.'

It was magnanimous of him to see it like that, Paniatowski thought – more than magnanimous.

The problem was, she was far from certain that the dossier would turn out to be *any kind* of lead at all.

'I'm not sure how much it helps us to know that he's a crook,' she said, because it had to be admitted sooner or later. 'It's true he might have some contact with all the dead men, because he's got his finger in all kinds of pies . . .'

'Like what?'

'Plumbing supplies, furniture shops, funeral parlours . . .' Paniatowski glanced through the list, 'and, apparently, agriculture.'

'Agriculture? That doesn't seem likely.'

'It says here that one of his dummy companies owns Moors' Edge Farm, which is somewhere out on Haslingden Moor.'

'Moors' Edge Farm,' Beresford repeated. 'I think I know where that is.' He closed his eyes and concentrated for a moment. 'Yes, I *do* know. I've walked past it on one of my moorland hikes.'

'I didn't know you were a hiker, Colin.'

'I wasn't – not when I had to look after my mother. But now she's in the residential home, I'm finding I've got a lot of time to fill.'

'So you joined a rambling group?'

'Not exactly,' Beresford said. 'I go on my own.'

'Poor Colin,' Paniatowski thought.

'It's sometimes good to get away on your own,' she said aloud.

'Anyway,' Beresford continued briskly, as if realizing he'd revealed a part of his private life he'd rather have kept hidden, 'it's not actually a working farm any more. I wonder what possessed Langley to buy it. I suppose he picked it up for a song, years ago, and planned to turn it into his country estate. Then he got richer, and decided to buy Ashley Court instead.'

'And so, instead of rising to great heights, as it might once have hoped, it's still just a shell – like any number of other abandoned cottages you find on the moors,' Paniatowski said.

'Actually, it's not a shell at all,' Beresford said thoughtfully. 'The roof is still in good condition, and you virtually never see that with abandoned cottages. There are heavy shutters up at the windows, too.' He frowned. 'In fact, thinking back on it, the place seemed pretty secure for what it was.'

Paniatowski looked down at the folder Forsyth had given her. 'What was it you said?' she asked. 'He probably picked it up for a song, years ago, when he was planning to turn it into his home?'

'Something like that.'

'Well, you're half-right and half-wrong. He did pick it up for a song, but he's only owned it for eighteen months. So I don't really see *why* he bought it. What possible interest could he have in an old farm in the middle of . . .' Paniatowski's face froze, but only for a second. Then her lips began to form themselves into a triumphant smile. 'I think we've just found the venue of the Thursday Night Club,' she said.

'I think we have,' Beresford agreed.

TWENTY-SIX

Paniatowski fought back the urge to jam her foot down hard on the MGA's accelerator, and instead navigated the rutted track which led to Moors' Edge Farm at a sensible speed.

From the moorland road which looped around it, the farm had looked as tiny and insubstantial as a doll's house, but the closer the car got to the actual building, the more she could appreciate just how solid and immovable it was.

'It's the ideal meeting place for people who don't want anybody else to even *know* they're having a meeting,' Beresford said from the passenger seat.

Yes, it was, Paniatowski agreed silently. The nearest village was at least six miles away, and since they had left the main road, they had not encountered even one other vehicle.

She parked the car, and got out, to take a closer look at the farm.

It was oblong, with a double frontage – which meant that it was slightly longer than it was wide – and, like most moorland properties, it had been built of local materials. Flat dressed stone had been used to tile the roof, larger, rougher blocks in the construction of the walls (which were probably at least two feet thick). The front door and window shutters were made of heavy planks, from an oak tree which must already have been more than a stripling when Francis Drake led his attack on the Spanish Armada. The farm had been built to withstand the harsh and unyielding moorland weather, and the fact that it was still there after more than two hundred years was ample proof that the anonymous, long-dead builders had known exactly what they were doing.

'See what I mean about it being in good condition?' Beresford asked.

She did. It was old, but it was cared for. There was not a roof tile out of place, and the mortar between the great stone blocks was so recent that it had hardly had time to discolour.

A blue van pulled up next to the MGA, and a man climbed

out of it. He was in his mid-forties, and had the sort of pinched features and shifty eyes which would have most bobbies on the beat instinctively reaching for either their notebooks or their handcuffs.

He grinned at Paniatowski and said, 'Well, well, another day, another forced entry, hey, Chief Inspector?'

'You're probably right, Roy,' Paniatowski agreed, 'but I'd better just check whether it's necessary first.'

She walked up to the front door, lifted the iron knocker, and brought it down against the metal plate which had been screwed into one of the oak planks. She counted to ten, then repeated the process. No one answered her knock, but she'd have been surprised if they had – because after the events of the previous few days, Moors' Edge Farm was the *last* place on earth that any member of the Thursday Night Club would want to be.

The police locksmith, observing her lack of success, reached into his overall pocket and produced a set of skeleton keys.

'My turn?' he asked.

'Your turn,' Paniatowski confirmed. 'How long do you think it should take you, Roy?'

The locksmith bent forward and examined the lock. 'Very modern, very expensive and very secure,' he pronounced.

'Does that mean you can't open it?'

Roy grinned again. 'There *may be* locks I can't open, but I haven't come across one yet. Can you give me five minutes?'

'Sure,' Paniatowski agreed.

She walked around the side of the house, where the rutted track which led from the road came to an end. The ground there was flatter and more regular than the rest of the land around the property, and looked as if it had only recently been excavated.

'This is where they parked the cars on Thursday nights,' said Colin Beresford, who had arrived at the spot before her.

And from the number of tyre tracks which Paniatowski could see gouged into the clayey earth, it was clear that he was right.

'How many vehicles do you reckon were parked here at any one time?' she asked.

Beresford shrugged. 'There's space for at least *twenty* cars, and I've spotted at least five distinct treads.'

No doubt the police technicians would be able to uncover

considerably more, Paniatowski thought. But even if there *were* only five, that was a lot of traffic for an abandoned farm house in the middle of the moors.

The air was suddenly filled with a loud mechanical screech, which seemed to be coming from the front of the house.

'Looks as if Roy's having more difficulty than he thought he would,' Paniatowski said.

He was. The locksmith had abandoned his delicate picks and was now attacking the lock with a heavy industrial drill.

'How thick would you say this door is, ma'am?' he asked, when he saw that Paniatowski had returned.

The chief inspector examined the solid oak boards – blackened by age and as hard as iron – which made up the door.

'About two inches?' she guessed.

'That's what I'd have estimated, too,' Roy agreed. 'But the lock itself is at least *four* inches long.'

'How's that possible?' Paniatowski wondered.

'The oak, as thick as it is, is no more than a veneer,' Roy explained. 'There's something bolted to the other side, and my guess would be that's a solid-steel plate. And as for the lock itself . . .'

'Yes?'

'Well, I've seen locks on bank vaults which were less sophisticated.'

'Wouldn't be easier to go in through one of the windows?' Paniatowski asked.

'You'd think that, wouldn't you?' the locksmith replied. 'But, you see, the wooden shutters are just like the door – no more than a veneer. And behind that veneer is a steel shutter which slides down into the stonework – and can only be opened from the *inside.*'

And this was supposed to be a moorland farm, Paniatowski reminded herself – a simple moorland farm.

'*Will* you be able to get the door open?' she asked. 'Or should we start thinking about going in through the roof?'

'Oh, I *can* get it open, ma'am,' Roy said cheerfully. 'I can open *anything*. It'll just take a bit longer than anticipated, that's all.'

Paniatowski turned away from him, and looked out at the bleak moors which surrounded the farm house, and at the distant road which had once connected the struggling moorland communities – and now merely connected their ghosts.

'What do you think we'll find once we're inside?' she heard Beresford say, from somewhere to her left.

'I don't know,' she admitted.

And she didn't.

She really had no idea at all.

But whatever it was, it would be significant. You didn't make a fortress out of an old stone cottage unless you had something to hide. And she would have known even without the evidence of the steel shutters – known because, of the men who had visited the place regularly on Thursday nights, four were dead and perhaps as many as a dozen had gone into hiding.

She lit up a cigarette, and found her thoughts drifting back – as they had the night before – to Bob Rutter, her long-dead lover.

If she'd never met him, what kind of life would she be having now, she wondered.

Would she be happily married to someone else?

She couldn't picture that, however hard she tried – couldn't throw off the feeling that the part of her life she'd shared with Bob had always been *meant to be*. And she knew that if she were whisked back in time, and given the opportunity to bypass the affair – with all its pain and all its guilt – she would turn that chance down without a second's hesitation.

'Cracked it, ma'am,' the locksmith called to her.

But when she returned to the front door, she found that it was still firmly closed.

'Thought you'd like to be the one to give the last push, ma'am,' Roy explained. 'You know, a bit like royalty cutting a ribbon to declare a place well and truly open.'

'How do I do it?'

'Just put your finger in the hole, and give it a good hard pull.'

Paniatowski did as instructed, opened the door, stepped inside the cottage – and gasped.

She had expected to find herself in a flagstoned corridor which ran right to the back of the house, where the kitchen – with its old copper boiler – would be located. She had expected there to be several doors leading off that corridor – doors which gave access to parlours and bedrooms and storage areas.

But it wasn't like that at all!

The retaining walls – which had originally both held the house together and supported the heavy roof – had all been removed, and steel joists put in their place, so what she had actually entered was not a cottage at all, but one very large room.

And a room designed with one specific purpose in mind!

There was seating around three of the walls, arranged in tiers. And in the centre was a pit enclosed by a two-foot high concrete wall.

Paniatowski shuddered.

She thought she knew why the killer had stripped his victims naked, ripped out their throats and posed them on their hands and knees.

She thought she knew why he had put his last two victims on display in Whitebridge Rovers' stadium, and had had them facing each other.

'Is this really what it looks like, boss?' Colin Beresford asked, in a choked voice.

'I'm afraid it is,' Paniatowski replied, still horrified – still not quite able to grasp the enormity of it all. 'I don't see what else it could be.'

The inspector from the Royal Society for the Prevention of Cruelty to Animals said his name was Bailey. He was probably only in his early forties, but his hair was greying and the frown lines on his forehead were showing signs of becoming a permanent feature. In many ways, he looked the epitome of the over-worked, undersatisfied official who could be found in every organization.

And then you looked at his eyes, Paniatowski thought.

The eyes were pale and washed-out, yet it was still possible to read in them the horrors he had seen, and despair it had brought him.

'Well, one thing I *can* say for certain is that they weren't trained here,' he told Paniatowski, after he'd glanced briefly around the room.

'How can you be sure of that?'

'If they'd been trained here, we'd have found the equipment. And we haven't.'

'Equipment?' Paniatowski repeated.

'They train the dogs almost like sports promoters train their boxers – except that it's a much more vicious process. Part of the training is to hang heavy weights around their necks, in order to strengthen the neck muscles. And they also have them running on treadmills.'

'Running on treadmills! How the hell do they make dogs do that?'

Bailey laughed hollowly. 'They give them an incentive, don't they?'

'What kind of incentive?'

'They have what they call the "bait" tied down at the end of the treadmill. It can sometimes be a wild animal, like a rabbit, but it's usually easier to use a domestic pet – a kitten or a small dog.'

'Where do they get them from?'

'Sometimes they'll snatch a pet off the street. Sometimes they'll answer newspaper adverts which offer an animal to anybody who can give it a good home. Anyway, the dog on the treadmill can see the bait, and he wants to tear it apart, as he's been trained to do, but the treadmill's moving so fast that he can't reach it however hard he runs. Later on, of course, when the training's over, the dog will often be given the bait as a reward.' Bailey grinned grimly. 'That enough detail for you?'

'No,' Paniatowski said firmly. 'I'm going to pay a visit to the bastard who's responsible for all this, and before I do, I want to know exactly what he's been up to.' She looked across at the pit. 'So there was no training in here. But there was fighting, wasn't there?'

'Undoubtedly. You can see the bloodstains in the concrete. Besides, if there hadn't been fighting, there'd have been no need for the tubs.'

'What tubs?'

'Those in the corner,' Bailey said, pointing.

'They look like baby baths.'

'And that's exactly what they are. Before the fight begins, each owner gives the other owner's dog a thorough washing down.'

'Each owner washes the *other* owner's dog?' Paniatowski repeated, to make sure she'd heard Bailey correctly.

'That's right.'

'Why?'

'To make sure the owner hasn't put poison on his dog's fur.'

'But surely that would poison his own dog as well,' Paniatowski said.

'Yes, it would. But it takes longer to absorb through the skin than it does through the mouth, and by the time the owner's own dog started to feel the effects, the fight would be over.'

'That's vile!' Paniatowski said.

'Isn't it just?' Bailey agreed. He walked over to the tubs and bent down. When he stood up again, he was holding two tapered pieces of wood in his hand. 'And then there's these,' he continued. 'They're what you call "bite sticks".'

'And what are they used for?'

'You can match up all kinds of dogs against each other – and the promoters often do. But the true "connoisseurs" claim that there's no fight like a fight between two Staffordshire pit-bull terriers – and Staffies have really powerful jaws.'

'So?'

'So sometimes one of the dogs gets its teeth deeply imbedded in the flesh of its opponent, and won't let go. Well, there's no "entertainment" in watching two dogs just standing there, is there – even if one of the dogs *is* suffering horribly. So they use the bite stick to prise his jaws apart and pull him off.'

'How long does one of these fights go on for?'

'Until one of the dogs is judged to be beaten. That can take hours – and I mean *literally* hours.'

'And when the fight's over?'

'Are you *sure* you want all the details?' Bailey asked.

'Yes.'

'It all depends on the condition of the dogs. If the winner's not too badly injured, then he might just live to fight another day, providing, of course, that he manages to survive his injuries without any proper medical care. If he is badly injured, then he's killed.'

'What about the dog that loses?'

'The very *fact* that he's lost usually means he'll never be of any use again. So they're almost *always* killed.' Bailey paused. 'The lucky ones are shot.'

'And the others?' Paniatowski asked, though she didn't really want to. 'The ones that *aren't* so lucky?'

'Listen, you don't really need to . . .'

'Yes, I bloody do!'

'If a dog loses, it's seen as a reflection on the poor animal's owner. He becomes a figure of ridicule to everybody else in the room. He didn't exactly *love* his dog before the fight, but he absolutely *hates* it now. So he doesn't *just* kill it – he makes it suffer for letting him down first. And he usually does that in front of all the other men who've been watching the fight. Sometimes he hacks it to death, sometimes he hangs it. Nobody there objects. Well, it's just a bit of fun, isn't it?'

'What kind of people *are* these?' Paniatowski asked.

'They are two kinds of animals involved in a dog fight,' Bailey said grimly. 'There are the ones fighting in the pit and the ones sitting in the seats watching it. And it's the spectators who are the *real* animals.'

TWENTY-SEVEN

The chunky security guard waited until the MGA had pulled up in front of the Ashton Court gatekeeper's lodge, and then opened the side gate and ambled over to the car as if he had all the time in the world.

Paniatowski, drumming her fingers impatiently on the steering wheel, watched his progress, and tagged him immediately as a slightly upgraded nightclub bouncer who confused swagger with intelligence.

The guard reached the car, removed his sunglasses, and leant casually against the bonnet.

'I don't know why you're here, but I've got strict instructions that nobody's to be admitted unless I've been notified in advance,' he said, chomping down on his chewing gum. 'In other words, sweetheart, you can't come in.'

'Guess again,' Paniatowski said, holding out the search warrant and her own warrant card.

The guard gave them no more than a cursory glance. 'Nobody's told *me* about this,' he muttered.

'Oh, haven't they?' Paniatowski asked. 'Maybe that's because they didn't think that *you* needed to be consulted.'

The guard shook his head uncertainly from side to side. 'I think we'd better wait until your boss arrives.'

'I *am* the boss, you moron, as you'd have seen for yourself if you'd bothered to look at my warrant card properly.'

'There's no need to take that attitude,' the guard said, tensing.

'Look, I'm having a bad day,' Paniatowski told him. 'And that's not an apology – it's a warning. I'm going to count to ten, and if the gates aren't open by the time I've finished, I'll arrest you for obstruction, and anything else I think I might be able to make stick.'

'Do you mind if I call through to the house, and tell Sir William you've arrived?' asked the guard, much more conciliatory now.

'Yes, I *do* bloody mind!' Paniatowski exploded. 'I want my

visit to come as a complete surprise to that bastard Langley – and, if doesn't, I'll have your guts for garters.'

'You really are in a bit of a bad mood, aren't you?' the security guard asked wonderingly.

'So would you be, if you'd just come from where I have,' Paniatowski told him.

As the guard walked back to the lodge – at a much more energetic pace this time – she revved her engine, and the moment the gates were open she shot forth from a racing start.

She'd knocked the mental stuffing out of the thug at the gate, she thought – but that was nothing to what she was planning to do to his boss.

Sir William Langley was in his study when he heard the sound of the car coming up the driveway towards the house – and immediately felt the taste of fear gushing into his mouth.

He was being irrational, he told himself angrily. He had six highly trained (and very expensive) guards patrolling the grounds of Ashton Court, and if the person driving the car had been thought by them to present any danger, they would never have let him get that far.

'Calm down!' he ordered his racing pulse and galloping heart. 'For God's sake, calm down!'

He looked around his study, and immediately started to feel better.

It was such a soothing room, he thought. It had so much obvious *class*.

His eyes swept along row after row of leather-bound books, all of them with the brown spines and golden lettering which chimed in perfectly with the rest of the colour scheme.

He let his gaze fall for a few seconds on the large oak table at far end of the study, which he had chosen instead of a desk because, he had been told, gentlemen always *preferred* tables.

A half-turn, and he was looking at the monumental fireplace he had bought from a derelict castle in Scotland, and the skin of a tiger in front of it, and which visitors always believed – erroneously, as it happened – had been shot by one of his ancestors.

The noise of the car's engine had died away, and Sir William assumed that whoever the driver was, he was probably being dealt with by one of his employees. But now there was a new distraction – the sound of two people walking rapidly down the passageway.

'I've told the staff, time and time again, not to run,' Sir William thought crossly. 'In the *best* houses, the servants wouldn't run even if the whole bally building was on fire.'

The study door flew violently open, and suddenly Monika Paniatowski was in the room, with a red-faced maid at heels.

'I . . . I told her you were busy, sir,' the maid wailed across at him. 'I said you weren't seeing anybody. But she just barged past me.'

Langley frowned at the unwelcome intruder.

'Really, this is *too much*, Chief Inspector,' he said haughtily. 'I'm all for cooperating with the authorities, but if you wished to see me, it would surely have been no more than common courtesy to ring and make an app—'

'Shut up!' Paniatowski said.

Sir William flushed, hardly able to believe what he'd just heard. 'I beg your pardon?'

Paniatowski swung round to face the maid

'Unless you want to be arrested, you'd better leave now,' she advised.

The maid hesitated for the briefest of moments, then took her at her word – and fled.

'This really is most unwarranted, and I shall certainly be lodging a personal complaint with your chief constable,' Langley said.

'Will you now?' Paniatowski asked. 'And will you be telling him about Moors' Edge Farm, as well?'

A hint of panic entered Langley's eyes for a second, and then was gone.

'Moors' Edge Farm?' he said. 'Where's that?'

'As its name suggests, it's a farm on the edge of the moors.'

'I assumed that to be the case, but . . .'

'Where's all the outrage gone?' Paniatowski wondered.

'I'm sorry, but I don't . . .'

'*A minute ago* you were furious that I'd had the audacity to tell you to shut up. *Thirty seconds ago* you were threatening me with the chief constable. I'm surprised that you've calmed down so quickly. Or maybe I'm not. Maybe that's what fear *does* to a man like you.'

'I assure you, I'm not in the least concerned,' Langley told her, with a creditable degree of conviction, 'and I have no idea why you should even have mentioned this farm.'

'I mentioned it because you *own* it.'

'I most certainly do not.'

'Not on paper,' Paniatowski agreed. 'At least, not at first sight. It's actually the property of United Holdings . . .'

'Well, there you are, then. I have nothing to do with any such company.'

'. . . which is a subsidiary of United Holdings (International), which, in turn, belongs to Enterprises Incorporated.'

How had she made the link, Langley wondered miserably. How had she – a mere policewoman – managed to wade through the acres of legal gobbledegook, navigate the scores of dummy companies set up by the best minds in the business, and arrive where she had?

'And who owns Enterprises Incorporated?' Paniatowski concluded triumphantly. 'Why, you do!'

'Perhaps you're right, and I do own this farm of yours,' Langley conceded. 'But I own a great deal of property, both here and abroad, most of which I've never even seen.'

'You've seen this,' Paniatowski said firmly.

'Are you calling me a *liar*?' Langley demanded, going onto the attack.

'Yes – and that's only for starters,' Paniatowski countered.

'But that's outrageous! If you repeated it elsewhere, I could sue you for libel – and I would.'

'You could sue me for *slander*,' Paniatowski corrected him. 'But only if I couldn't prove it – and I *can* prove it!'

Of course she could prove it, he thought. It would take her no time at all to track down the builders and security consultants who'd done the work on Moors' End Farm – and they would lead her directly back to him.

'I . . . I need to sit down,' Langley said shakily.

'Good idea,' Paniatowski agreed. She walked over to the expensive leather sofa and gently patted the arm with her hand. 'This looks very comfortable – and you might as well grab a bit of comfort while you still can.'

'What do you mean?'

'You *know* what I mean.'

Paniatowski stepped aside, and Langley slumped down onto the sofa.

'Dog fighting is a sport, just like any other,' he said weakly, now it was clear the game was up. 'It's been patronized by the aristocracy – and even the monarchy. The dogs enjoy it, too.'

'Enjoy it?' Paniatowski repeated.

'Fighting comes naturally to them. It's what they're born for.'

'It's barbaric and it's illegal. And you're going to jail for it.'

Langley's lower lip quivered. 'I'm more than willing to pay the fine. I don't care how much it is.'

'You're . . . going . . . to . . . jail,' Paniatowski repeated. 'The only question is, how long are you going to be inside? That will partly depend on what *I* say at your trial. And what I say at your trial will depend on how much you cooperate with me now.'

'I'll tell you anything you want to know.'

Paniatowski nodded. 'Good. Begin by telling me how it all got started.'

'I suppose it started with the hunt,' Langley said. 'No, it began even before that, with the Golf Club.'

'What the bloody hell has any of that got to do with dog fighting?' Paniatowski demanded.

'Please, let me tell it my own way, so you can see what tremendous pressure I've been under,' Langley begged.

'So that you can make excuses for yourself as you go along, more like,' Paniatowski thought.

But why *not* let him tell it his own way? If she gave him enough rope, he would probably reveal more than he'd ever have done under direct interrogation. Besides, when she explained what a grovelling wreck he'd been in open court, it would only add to his humiliation.

'Go ahead,' she said.

'My difficulty has always been that some of the people who matter in this town knew me before I was rich, so they'll never really accept me for what I've become – what I've *grown into*,' Langley said. 'Oh, they're nice enough to me at the Golf and Country Club. They even co-opt me on to their charitable committees, if I promise to make a big enough donation. But they don't *like* me. They don't *respect* me.'

'I find that very hard to believe,' Paniatowski said.

'And for quite some time, so did I. If I got the occasional hint of it, I managed to persuade myself that I was only imagining things. And then, one day, I overheard one of the other members, who I'd always thought of as one of my closest friends, refer to me as Bumptious Billy.'

'Shocking!' Paniatowski said.

'Yes, it is, isn't it?' Langley agreed. 'I told myself it didn't really matter. They were just townies – no more than jumped-up members of the bourgeoisie. My true friends, I now realized, were my *country* friends – the people who are the real backbone of England.'

'The landed gentry, like yourself,' Paniatowski suggested, and could hardly believe her eyes when Langley nodded.

'I had been riding with the Lea Vale Hunt for some time when it was suggested to me that if I financed the new stable block I was virtually guaranteed to be elected as its next master.'

'And, naturally, you were delighted,' Paniatowski said.

'Of course I was. Who *wouldn't* want to be the master of the hunt. Unfortunately, things didn't work out as they were supposed to. There was a small dissident element on the committee, and while most of the members *wanted* to elect me as master, they were forced to accept a compromise candidate. It was a big blow, and I don't mind admitting it – and that was when I started developing an interest in dog fighting.'

It is the day after the hunt has appointed its new master. Edward Dunston – accountant and dog-fight aficionado – is amusing himself by sitting at the bar in the Golf Club and watching Sir William Langley, all alone, at a table near the window, getting quietly and desperately drunk. And then it occurs to him that there is perhaps more to be gained out of this situation than the mere sport of observing another man's misery – that if he plays it cunningly, he can solve one of his own little problems.

He gets up and walks over to Langley's table.

'Mind if I join you, Sir William?' he asks.

Langley looks at him through bleary eyes. 'No, I . . . sit down.'

'I was sorry to hear that the hunt elected someone else as its master,' Dunston says, taking the seat opposite him. 'You must be pretty cut up about it.'

'Not at all,' Langley replies, unconvincingly. 'I was the popular candidate, of course . . .'

'Of course.'

'. . . but I was more than willing to step aside for the good of the hunt.'

'Bloody liar!' Dunston thinks.

'Well, I think the hunt's made a big mistake and will live to regret it,' he says aloud. 'But you can't entirely blame the members.'

'You can't?'

'Certainly not. Ensuring that the right man's slotted into the right job is always a tricky business, and, more often than not, people get it wrong.' He pauses for a moment. 'In fact, it's because we're so aware of that particular difficulty that my own little group is taking so long over selecting a leader.'

'Your own little group?' Langley asks, with some signs of interest. 'And what little group might that be?'

'We're planning to establish a dog-fighting club.'

'But isn't that illegal?' Langley exclaims.

'Keep your voice down,' Dunston says, glancing across at the barman. 'Yes, strictly speaking, I suppose it is illegal. But that says more about how our rights as Englishmen have been eroded than it does about anything else. Dog fighting is as much a part of the English tradition as fox hunting.'

'I suppose it is,' Langley says thoughtfully.

'Anyway, we have most of the elements in place to start the club, but what we're lacking is a master.*'*

'Do dog-fighting clubs have *a master?' Langley asks.*

'Of course they do,' Dunston lies. 'As I said, they're as traditional as hunts. And let me tell you, the master of a dog fight is accorded just as much respect as the master of a hunt – if not more. That's why it's so important to elect the right *man.' He paused for a second time. 'Perhaps you can help us out here. Could you – with your wide range of contacts – think of anyone who might fill the role?'*

* * *

'Didn't you find it strange that while he was asking your advice on who to appoint, Dunston couldn't see that the solution to his problem was sitting right there opposite him?' Paniatowski asked.

'Not really,' Langley said dismissively. 'The man's a *book-keeper*. He's got a good head for figures, but he's rather lacking in imagination. At any rate, when I proposed myself, he was delighted. He said he already had a property in mind for the venue – Moors' Edge Farm – and that now things could finally get moving.'

'And you bought the farm with your own money?'

'Well, yes, as the Master, it seemed only appropriate that I should do so.' Langley paused for a moment. 'But you do get the point, don't you?'

'What point?'

'The whole thing was Edward Dunston's idea, so if anyone's going to be punished for it, it should be him.'

The man was beneath contempt, Paniatowski thought.

'What did *you* get out of it?' she asked aloud. 'Did you enjoy seeing dogs being ripped to shreds?'

'No, not really,' Langley admitted. 'Sometimes it got so bloody that I had to turn away. But once the fighting was over – once the blood had been spilled – ah, that was bliss!'

'What happened then?'

'That was when they had the loyal toast. Everybody there – and I mean every single man-jack of them – would raise his glass or his can of beer in the air and shout, "To the Master!" They were drinking that loyal toast to *me*!'

'They were laughing at you, just like the men in the Country Club and the hunt,' Paniatowski thought. 'They were taking your money, and *laughing* at you.'

'How did Andy Adair come into the picture?' she asked.

'Adair had only just moved to Whitebridge, but Edward Dunston knew him from dog fights they'd both attended in other parts of the country, and he said that with Adair's experience, he would be the ideal chap to run things for us.'

'And even though Adair was already working for Forsyth, he couldn't resist the opportunity to make a little bit extra on the side,' Paniatowski thought.

'One of my bright young officers pointed out that there were no Catholics amongst your members,' she said. 'Was that Adair's doing?'

'Yes. He hated Catholics with a vengeance, and he'd only agree to take on the job if we promised to keep them out.'

'Tell me about Simon Stockwell.'

Langley looked puzzled. 'There's not much to tell. He was just an ordinary member.'

'So why did the killer single him out for execution?'

'I don't know. I didn't give it much thought. Some maniac had killed a member of the club and left his body in my grounds. That alone was *more than enough* to think about, thank you very much.'

'And Len Gutterridge?'

'Why are you asking about him?'

'Because he was killed last night – and so was Edward Dunston. We found them both in the Whitebridge Rovers' stadium this morning – naked and on all fours, just like the others.'

'Oh, my God,' Langley moaned. 'This is terrible.'

'Yes, you're probably right,' Paniatowski agreed. 'At any rate, Dunston and Gutterridge didn't look too pleased about it. But you still haven't answered my question.'

'What question?'

'I can understand why the killer chose Adair and Dunston as his victims – Dunston set the club up, and Adair ran it – but what reason did he have for singling out Stockwell and Gutterridge?'

'I don't know,' Langley admitted. 'Unless it had something to do with the dog.'

'What dog?' Paniatowski demanded.

Len Gutterridge walks into the club with a Staffordshire bull terrier on a lead. The dog seems bemused by the whole situation, yet eager to please the man who brought it out for a walk – and, even to Langley's untutored eye, it doesn't look like the usual fighting dog at all.

Gutterridge brings the dog over to where Langley and Dunston are standing.

'You're never planning to enter that thing in the fight, are you?' Dunston asks. 'It's not got the instinct. It'll not last five minutes'

'It's a good dog, this,' Gutterridge protests. 'Full of fighting spirit. But no, I wasn't planning to enter it into the fight myself.'

'Well, then?'

'I thought the club might like to buy it off me. I thought the club *might like to enter it.*'

Dunston and Langley exchange glances. Neither of them wants the club to buy the dog, but Gutterridge – for all that he is as guilty as anyone else in the room – is still a policeman, and it might be wise not to cross him.

'How much do you want for it?' Dunston asks finally.

Gutterridge shrugs. 'Thirty quid?'

Dunston pays him the money, and fifteen minutes later the dog is sent into the pit. It puts up a poor show, and the fight is over even quicker than Dunston guessed it would be.

The badly injured animal is dragged away.

'What do you want us to do with your useless bloody dog, Len?' Simon Stockwell calls out mockingly.

'It's not my dog,' Gutterridge says. 'It's the club's dog. Do whatever you bloody well want with it.'

Stockwell brings a rope and throws it over a large hook, which has been set in place for just this purpose.

And even as he is putting the noose around the badly mauled animal's neck, Langley notices the dog is looking up at him, with hope in its eyes that it will yet be shown some kindness.

Stockwell begins to haul on the rope, and Langley has to turn away. Behind him, he can hear the other men shouting and jeering as the dog gasps and struggles as it tries to hold on to its life.

'This is horrible,' the Master thinks. 'This is the worst thing I've ever seen.'

'But you didn't try to stop it?' Paniatowski asked.

'No, I . . . I was the Master. I didn't want to seem weak in front of men who had so much respect for me.'

Paniatowski sighed. All the hints she had been given throughout the investigation had finally slotted into place, and though she didn't know *everything* yet – though there were a few pieces of information to collect before the picture was complete – the case was as good as over.

'What happens now?' Langley asked.

'When my inspector gets here, he'll take you down to police headquarters where you'll be formally charged, photographed and fingerprinted.'

'Like a common criminal,' Langley said mournfully.

'Not *like* one – you *are* a common criminal,' Paniatowski pointed out.

Langley's lip quivered. 'Will I . . . will be let out on bail, once I've been charged?'

Paniatowski nodded. 'Unless, of course, the magistrate refuses bail – and there's no reason why he should.'

'But I *will* go to prison?'

'Yes, you will.'

'And what about when I *come out of* jail?'

'*What* about it?'

'No one who matters in this town – who matters *anywhere* – will want to have anything to do with me, will they?'

Paniatowski laughed. 'Oh, I don't know about that,' she said. 'You might be something of a hero with the dog-fighting set.'

Langley bowed his head. 'My life is over,' he pronounced mournfully.

'It doesn't have to be,' Paniatowski told him. 'Not if you show a little backbone – not if you finally start acting like a *man*!'

'Could I ask you a small favour?' Langley asked.

'What is it?'

'Before you actually arrest me, I'd like to spend a little time by myself, in my trophy room.'

'In *where*?'

'My trophy room. It's where I keep the heads of all the animals I've shot. I've got a very fine elk, and a stag with antlers that . . .'

'I'm not interested in hearing about all the helpless creatures you have slaughtered,' Paniatowski said harshly. 'But I *would* like to know where you keep the guns you used to carry out that slaughter.'

'They're . . . they're safely locked in a cabinet.'

'And is that cabinet in the trophy room?'

'Yes, it is,' Langley admitted, looking down at the floor.

'In that case, I can see no objection to you spending a few minutes with some of your victims,' Paniatowski told him.

The guard at the gatehouse of Ashton Court was still, in theory, on duty, but he gave Beresford's warrant card no more than the most cursory of glances before waving the inspector through.

It was amazing how quickly word got around, Beresford thought, as he drove up the driveway towards the house. It was like throwing a stone into a pond, and watching the circles spread out from it. Already – though Monika had probably not even arrested the merchant banker yet – his security staff knew that he was finished. And by the afternoon, when the circles had spread almost to the edges of the pond that was Whitebridge, there wouldn't be a single person in the town with a good word to say about Sir William Langley.

He parked in front of Ashley Court, and was shown into the study by the same uniformed maid who Paniatowski had barged past earlier. He had expected to find Langley there, but the only person occupying the vast, pretentious room was his boss, who was gazing out of the window with a preoccupied air about her.

'Where's Langley?' he asked.

Paniatowski turned to face him. 'Langley is elsewhere,' she said. Then, more crisply, she added, 'What have you got to report, Colin?'

'We've sealed off the farm, and the forensic boys are getting to work on it even as I speak,' Beresford said. 'In addition, I've arranged a press conference for this evening, but I've warned the hacks that you may have to cancel it if . . .' He paused. 'I'm sorry, boss, what did you mean by "elsewhere"?'

Paniatowski smiled, though it was not a happy expression. If anything, Beresford thought, he would have called it *tortured*.

'The Lord of the Manor is in his trophy room,' she said.

The words exploded inside Beresford's head.

In his trophy room!

'But good God, boss, there are probably guns in there,' he said.

'There *are* guns in there,' Paniatowski replied calmly.

'And don't you think there's a danger he might . . .'

'Blow his own head off?'

'Well, yes.'

'That course of action must certainly have an appeal for him. With that last final gesture, he'd confirm – at least to himself – that he really is an English gentleman.'

'Then how could you . . . what ever possessed you to . . .?'

'Let's go and see how he's getting on, shall we?' Paniatowski suggested.

The doors to the gun case in the trophy room had been thrown wide open, and several expensive customized shotguns were there for the taking by anyone who cared to reach into the cabinet. But Sir William Langley couldn't take advantage of the opportunity, for though he could almost touch the guns with the fingertips of his left hand, his right wrist was firmly manacled to one of the substantial heating pipes.

It had been a fine calculation on Paniatowski's part, Beresford thought. There was no way that Langley could actually get his hands on one of the guns, but she had tethered him close enough for him to still live in the desperate hope that – with a little more effort – he just *might*.

Langley noticed them looking at him from the doorway.

'So you've brought your underling to observe me in my humiliation, have you, Chief Inspector?' he asked angrily.

'That's right,' Paniatowski replied, in a cheery voice. 'I thought he could use a good laugh.' She turned to Beresford. 'Seen enough, Colin?'

'More than enough,' Beresford said, sounding troubled.

They walked back down along the corridor in uneasy silence, and it was not until they were back in Langley's study that Beresford said, 'Why did you do that, boss?'

'You're supposed to be a detective,' Paniatowski replied, in a tone he couldn't quite pin down. '*You* work it out.'

'You wanted to make him suffer?'

'Full marks – go to the top of the class.'

There had been a frown on Beresford's face since he'd first seen what she'd done to Langley, and now that frown deepened even further.

'This isn't like you, boss,' he said. 'It isn't like you at all.'

'Isn't it?' Paniatowski demanded – and now he had her tone pegged as *anger*, a deep, boiling anger he'd never seen in her before. 'Why *shouldn't* I want him to suffer, after what he's done? Why shouldn't he pay for standing by while poor dumb suffering animals were ripped to shreds? But that's *nothing* compared to what *else* he's done. Through his vanity and his insecurity, a *good* man has been destroyed – and there can never be *enough* punishment for that!'

'A good man?' Beresford repeated, mystified. 'Who are you talking about?'

'Oh, for God's sake, who the hell do you *think* I'm talking about?' Paniatowski countered.

TWENTY-EIGHT

Paniatowski found Cousins in her office, sitting in Beresford's chair.

'Sorry to have come in here without asking your permission first, ma'am,' the sergeant said.

'That's all right, Paul,' Paniatowski said, seating herself down opposite him.

'I wouldn't normally have done it,' the sergeant continued, 'but when I heard that you'd been out to Moors' Edge Farm I suddenly felt so *tired*, and I knew I had to find a place where I could be on my own for a while.'

'I understand.'

Cousins reached into his wallet, took out a photograph, and slid it across the desk to Paniatowski.

'I'd like you to take a look at that,' he said.

The picture had been taken in a garden, and in the background Paniatowski could see honeysuckle climbing a trestle. The two people in the shot were sitting down on plastic chairs. The woman was smiling at the camera, but even though she was making a great effort to hide the fact that she was in pain, she was not being entirely successful. The man was smiling too, but his eyes, filled with concern, were fixed not on the camera but on the woman. A ginger cat sat on the woman's knee, and a dog – a Staffordshire bull terrier – was curled up contentedly at her feet.

'That's us,' Cousins said. 'That's the family.'

Paniatowski smiled. 'I guessed as much.'

'We always thought Mary would be the first to go. But she wasn't. A few weeks before she died, Ginger was run over in the street. It was nobody's fault but his own – he was always a reckless bugger – but it hit Mary hard. She said there seemed to be a curse on the family.' Cousins paused. 'You have to laugh, don't you, ma'am? There she was, dying of cancer herself, and the first time she mentions a curse is when the bloody cat gets killed!'

'It must have been awful for her,' Paniatowski said, sympathetically.

'But she was right – as usual,' Cousins continued. 'We *were* cursed.' He paused again, as if this was all very difficult for him. 'Mary had always been close to Davie, but she grew even closer to him after Ginger was killed.' He laughed. 'Davie! Funny bloody name to give a powerful animal like a pit-bull terrier, isn't it?'

'I think it's a nice name,' Paniatowski told him.

'But my Mary was most insistent that was what we call him. She said he'd got "Davie" written all over him. That was the thing about her. She had her own way of looking at everything and everybody, and she saw qualities in them which other people didn't. She certainly saw qualities in me I never knew I had, but because *she'd* seen them, I believe I actually did start to develop them. Does that make any sense at all?'

'It makes a lot of sense.'

'When she first got ill, I did everything I could to help her. I took medical books out of the library, to see if I could find a cure that her doctor had somehow missed. But of course there wasn't one. I got her to take some of those "alternative" medicines, but they either had no effect at all, or they made her feel sick. I hadn't prayed for years, but I prayed then – down on my knees until it hurt so much that I could hardly stand up again. None of it did any good. I failed her.'

'You didn't fail her,' Paniatowski said softly. 'You loved her and you cared for her right to the end – and that's all anybody can ask.'

'She was worried about what would happen to Davie after she'd gone,' Cousins said. 'She'd had him from a pup, you see. She loved him with all her heart, and one of the last things she did before she died was to make me promise I'd look after him.'

'But you couldn't cope,' Paniatowski said. 'You were having a mental breakdown, so you were forced to give him to your old friend Len Gutterridge to look after.'

'You know about that, do you?'

'Yes. His widow confirmed it, not half an hour ago. And I also know that Gutterridge used to go to Moors' Edge Farm on Thursday nights.'

'If Len had thought there'd be a possibility I'd be coming out of the nut house soon, Davie would have been quite safe,' Cousins said sadly. 'But he believed I'd be in there for the duration, so he took the dog to the fight. He sold our Davie – and then he stood there and watched him being ripped to shreds.'

'How did you find out what had actually gone on?' Paniatowski asked.

Cousins shrugged. 'It wasn't difficult. The first time I spoke to Len after I'd been released, he seemed very nervous. When he told me that Davie had died of distemper, I knew he was lying, so I checked with all the vets in Whitebridge, and none of them had treated my dog. You can fill in the rest for yourself, can't you, ma'am.'

'I think so. You started watching him closely, and one night you followed him out to Moors' Edge Farm?'

'And once I saw what was going on there, I *knew* what had happened to Davie. There were still a few details that needed to be filled in, but Andy Adair was most forthcoming, once I'd given him the blow-lamp treatment.'

'You decided that the four men most closely connected with Davie's death had to die themselves.'

'That's right, ma'am. Len had betrayed Davie – and me – for thirty pieces of silver, Dunston had paid the money, Adair had managed the fight, and Stockwell . . .' A sob came to Cousins' throat. '. . . Stockwell had hanged my poor, sweet little dog when it was all over.'

'You led this investigation on a merry dance,' Paniatowski said. She paused for a second. 'When Stockwell's van burst into flame, you weren't even there. How did you manage that? A timer?'

'That's right, ma'am.'

'And it was you who first introduced the idea of IRA involvement, and sent us off in entirely the wrong direction.'

'I didn't *like* doing it, ma'am, because I respect you as a bobby. And, as a member of your team, I wanted to do all that I could to help you. But I needed time to finish my work.'

'You could have killed them all in one night, if you'd really put your mind to it,' Paniatowski pointed out.

'Yes, I suppose I could,' Cousins agreed.

'Or you could have hidden the first few bodies until you'd finished the job – so we wouldn't even have been sure there'd *been* any murders.'

'True.'

'But you didn't do that. You slit their throats with the closest thing you could find to a dog's teeth, you stripped their bodies, you posed them like fighting dogs, and then you put them on public display. Why?'

'You know the answer to that, don't you, ma'am?' Cousins asked.

'Yes, I rather think I do,' Paniatowski admitted. 'But I'd still like to hear it from you.'

'I couldn't kill all the members of the club – I knew my luck wouldn't hold out that long – but I *did* want to make all of them suffer. I wanted them to know what it was like to feel naked and afraid.'

'So you left Stockwell's body at the home of the man who was financing the fights?'

'That's right.'

'And you left Dunston's and Gutterridge's facing each other in the Rovers' stadium, because that was like the dog pit writ large?'

'Exactly.'

'But what I still don't understand is why you left Adair's body in the woods. Was the kennel owner – Toynbee – a member of the dog-fighting ring?'

'No, ma'am. As far as I know, he's exactly what he seems to be – a decent man who loves animals.'

'Well, then?'

'I didn't do it for his benefit – I did it for his dogs.'

'For his dogs?'

'Dogs can sense evil. They can sniff out their natural enemies. I thought that I'd show them that – just once in a while – cruelty *wasn't* triumphant.'

'You do *know* that you're insane, don't you?' Paniatowski asked.

'Oh, yes, ma'am,' Cousins agreed easily. 'In fact, I'd go further than that.' He smiled. '*I'd* say I was barking mad!'

EPILOGUE

It was an unseasonably cold September morning, and even the birds in the elm trees seemed less enthusiastic about the start of the new day than they would normally have been.

Three people – a man, a woman and a Catholic priest – stood next to the newly re-opened grave and watched the coffin being slowly lowered into it.

'It was kind of you to come with me, Colin,' Monika Paniatowski said, in a voice which was thick with emotion.

'Think nothing of it,' Beresford replied.

'Did I do the right thing?' Paniatowski wondered, and now there was anguish in her tone. 'Would he have wanted to be buried in foreign soil, so far away from his beloved Poland?'

'From what you've told me about him, he'd have wanted anything that he knew would bring you some comfort. And this does.'

Paniatowski sniffled. 'Yes, it does.'

'Besides, after all these years, he's finally been reunited with his wife, and I think that would have mattered to him much more than a line on a map.'

'I'm not sure that's true,' Paniatowski said. 'But thank you for saying it, anyway. You're a true friend.'

'I'm better than that,' Beresford told her. 'I'm a true *mate*.'

'Yes,' Paniatowski agreed, sniffling again. 'Yes, you are.'

Two men stood watching the scene from a distance. One was tall and chunky, and had ginger hair. The other was more compact, with silvery hair atop a face which gave away nothing of what he was thinking.

'What made you go to all this trouble?' asked the chunky man, Chief Constable George Baxter.

'I knew it would mean a lot to Monika,' Mr Forsyth replied.

'If I'd never seen the way you operate, I might almost believe you,' Baxter said. 'But since I have, I don't.'

Forsyth shrugged. 'Believe what you wish.'

'I think she's got something on you. You probably made her sign the Official Secrets' Act . . .'

'I did.'

'. . . and you were also probably very explicit about what would happen to her if she ran foul of it. But knowing Monika as you do, you weren't sure *that* was enough. You thought you needed an additional hold on her, and that's what returning the bones gave you.'

'Possibly,' Forsyth conceded.

'She's *grateful* to you now – she might hate herself for that, but there's nothing she can do about it. And, for the record, I hold you in nothing but contempt for ever putting her in that situation.'

'Without wishing to be impolite, I should tell you, again for the record, that your opinion of me is not something I will lose any sleep over,' Forsyth said. 'I do what needs to be done in order to keep my country safe.'

'You do it because you *love* doing it,' Baxter said harshly. 'The dirty tricks, the double-crossing, the intimidation, the assassinations – it's all meat and drink to you.'

'That, too,' Forsyth agreed. 'I am most fortunate in having a talent and a temperament which fit so well together.'

Paniatowski had turned, and begun to walk away from the grave. Beresford, by her side, held out his arm in case she felt a need for support, and she took it gratefully.

'Just tell me one more thing,' Baxter said to Forsyth. 'Are they *really* her father's bones in that grave?'

'Why don't you ask Monika?' Forsyth replied. 'I'm sure *she'll* tell you they are.'

Baxter grabbed him by the lapels, and shook him furiously.

'I know what *she'll* tell me,' he growled. 'But I'm not asking her. I'm asking you, you bastard.'

He released his grip and took a step backwards. Forsyth brushed his lapels lightly, as if he'd just noticed a few specks of dust on them.

'*Are* they his bones?' he asked. 'Why wouldn't they be? They come from the battlefield on which he died, so there's as much chance they're his as there is that they're anybody else's.'